THE CRADLE ROBBER

THE PAISLEY STERLING MYSTERIES

Cemetery Silk
The Plague Doctor
The Paper Detective
The Cradle Robber
The Poisoned Pen
The Sow's Ear

Published by Wildside Press

THE CRADLE ROBBER

The Fourth Paisley Sterling Mystery

by

E. JOAN SIMS

The Borgo Press
An Imprint of Wildside Press

MMVII

CONTENTS

DEDICATION

To my lovely sister Jeanie

This one's for you in the hopes that you will forgive me for covering you with mud, terrifying you with scary stories, talking you in to burning down the outhouse, and all the rest of the mischief of our childhood.

ABOUT THE AUTHOR

E. JOAN SIMS was born in a delightful small town in Kentucky not unlike the fictitious "Rowan Springs" which is the home of Paisley Sterling, the heroine of her mystery novels.

After completing her graduate and postgraduate work at Emory University in Atlanta, Georgia, she became the Director of Medical Records at the newly built Holy Family Hospital, where she worked until she and her new husband left for a year in Barcelona, Spain. They returned to Georgia to pursue their careers, and then moved again—this time to Caracas, Venezuela, where they spent fourteen wonderful and exciting years.

When the family returned to the United States, Joan resumed her interesting work in disease surveillance at the Centers for Disease Control and Prevention, where she is still employed.

Writing is in her in blood. Joan's father published many short stories and poems in the popular magazines of the forties and fifties. Her dream was to place her own works next to his on the bookshelf in the family library. The publication of the Paisley Sterling Mystery series is the realization of that dream. Joan notes that there is plenty of room remaining on the bookshelf, and lots of mysteries waiting for Paisley to solve.

Be sure to visit her web site at:

www.ejoansims.com

CHAPTER ONE

It was still not quite the middle of May, but the temperature had been hovering in the mid-to-upper eighties for the past week. This morning had started out a bit cooler than the others, and encouraged by the dewy freshness in the air, I set out for a brisk walk carrying a picnic basket and a sweater. The cotton cardigan that was a necessity at seven had been discarded by nine and the picnic basket had been emptied before eleven.

The early morning breeze had been sweet and just strong enough to keep the insects at bay, but shortly after noon the wind died down, and June bugs, their beautiful iridescent bodies shining like emeralds, began to dive dangerously close to my resting place beneath the hickory nut tree.

Curious dragonflies hovered over my face, daring me to reach up and touch their fragile wings. Scores of dainty yellow butterflies, looking for all the world like real pats of butter, swirled around me and the remains of my picnic lunch.

A hairy little leg tickled the back of my sweaty neck, but I was too lazy to move. After a few moments, the tiny green grasshopper traversed my shoulder and hopped on the red and white calico square of the quilt underneath my cheek. For a full minute, the two of us stared into our various eyes trying to size each other up. He won when I blinked first. Waggling a slender antenna in farewell, he hopped off into the grass with a triumphant bounce.

I heard the sound of a plane in the distance and raised up on an elbow to peer through half-closed eyes in the direction of the airport that bordered our back field a half mile away. Twenty years ago, the "powers that be" had forced my father to sell them the land where the Lakeland County Airport now proudly boasted its one runway. We hadn't been happy about it at the time, and even though it was used only occasionally, Mother and I still resented having our quiet afternoons disturbed by noisy little airplanes practicing takeoffs and landings.

The single engine aircraft circled slowly above the end of the runway in preparation for landing. The plane waggled its wings, and for one brief moment I thought I saw a something fall to the ground. I wiped the sweat from my forehead and blinked against the bright sunlight. When I looked again, all I could see was a solitary buzzard wheeling in slow, indolent circles over the distant field.

I plopped back down on the quilt and tried to shut out the harsh sound of the engine as the plane landed and taxied to the other end of the runway. When the blessed peace and quiet finally returned, so did the insects.

"I guess you're all trying to get me to leave," I mumbled drowsily. "I should have brought Aggie. She'd chase you away."

Aggie was my daughter's foul-tempered Lhasa Apso. Cassandra had talked her grandmother into letting Agatha Christie become a part of our little family here on Meadowdale Farm three years ago. Our lives haven't been the same since.

Aggie is a soft cottonball of a dog with the teeth of a piranha. I had the scars to prove it. The last time she bit me I had to get a tetanus shot. Cassandra was coming home tomorrow. I didn't know what her post-graduation plans were, but I was going to make sure they included taking Aggie with her wherever she went.

I tried to put the possibility of Cassie's moving away out of my mind. I had missed her terribly during the four years she had spent at Emory University—and Atlanta was close enough for us to spend most vacations and holidays together. What would I do if she did something crazy like I did and move to South America? I knew one thing for sure, I couldn't argue against it.

My parents had let me marry Raphael Luis DeLeon twenty-two years ago and then move to San Romero without a squawk because they knew how very much in love we were. They trusted Rafe to take care of me, and a year later, our baby daughter. What none of us counted on was his disappearing into the jungle when Cassie was eight. By then, San Romero was torn by a bloody revolution, and Cassie and I barely escaped to New York with the clothes on our backs.

Without hesitation, my best friend from college took me under her wing. She gave us a home for the first few months and even helped me find a way to support myself. Pamela is a literary agent. She convinced me to write down the bedtime stories I told Cassie each night. From those stories, we created a best-selling series of children's books. With the income from my writing, Cassie and I were able to shape a decent, if not completely content, existence in Manhattan. When America's children finally got fed up with my stories, I started writing murder mysteries under the *nom de plume* of Leonard Paisley, hard-boiled detective. "Leonard" was a great success, and soon I was financially stable enough to move back to my hometown in Kentucky. Life suddenly became a real pleasure again.

I loved Meadowdale farm. It had been in my family for generations. I loved the rich brown dirt that squished up between my bare toes as I walked, the smell of the honeysuckle blooming haphazardly on the back fence, and the buttery yellow Anjou pears in my grandfather's orchard. I was convinced that the sun shone brighter from a sky more beautifully blue over our hundred acres of rolling fields and woods than anywhere else on God's earth.

My mother's house was over 150 years old. It had originally been a log cabin. Succeeding lords of the manor had built on room after room until it was a strange hodge-podge of various roofs and walls. I loved every capricious inch of it. If I could summon up enough energy, I would gather up my picnic debris, trudge over the fields to the big screened-in back porch, and collapse in the chaise lounge for the rest of my nap. Maybe Mother would have some fresh sweet tea in the fridge. The ice had long ago melted in my thermos, leaving nothing but unappetizing flecks of lemon pulp floating on a sea of tepid brown.

A bumbling black carpenter bee bombarded my right ear and forced me to my knees. I swayed for a moment in the heat and glare of the sun, then stumbled to my feet. I was ready for air-conditioning and a nice cool shower with some of that fancy lavender-scented soap Cassie gave me for my birthday.

CHAPTER TWO

My shower was not the luxuriously indulgent affair I had envisioned. I barely had time to dry off, much less put on lipstick or float face powder over the freckles on my nose. The only thing I could say for myself was that I was clean and fresh when Mother packed me into her new Lincoln Continental and headed for town. She decided that our larders needed replenishing and insisted that she needed my knowledge of Cassie's likes and dislikes to make sure of pleasing her returning granddaughter's palate. I argued that she was well aware that Cassie ate almost everything except celery and oysters, but to no avail.

Mother is a good driver, even if she does get distracted on occasion. My grandfather Howard taught her how to drive his vintage 1939 Ford coupe when she was eleven. Five years later, when she got her license, he gave her the car, which by then was only four years shy of twice her age. Our family album has almost as many pictures of "Mr. Peabody" as it does of the non-motorized members of our clan.

She babied the old car through college and into the fifth year of her marriage to my father. When it was apparent that Mr. Peabody was on his last cylinder, my father bought his bride her first Continental to ease the loss of a beloved and faithful friend. Cassie or I would have been inconsolable. Mother was ecstatic. She has sported a new Lincoln every five years since then. The latest one—baby blue with white leather seats, was a mere four months old when the ramshackle, mud-spattered farm truck broadsided us at the corner of Harrison and Oak streets.

"Damn it, Mother! Didn't you see that stop sign?"

"I most certainly did! But I stopped twice back there for that silly squirrel. How many times do I have to stop in one block?"

I shook my head in bewilderment rather than answer her in the mood I was in, and tried to open my door. I pushed and pulled, but even though the truck had bounced back after the impact, I was unable to budge the door an inch.

"Get out, Mother."

"The manual clearly states that the driver should always remain in the car after an accident unless the vehicle is in immediate danger of another collision or fire," she pontificated.

"Get out of the bloody car, please."

"Really, Paisley, watch your language! I know you're under some stress. I don't like being involved in a traffic accident either, but..."

"Being involved? You caused the accident! And I can't open my door. Please let me out!"

"I cannot believe you wish to flout the rules by exiting the car before the authorities arrive."

"Mother!"

"Very well, then, if you insist on rebelling."

As she opened her door, she noticed for the first time the crowd that had gathered to watch our predicament.

"Oh, dear! Paisley, where is my handbag? Is my makeup on straight?"

By the time I finally got us out of the car, Andy Joiner and his deputy chief of police had arrived. They took one look at the mess of metal and chrome that had been Mother's pride and joy and promptly arrested all three Mexican laborers in the other vehicle.

"But, Andy," I argued heatedly, "the accident wasn't their fault."

"She's quite right for once," agreed Mother. "I was trying to avoid hitting one of God's smaller creatures, and I'm afraid I was too distracted to remember to stop at the corner."

"Sorry, Miz Sterling. But I have to take them in. There's not a valid driver's license between the three of them, and I'm almost positive what little documentation they do have is fake. Besides, one of them was drinking a beer. There's a law against drinking alcohol in this county."

"Then you'd better hurry on out to the Country Club. It's just about time for cocktails."

"Don't be cheeky, Paisley."

"It's true, Mother, and you know it. This whole town is in on the secret. I guess you only get arrested for drinking if you're too poor to hire one of the lawyers that gets drunk at the Rowan Springs Country Club every night."

"That's quite enough, dear," whispered Mother in my ear. "You're making a spectacle of yourself."

"Well, damnit! It's just not fair. Those poor guys probably haven't got a pot to pee in, and we come barreling along in your fancy car to ruin their day and maybe even get them deported."

I watched as Andy's deputy handcuffed the three men and pushed them roughly into the back seat of the police cruiser. The Mexicans weren't a pretty sight. They had obviously been working in the tobacco fields all day. Their clothes were sweat-stained and dirty, and they all were in need of a shave and a haircut. I thought I would see my outrage mirrored in their faces, but instead they seemed only weary and resigned to their fate, as though being hauled off to prison were not a new experience for them.

"Looks like we'd better call a tow truck for your car, Miz Sterling. I can drive you home when Jimmy returns with the cruiser, if you don't mind waitin'," offered Andy.

Under the gentle insistence of their Chief of Police, the crowd gradually dispersed. Once they were gone, and Mother no longer felt like she needed to put up a front, she sank gratefully into the backseat of her ruined car and closed her eyes.

"Mother, are you okay?" I asked in alarm. "You weren't hurt, were you?"

"No, dear. Only my pride is a bit wounded. You were quite right to chide me. It was my fault. I was driving carelessly. And now look at my beautiful car."

I knew better than to think she would cry outside the confines of her own bedroom, but this was as close to it as she would come. I slid in beside her.

"Never you mind," I said, patting her hand. "The car will be as good as new before you know it."

"Am I getting too old to drive, Paisley? Tell me the truth. Am I getting senile?"

"Senile? You?"

I started laughing. I guess it was the reaction setting in from the accident—hysteria perhaps—but I laughed until my sides were hurting, and my mother was about as mad as she ever gets. She looked at me with fire in her eyes and whipped out her makeup mirror. Once she was assured that every silver-white hair was neatly pulled back into the soft French twist and the makeup was perfect on her patrician features, she climbed out of the car and went into the drug store to call the town's only taxi. When it came, she left without even waving goodbye.

When Jimmy returned with the cruiser, he supervised the towing of the Lincoln so Andy could take me home.

"Sorry 'bout you havin' to ride in the back, but it's the law," Andy apologized. "Hope it doesn't smell too bad back there."

"It is a mite rank," I admitted. "Those men, how long will you keep them in jail?" I asked, trying not to breathe too deeply.

"I'll have to run a check on them. See if any of them have a sheet. And we'll have to look into those bogus-looking papers." He glanced at me in the rearview mirror. "Don't you worry about those guys, Paisley. I'll see they get a fair shake; but if they're here illegally I'll have to send them back. You know that, don't you?"

I sighed and lifted the hair off my forehead. I didn't have time to dry it before we left for town and now the auburn curls were tangled and messy. I had stuck a rubber band in my jeans pocket before we left the house. I pulled it out to make a pony tail and promptly dropped it in the seat.

"Damn!"

"What's that, Paisley?"

"Nothing, I just...never mind, I found it."

I pulled the hair off the back of my neck, vowing once again to have a haircut in the immediate future, and looked at the other object my searching fingers had encountered. It was a small, well-worn, silver medallion of the Virgin of Guadalupe—the patroness of Mexico. I knew then that somehow I would have to help those men. They were a long, long way from home and friendless. I knew what that was like. I, too, had once been a stranger in a strange land.

CHAPTER THREE

Mother wasn't home when Andy dropped me off. I decided to try and get back into her good graces by taking my Jeep and fetching the groceries myself. I walked down through the orchard to the carriage house, pausing on my way to examine the young buds on the peach and pear trees. From the looks of the abundant blossoms, we would have a bumper fruit crop by late summer. The plum trees were already in full bloom, and the honeybees were making merry on the first nectar of the season. I smiled. The orchard had been my grandfather's pride and joy. Every spring a little bit of him came back to life as each tree awakened and was reborn.

I could hear Aggie barking inside the house. If she recognized me, I couldn't tell. She wasn't the most astute watchdog in the world. I daydreamed for a moment about the new puppy I would get when Cassie took her away. Maybe a friendly, happy-go-lucky Lab, or a little Jack Russell with all the smarts Aggie was missing. Big or small, the new canine would have to be a lot easier to get along with. I was tired of being a pincushion.

Since Mother had taken possession of her new car, I hadn't driven my Jeep Cherokee very much. At least for the next couple of weeks I would get to be the chauffeur again. I opened the garage door and admired the big hunky fenders and the bilious green body. I loved Watson. Cassie had named him when I first came home with him two years ago. I thought at the time that we would be bouncing over hill and dale in search of evil-doers for my stories and have need of a four wheel drive. So far I had been disappointed. All the villains we had encountered were either city dwellers or hidden so deeply in the forest that they could only be tracked on foot.

The big engine started up on cue and hummed merrily as I backed out of the garage and circled the carriage house to make sure everything was in working order. The late afternoon sun was courting the western horizon, but it was still strong enough to make the air above the fields shimmer with heat. I looked up and noticed that the lone buzzard I had seen earlier was now in the company of almost a dozen of his predatory fellows. They were spiraling over the end of our farm just beyond the airport runway—right where I thought I had seen something fall from the airplane earlier.

"Hey, wha'cha' say, Watson! How about a little adventure?"

I barreled down the lane toward the field with little more thought about what I was doing than if I had a cabbage for a head. If I had ruminated a bit, I might have realized that my dog with no brains and I had more in common than I knew.

Billy, our farm manager, had cleaned out the lane last fall. The overgrowth of blackberry and honeysuckle had been cut back and pruned so that the snaking vines no longer grasped wickedly for arms and hair.

I cut across the field at the little pond, but not before seeing two turtles and several big bullfrogs jump for their lives into the cool depths. From a distance, the field looked smooth and even, a carpet of green velvet, but the ride was rough. I had a grand old time.

The circling buzzards created something of an optical illusion. The closer I got, the farther away they appeared. Seeds from the tops of the tall growth of fescue splattered across the windshield and gathered in little rivulets above the wiper blades. I made the mistake of trying to wash them away. Even Watson's mighty wipers couldn't clear off the mess of dried hulls and fine, chocolate-colored dust. I pulled up on the highest point in the middle of the field and rummaged around in the backseat hoping to find some glass cleaner and paper towels. What I found instead was a half-empty plastic bottle of Evian and three used paper napkins from the Dairy Queen.

I opened the car door and stepped gingerly down into the waist-high grass. Visions of copperheads and giant ticks with ghoulish appetites crossed my mind and encouraged me to hop up on the fender and crawl up on the hood.

I cleaned off the windshield as best I could and sat back on the top of the car. The squadron of buzzards was now off somewhat to my right. The fading light of the setting sun cast confusing shadows, and it was hard to tell if they were over the airport or still flying over the edge of our field. The tall grass danced and swayed to the whispering tune of the evening breeze and hid the perimeter fence from view. I finally gave up the search with a disappointed sigh and stood up to brush off my jeans.

The bullet whizzed past my shoulder like an angry hornet. I dropped like a rock and flattened my body on Watson's hood. I didn't hear a report, and for a moment I doubted my first impression that someone was trying to kill me. When a second bullet whizzed overhead, I slid off the hood and climbed back in the driver's seat as fast as I could. Out here in the middle of the field I was too good a target. I turned on the engine and headed toward the protection of the trees at flank speed.

I bounced madly up and down in the seat as I cut across the furrows, tasting the hot salty rush of blood as my head came up against the roof and I bit my tongue. I was well aware that if I lived to see the next day my nether parts would be black and blue.

By the time I reached the trees, darkness had fallen, and it was difficult to see the entrance to the lane. Turning on the headlights would make me a sitting duck. Instead, I slowed down and inched my way forward. I almost drove into the pond, but I saw the dark outline of flat, still water just in time.

I circled the narrow shore until I found what I was looking for. The dark tunnel of trees seemed overwhelmingly foreboding, but it was my best chance, unless someone was waiting inside. With some difficulty, I shut off my imagination and headed blindly for home.

The moon came up over the treetops as I drove up to the garage. The sprawling silhouette of the house was dark against the moonlit sky, and I knew Mother wasn't home yet. For a moment I considered heading straight into town and Andy Joiner's office. I wanted to tell him what had happened as soon as possible, but I was afraid to leave and have Mother arrive alone. I decided to park the car and go inside to call Andy.

Just as I ran across the driveway, two headlights appeared at the bottom of the hill. With a pounding heart, I threw myself behind a lilac bush and waited to see who was coming. When I heard the expensive hum of Horatio Raleigh's Bentley, I relaxed and crawled out from my hiding place.

"Paisley Sterling! What in the world are you doing? Don't you think you're a bit old to be playing cat and mouse in the dark?" asked Mother as her old friend helped her gallantly out of the car. It was obvious that she hadn't forgiven me for laughing at her earlier that afternoon.

Horatio, who was much more astute, divined immediately that something was amiss, and ushered us politely but quickly into the house.

"Anna, my dear," he said. "Our Paisley looks to be in need of a small libation, and perhaps some of that wonderful tomato bisque you prepared last night. If you have any left, that is?"

Mother was instantly contrite. "Oh, dear! Paisley, darling, are you all right?"

"Of course, Mother," I lied. "But I would like some soup."

"Bisque, dear. Tomato bisque. And you have a leaf in your hair."

"Yeah, soup. Hot. With crackers."

Horatio led the way into the library and turned on the small Chinese porcelain lamps on each of the sofa tables. I crossed over to the French doors, and after a cursory look at the empty backyard, pulled the new red-and-yellow-striped silk draperies over both doors.

"Someone chasing you again, my dear?" asked Horatio with a lift of one elegant eyebrow.

Horatio Raleigh had been a friend of our family for years. And while he had always been in love with my beautiful mother, he didn't make it known until after my father's death over a decade ago. Since then, he had been Anna Howard Sterling's constant and ever-admiring companion.

Horatio had retired from the family mortuary business years ago and only went into "the shop" when someone of importance died and the relatives needed to part with an extra ten grand for a "bereavement consultation." Horatio's taste was exquisite, expensive, and worth every penny.

I had consulted with him in the past because of his knowledge about more clandestine matters. It was rumored, and not without some basis, that he had held certain high positions in very hush-hush circles during the war. And although he never admitted to it, I was positive that he was still well-known in those august groups. I had always found his advice invaluable. I didn't hesitate to tell him what had happened the minute we sat down.

"Some asshole tried to kill me!"

Both eyebrows went up now. And the pipe came out. That was a sign that Horatio was in full attention mode even though he appeared to be distracted by preparing a smoke. He patted the pockets of his smart navy blazer to find his tobacco pouch and sterling silver tamper. Once he had all of his tools at hand, he started questioning me.

"Which, er, asshole, is this, Paisley, dear?"

"I have no idea," I answered, flopping back on the soft down cushions of the red chintz sofa. "But somebody took at pot shot at me. Twice!"

I slipped off my beloved old Cole-Haan moccasins and watched in dismay as grass seeds puddled on Mother's priceless Oriental carpet.

"Oh, well," I sighed. "I'll vacuum later."

Horatio chuckled and drew the first fragrant puff from his pipe.

"Just like a woman to worry about housekeeping even when her life is in jeopardy."

"Worried about Mother's wrath is more like it," I laughed.

"Well, it's good to see that you're not that upset about your adventure."

"I'm beginning to think I imagined it. Perhaps it was a hornet after all, or maybe a nest of yellow jackets. I was driving pretty fast. I could have stirred something up without even realizing it."

"Yellow jackets?" echoed Mother as she came into the room carrying a small tray with a steaming bowl and a plate of crackers. "No wonder you were upset. Were you stung, dear?"

I winked at Horatio and accepted the dinner tray from my mother. No use upsetting her by letting her in on what I thought had really happened.

"And when was this," she asked, "before, or after someone shot at you? By the way dear, try not to use vulgar terminology. It's so unladylike."

Horatio smiled and shook his head in amazement. I laughed and happily slurped Mother's divine bisque. She was right. Something so delicate and delicious couldn't be called simply "soup."

CHAPTER FOUR

Horatio and I sat up until after midnight discussing the possibility that some poor misguided soul had, as Leonard would say, the desire to take me out. Horatio found it very hard to believe that I had an enemy with a murderous bent, and I had to agree with him. Since I'd returned to Rowan Springs, I had kept a very low profile. Mother was the social butterfly. My social life consisted of going to the drive-through at the Dairy Queen, with perhaps an occasional visit to the library and grocery.

Mother was always trying to entice me to the country club, the First Baptist Church, or one of her bridge games. She raved about the chicken and almond salad at the Rose Tea Room and extolled the artistic virtues of belonging to the Creative Guild, but thus far, I had managed to avoid being drawn into any of the social activities of our fair city.

People in Rowan Springs ask first what your husband does for a living, then what church you attend. Since I have neither husband nor church, I am a pariah. The only standard "little southern town" question I can answer with some assurance of being held in any regard at all is, "What was your name before you married?" The fear of this serial interrogation alone was enough to keep me off the social merry-go-round. And while I hadn't bothered to make friends, I certainly hadn't put out the effort to make any enemies.

Around one-thirty in the morning, I walked Horatio to his car. Thanks to our rational conversation and his reassurances, my fear of assassination had vanished. I was even relaxed and comfortable enough to let Aggie have a run in the orchard after Horatio drove away.

There had been a full moon earlier in the evening, but it had gone to sleep behind the tall cedars on the faraway hills hours ago. The night sky was dark and full of clouds that were darker still. I heard the dry whisper of leathery wings as scores of bats fed on insects and returned to roost in the eaves of the outbuildings when they were replete.

I strolled beneath the spreading limbs of the fruit trees enjoying the coolness of the night breeze and the privacy the darkness afforded. Aggie ran back behind the raspberry patch and I lost sight of her. Rather than call out and break the magic of the moment, I followed.

A bright flash of lightening, followed by a loud clap of thunder took me completely by surprise. I yelped and Aggie barked. We both jumped about a foot. The first thunderous explosion was quickly succeeded by a second, and an even louder third. The night was suddenly filled with unfriendly fire and a barrage of hard-driving wind and rain that stung my unprotected face and quickly drenched my clothes.

Aggie didn't need any urging. She ran beside me through the orchard toward the house. By the time we crossed the driveway, hail the size of marbles was falling with bruising force against my shoulders and head. The backyard was already full of the icy little balls. As I ran across the patio, my feet slipped out from under me and I fell backwards. Stunned, I lay there until it ceased to hail with the same sudden abruptness and I could hear Mother's frightened voice calling frantically over the wind and rain. I got to my feet and staggered to the back porch where she was struggling to hold the screen door open for me. The wind billowed the skirt of her housecoat up around her knees and pulled tendrils of silver white hair from the sleek French twist.

"Paisley! Thank God! Are you all right?"

"I...I think so. My head hurts like hell. What in the world is going on?"

"Tornado warning!" she shouted over the increasing roar of the storm. "We'd better get inside quickly and take cover."

She grabbed my hand and led me through the kitchen. The house was in total darkness. All the comforting little lights that normally twinkled from the coffee maker, microwave, and refrigerator were gone, but Mother had a flashlight. I followed her quickly through the house to the utility closet under the stairs. She opened the door and pushed me unceremoniously inside.

We sat huddled together on the dusty floor like two terrified children while Mother Nature threw a fierce electric temper tantrum all around us. The old house creaked and shivered. The logs that formed the inner walls of the rooms in the front were more than a century and a half old. I was uncomfortably reminded of that fact as I felt them shift ever so slightly with the wind.

It was impossible to be heard over the fury of the storm, so we didn't even try to speak. Suddenly it went dead quiet. It was an unnatural and unhealthy silence. A sharp pain in my ears told me the atmospheric pressure had changed. Then we heard something strange. Not the roar of a freight train, but the splitting of trees as the tornado passed over us. I had heard that sound before. One winter when I was ten, I quite recklessly walked across the thin sheet of ice on the pond at the end of the lane. The ice had cracked beneath my feet with the same hollow sound as I hurried, breathless and strangely excited, to the other side.

There was no excitement now, only terror. Mother and I held hands tightly and stared up at the cobwebbed underside of the staircase. Dust sifted through the cracks and floated like a cloud in the beam of the flashlight as the floor swayed and creaked loudly above us.

"Oh, my God," breathed Mother, prayerfully.

"Amen," I whispered.

There was a great rustling sound, like a mighty sigh, and as quickly as it had begun it was all over. The dust continued to fall, but the house was still and at rest once again. Mother dropped the flashlight and covered her face with her hands. For a brief moment I thought she was going to cry, but she straightened up and gave me a slightly crooked little smile.

"Wow!"

"You can say that again," I laughed hoarsely. "You okay, Mother?"

"I think so, but we need to get you some dry clothes. You must be freezing."

I sneezed right on cue, then got to my feet and helped her up. We had to bend over to avoid bumping our heads on the stairs. That's when I noticed that Aggie wasn't in the closet with us.

"Mother! Where's the dog?"

"Why, I don't know. Wasn't she with you?"

"Damn! What if she didn't come back in the house?"

Mother didn't even correct my vulgar language in her distress.

"Oh, my goodness. I'm almost positive she did. Poor little thing! She must be terrified. We have to find her quickly."

We found two more flashlights in the kitchen and some extra batteries when the original ones died. For two hours we searched every room in the dark house. We looked under all the beds and in the closets. Mother suggested that Aggie was so frightened she might not come when we called. I reminded her that Aggie never came when she was called.

"Oh, Paisley, don't speak ill of the sweet little thing. Have you thought of what you're going to tell Cassandra when you pick her up at the airport tomorrow without her puppy?"

"Rats! I forgot about having to pick up Cassie. I have to get some sleep or I'll never make it."

But I couldn't.

I lay in the bed with my eyes closed while the sound of splitting trees played over and over again in my memory. Occasionally I heard the fire siren going off in town, but there was no sound of cars on the road. The electricity was still out, and I found that very disconcerting. There is a big difference between going to bed in the dark and going to bed in a house where there is no light. I was musing over the possibilities of a world where the lights never come back on when I finally dozed off. I slept soundly for a full twenty minutes until the alarm sounded.

"Damn and drat!"

I hated not getting enough sleep. My stomach felt queasy and my head ached. I stumbled to the bathroom and stared into the mirror at the exhausted green eyes and freckles that stood out boldly on my pale face. I splashed on some cold water and sighed into the towel as I dried my chin and looked out the window.

"Holy cow!"

I couldn't believe my eyes. For a moment I considered the possibility that I was still asleep and having a nightmare. I discounted that when a sharp pain sliced behind my eyelids and throbbed in my temple. I was awake all right, and looking out at the ruin of what was once the most beautiful place on earth—at least to me.

Hot tears flooded my eyes as I stared unbelievingly at the huge maple that had provided summer shade for generations of Sterlings. It had been torn out by the roots and cast down across the patio. The hole it left in the raw earth was easily ten feet across and four feet deep. Maple leaves embraced the lawn almost across the whole width of the backyard, yet the tree had miraculously missed falling on the back porch. I wondered sadly if a small furry body lay smashed beneath its limbs.

I ran back to my bedroom and knelt on the window seat. The oak trees in the front yard hadn't fared much better. One lay across the driveway and the others were missing the top half of their limbs. It looked like a giant scythe had whacked them off about twenty feet above the ground.

I shrugged into my jeans and a sweatshirt and slipped on my Cole-Haans even though they were still damp from the night before. I steeled myself as I opened the French doors in the library and stepped outside.

The sky was clean, freshly washed, and a brilliant blue. Fluffy white clouds preened in front of a golden sun. It was a beautiful day. The ground was still soaked from the rain. I felt it sink through my jeans as I fell to my knees when I saw the devastation the storm had wreaked on my grandfather's orchard.

Limbs were everywhere. Peach, plum, and apple trees were scattered about like pick-up sticks. Everything was destroyed except for one lone sapling—the little cherry tree we planted last summer. I wept.

When I was spent, I pulled myself up and climbed over limbs and tree trunks to the other side of the house. My moonlight garden: the white roses, my gardenias and paper whites, even the tiny lilies of the valley were crushed by storm debris. Incongruously, in the middle of the garden stood the glass reflecting ball without a scratch to mar its shiny silver surface.

I climbed over scattered limbs searching for Aggie, knowing that if I found her it would be too late. If she had been anywhere in the yard during the storm, she was a goner. Somehow the falling trees had missed the house, but there wasn't a square foot of lawn that was not covered by debris. Aggie wouldn't have been able to run fast enough to escape. Poor little puppy. I cried again when I imagined the terror and helplessness she must have felt. And I was miserably sorry that yesterday I had been happy thinking I would soon be rid of her. Now, I would miss her always.

I slipped and skinned my hands and knees as I climbed over limbs and tree trunks. I was cursing like a sailor before I made it back to the driveway. I kicked aside the cans and plastic bags from someone else's garbage that had flown through the air and landed in our yard and made my way down to the carriage house.

I held my breath and said a small prayer as I rounded the corner and looked inside. Watson was unscathed, but the back of the roof over the garage had caved in underneath the weight of a huge broken limb from a walnut tree. There was no way I could get the Jeep out without some help. The limb was as big around as twice my waist. It didn't even budge when I tried to move it.

"Well, damn and double damn. This is a fine kettle of fish!" I swore, wiping the sweat from my upper lip with a skinned knuckle.

"Indeed it is," answered Mother as she picked her way around the stump of the walnut tree and came up behind me.

"Mother! You scared me half to death! What are you doing out here?"

"The same thing you are, I imagine. Crying a bit, and wondering how long it will take us to clean up and get everything back to normal."

She looked calm and collected in her neatly pressed Ralph Lauren chambray shirt and navy slacks. Not a silver hair was out of place. It made me furious.

"And Cassie?" I snapped. "Just how am I going to pick up Cassie?"

"I called the Nashville airport and left a message at the Delta information desk," she responded calmly. "I also reserved a rental car for her. She is perfectly capable of driving herself home—and I need a rental car until mine is out of the shop. It all works out perfectly."

"Yeah, just hunky dory," I muttered sinking down on the walnut limb. I stared morosely at the tall pole of the martin house that my father had built. It leaned at a drunken forty-five degree angle, spilling bits of straw from each tiny doorway.

"What a mess!"

"I quite agree, darling, but it could be worse. Horatio called me from his, er, office. At least six people didn't make it through last night."

"You're kidding?"

"Well, dear, look around you," she said pointing at the swath the tornado had cut through the orchard. "We were really quite fortunate. Imagine if the path of the tornado had taken it a few feet in another direction. Our house would be mixed up in all this mess, and you and I might be in heaven's equivalent of Kansas."

"Yeah, I guess you're right. Wow, six people. Do we know anyone who was killed?"

"I don't think so, dear. At least Horatio didn't think so. Or he may have been protecting me until he could tell me in person."

"Great!" I grumbled, "Something else to look forward to,"

CHAPTER FIVE

Mother finally convinced me there was nothing more we could do until we got some help. She had already called Billy to make sure his family was all right and to enlist his aid in procuring some heavy equipment to move the fallen trees. Until the driveway was cleared and the walnut tree was lifted off the garage, we were trapped. The very thought made me crazy to get away, even though Cassie was coming home on her own and I really had nowhere to go.

Somewhere deep inside, my rational self recognized that my impatience and irritability were aftereffects of the storm, but that didn't keep me from behaving like a spoiled brat all afternoon.

Mother went to a great deal of trouble to make lunch for us in a kitchen with no electricity. She dragged the gas grill out of the corner and prepared shrimp kebabs with pineapple chicken and coconut rice.

"Why in the world did you fix all this food?" I asked petulantly. "It was just a tornado, not the end of the world."

She smiled pleasantly at me over the lovely table she had set in the corner of the back porch. The sunlight painted rainbows on the heavy white damask tablecloth as it passed through the stems of delicate Waterford goblets. Her best silver cutlery gleamed next to the finest Wedgwood porcelain. I stared at the plump, perfectly grilled shrimp on my beautiful plate and burst into tears.

Thoroughly ashamed and undone, I hung my head until my chin almost touched my chest and whispered an apology.

"I'm sorry, Mother. I don't know what's wrong with me."

"You should. You've been through this before," she said matter-of-factly.

"What do you mean?"

"Post-traumatic stress—from your experiences in San Romero."

"Don't be silly," I hooted. "There's a big difference between rescuing your daughter from a bloodthirsty mob and spending a night under the stairs because of a little storm."

"Not such a little storm," answered Horatio as he climbed over a limb and opened the screen door.

He walked around behind my mother's chair and gently kissed her behind the ear. She closed her eyes and clasped his hands. Tiny lines of stress eased around her mouth and eyelids as she smiled. She sat back in her chair, and I realized for the first time what an effort it had been for her to remain calm and collected. This meal, the elegant place settings, and the elaborate food had been her attempt to exert some control over the chaos that nature had created. I felt even more embarrassed by my childish behavior.

"Please sit down, Horatio," I said. "I'll get another place setting. You sit in my chair and eat while everything is still hot."

I hopped up and urged him into the chair against his protests. His arguments were feeble, and I could tell he was nearly exhausted.

"How about a glass of champagne, Mother? Don't you think it would be the perfect touch?"

"Absolutely, Paisley, darling! That's the spirit!"

Horatio thought of our toast, "Here's to high winds and higher hearts!" but he took no more than a token sip of bubbly.

"Sorry, m'dears, but I have to get back to the shop. The highway patrol called shortly before I left for lunch. Another casualty of the storm, I'm afraid. A pilot radioed that he spotted a body just past the end of the runway as he was taking off."

"You're kidding! That must have been the reason for the buzzards."

"I suppose you're right, Paisley," he said, raising his eyebrows in surprise. "I cannot believe I didn't make the connection myself." Horatio covered Mother's hand with his. "Anna, you might have to trade me in on a new model. I seem to be getting somewhat dull of wit."

"Nonsense, Horatio," protested Mother. "Nevertheless, we must all husband our energies during the next few days. We still have a long way to go to reach normalcy again. My friends report more damage to Rowan Springs than I ever imagined. Is it true, Horatio?"

"I'm afraid so, my dear. The high school gymnasium is destroyed. And part of the roof of the adjacent classroom building is at present in the middle of the football field. The courthouse is virtually the only building downtown without any damage. Oh, and Celestine's building. Of course, she has had to close down like everyone else until the electricity is restored, but she was the luckiest one on Main Street. The sporting goods store on the corner is a total loss. And from what I hear, Bruce Hawkins is about the only one on Main Street who had enough insurance to cover his losses."

Hawkins was Mother's lawyer. Several years ago, he remodeled the old Capitol Theater and made his offices an homage to movies of the forties and fifties. He actually had old movie posters and publicity stills with autographs of the stars. I was really glad none of his treasures had come to harm, but the thought of all the damage Horatio had described made me tear up again.

"Paisley, are you all right, dear?"

"Of course, Mother." I got up and fussed with the food still warming on the grill to hide my emotions. "More shrimp, Horatio? There's plenty left."

"Thank you, but no. Miles to go before I sleep and all that, you know. Thanks for the luncheon, Anna. It was exquisite as always. And just the perfect touch." He winked broadly. "You always rise to the occasion." Horatio gallantly touched the back of Mother's extended hand with his lips and headed for the back door. "Call me if you need me, my dears. And please let me know when our Cassandra arrives. I cannot wait to see her."

I watched the old man pick his way through the fallen limbs. He was almost twice my age, but he was still strong and agile. As I turned back around to help Mother clear the table, I felt my heart flip-flop in a hollow chest. Suddenly all the air was gone from my lungs and my vision was full of sparkling black dots. I grabbed one of the center posts of the porch and fought for a clear head. Mother's voice echoed in my ears making no sense whatsoever for a full minute.

"...might need some help. What do you think, dear?"

"Oh, er, sure. Whatever, Mother," I answered, hoping that would be sufficient for the moment. Eager to cover up my near lapse of consciousness, I grabbed the plates and silverware and headed for the kitchen. She followed, prattling on, and thankfully giving me more clues as to what I had agreed to do.

"We can start by visiting Miss Lolly and her sister. They seem to be quite self-sufficient and very capable of taking care of each other in a crisis, but they are getting on in years."

"That's an understatement if I ever heard one," I snorted. My head had cleared and I was beginning to feel like my old nasty self again. "Miss Lolly is eighty if she's a day, and her sister is older than that."

Mother ignored me. "Some nice cream of potato soup and homemade corn muffins would be nice, I think."

"And just how are we going to accomplish that little culinary miracle without any electricity?"

"You were a Girl Scout, dear. There are ways."

I grumbled and mumbled as I washed and dried her china and silver. The last thing I wanted to do was play Lady Bountiful to a bunch of Mother's crotchety little old lady friends. I had too many other things to worry about.

29

A precious porcelain cup almost slipped out of my hands as my heart lurched and fluttered wildly against my ribs once again. I leaned against the sink and held on for dear life. This time I was frightened out of my wits.

"Cassie's here, darling!"

I wiped the cold sweat from my brow with the dishtowel, then threw it towards the sink as I hurried to the back door. If I were having a heart attack, I wanted my daughter's sweet face to be the last thing I saw.

Cassie was standing up on one of the bigger limbs looking around at the storm damage. In spite of the warm weather, she wore her dark hair down. It hung straight and shining past her shoulders. And somehow between final exams she had found the time to get a really terrific tan. Her slim arms and long legs were the color of cinnamon. She looked like a million dollars in khaki Bermuda shorts and a simple white cotton tee shirt.

"Oh, dear," murmured Mother. "I hope she didn't travel like that."

"Mother, please don't start!"

"But Paisley, someone has to tell her," she whispered. "You obviously don't care, but, thank heaven, some of us still have standards."

"Oh, for Pete's sake!" I hissed.

"What are you two fighting about?" called Cassie, gaily. "I should think you'd be so happy to be alive after all this you'd cut out that silly crap."

She jumped off the limb and picked up a dilapidated old backpack that had definitely seen better days. One strap was hanging loose, and the zipper was half open, allowing her clothes, including several pieces of lacy underwear, to peek out unashamedly.

Mother opened her mouth again, but I flew out the back door and down the walk before she could utter another critical remark.

I hugged my beautiful daughter as hard as she would let me. Her hair smelled like fresh flowers and her skin really did have the scent of cinnamon.

"Wow, honey! You look gorgeous," I said with a happy smile.

"That's not what Gran thinks? That's what you all were arguing about, isn't it?"

She untangled herself from my arms and picked up an even rattier leather bag that was old enough to vote when we escaped from San Romero with her dolls packed inside.

"Never mind," she sighed when I didn't answer. "I know. And honestly, I'll try to be patient with her this summer; but you gotta understand, in some circles I am considered quite a terrific looking broad."

"Darling, she thinks so, too. It's just that she believes you should dress more conservatively when you travel. And she doesn't like old, well...old beat-up things. Didn't she send you some new luggage?"

A look of distaste distorted Cassie's perfect features for a moment.

"Yuck! Burgundy tapestry with big, ugly, green leaves! I sent it right back to Macy's and told them to credit her account."

"Cassie, that's rude!"

"Don't you start, Mom! And it's no more rude than having the impertinence to pick out something as personal as luggage and force it on me under the guise of a gift."

I smiled. At least I was familiar with the way this wind blew. Cassie and her grandmother had been fighting the same old battle since she was old enough to talk.

Cassie had to park the rental car down on the road because of the fallen tree across the driveway. I helped her unload her things and carry them up the hill without giving any thought to the effort it took. It wasn't until we had finished and were sprawled out on the back porch enjoying some iced tea that I remembered I was supposedly having a heart attack. I was hot and sweaty, but the old ticker was beating with a calm regularity beneath my breast.

"You're really good for what ails me, sweetie," I grinned.

Cassie looked at me with quick concern.

"What's wrong, Mom? You're not sick are you?"

I knew better than to alarm her. It had taken quite a few therapy sessions before she had overcome the fear of losing her remaining parent the way she had lost her father. I was sure that fear was still there, not far beneath the surface.

"No, of course not, darling. Slightly shaken, only. The tornado threw me a bit, that's all. We were really lucky. It could have been a lot worse."

"Absolutely! And that's what scared you half to death. You realized how random the world is—that really bad things can happen without any rhyme or reason—and you have no control whatsoever."

I sat up closer to the edge of my chair and leaned towards her.

"Then why didn't Gran react the way I did? Why isn't she having aftershocks like me?"

"Are you kidding," laughed my daughter. "Gran would never admit that she doesn't have absolute control over everything all the time. I'm sure she thinks she either prayed or willed away the storm and saved the day."

I lay back in the chaise and took a long sip of tea. What Cassie said made sense. In San Romero we had been in great physical danger, but there was something we could do to save ourselves. I had been too

31

busy saving our hides to worry about anything.

"I was scared, too," admitted Cassie in a quiet little girl's voice. "I heard about it on the radio this morning. When they said six people were killed...."

I hopped up immediately and hugged my child. My fears were silly next to the memory of her childhood terror.

CHAPTER SIX

It didn't occur to Cassie that Aggie was *in absentia* until that night before we went to bed.

"When can we pick puppy up from the kennel?"

"Uh, we need to talk about that, pumpkin, but let's wait until tomorrow morning after breakfast," I added hopefully.

"Okay, Mom. Come clean. What's going on? What did Aggie tear up? I'm sure she was terrified during the storm. Did she ruin one of Gran's holier than holy, more precious than gold, oriental carpets?"

I was helping Cassie unpack. I sat down on the edge of her bed with an armful of tee shirts.

"You still have my old tee from Elton's concert?" I asked, admiring Versace's beautifully intricate silk-screened design of the shirt on top of the stack.

"Don't change the subject, Mom. How much crow am I going to have to eat to get Aggie back in Gran's good graces? I really missed that silly puppy. And I know she'll go crazy when she sees me. It's been over six months."

"Cassie, she disappeared during the storm," I said quietly.

"Oh, yeah, just like Toto! And Gran thought I would buy that?" she laughed. "You all will have to do better than that."

"It's true, honey. We were outside taking a walk. I didn't even know a storm was coming until it was practically on top of us. I was running back to the house when I slipped and fell on the patio. I guess it knocked the stuffing out of me because things got kind of fuzzy after that. Your grandmother grabbed me and took me to the closet under the stairs. We both thought Aggie was with us. We didn't notice she was missing until the tornado had passed," I finished miserably.

Cassie stared at me for a long moment until the truth of what I was saying sank in.

"Oh," she whispered. Huge tears slid down her cheeks and made big wet splotches on the front of her nightgown. "Oh."

"I'm so sorry, Cassie. Your grandmother...."

"Don't tell me Gran is soooo sorry, too," she crooned sarcastically through her tears. "You and I both know she hated Aggie from the minute we brought her home!"

"That's not fair, Cass. Your grandmother was more than patient with Aggie, and you, too. You never trained her properly, you know."

"That's right! Turn it around on me! You lose my wonderful little dog, and it's all my fault!"

She slammed her closet door shut and grabbed the shirts from me.

"I'm suddenly very tired, and I want to go to bed. I can finish unpacking by myself. I know how to take care of my things and it's obvious that you don't."

"Cassie, please, you're being unreasonable," I pleaded.

"Unreasonable? Is it so unreasonable to expect your own mother to take care of the most important thing in your life? I trusted you!" she cried. "She was just a tiny little puppy. So helpless and innocent!"

"Innocent as a viper!"

"That's right! Vilify her, now that she's gone!" snarled Cassie.

"Hell! I vilified her when she was here and peeing on the carpet, but I never mistreated her. Even when she was using me for a chew stick."

"She only snapped at you a couple of times."

"Cassandra, your precious little canine sent me to the doctor twice. Do you know just how foolish I felt when I had to admit my own dog bit me?"

"Well, you'll never have to do that again, will you? You should be ecstatic!"

She was sobbing for real now, her face crumpled in misery. I stood up and made a move to approach her, but she ran into her bathroom and locked the door. I knew from long experience that we were done for the night, maybe even for the next few days. Cassie had grown up a lot, but she could really hold a grudge when she was mad enough.

I trudged off to my bedroom, shaking my head and wondering how things went so wrong so quickly. Tonight should have been a relieved and happy one for us. Instead, I felt a leaden sadness that weighed down my limbs and pulled at my lower lip.

What I missed the most when Cassie was gone were the late night chats full of giggles and grins that lasted sometimes until dawn. I had thought tonight would be one of those happy times when we would laugh and share the joys and misfortunes of what had taken place when we were apart. I certainly hadn't anticipated this turn of events.

I looked forlornly in the mirror while I brushed my teeth. The reflection of the silly woman who had so mismanaged a delicate situation with her hurt and disappointed child stared back at me.

"You old fool!" I snapped angrily.

By the time I put on my pajamas and crawled into bed, I was mad at Cassie again. After all, she was a grown woman. She shouldn't have placed the blame for Aggie's demise solely on my shoulders. But then, I thought, that's exactly where it did belong. I was responsible. I had taken the dog outside. I should have exercised more caution with the poor creature.

I cried myself to sleep.

I slept late the next morning. By the time I got up, Cassie was already gone, leaving us stranded once again. It was Mother's turn to be angry.

"It certainly appears as though your daughter hasn't learned anything about consideration in the last four years. I rented that car for myself. Didn't you tell her that it wasn't hers to take?"

"So it's my fault, now?" I asked, echoing Cassie's question of the night before. She had to have learned to fight somewhere. Why not at her mother's knee? The absurdity of it all made me laugh. I laughed until tears filled my eyes and the image of my absolutely enraged mother blurred as she slammed down her linen napkin and left the kitchen in a huff.

Feeling better, I dressed quickly and hurried outside. Billy was supposed to bring a small front-loader and two men with chain saws out to help us. I wanted to help them.

I turned out to be as useful as a pyramid roofer. Billy showed up right on time, but the front-loader didn't come lumbering down the road for another hour. When it finally pulled up out front, the driver gave us the bad news. Things were so awful all over town that he could only spare the time to move the trees out of the driveway. All the rest would have to wait until other more pressing emergencies were taken care of. In five minutes flat, the big oak was hoisted up and away. The driver gave a cheery wave and departed.

Since there was little else he could do at the moment, Billy made a survey of the damage to the house. He noticed more than a few shingles missing from the roof and a precarious loose brick or two on the older chimneys.

"I can take care of that myself, Paisley—this week if the weather holds. But all the rest..." He looked sadly at the panorama of limbs and debris piled about. "You're going to have to wait until I can find some men who have the time to come and cut these trees and carry all this mess away. Every man jack around town is busier than a bucket of red ants right now. There's hardly a house in the county without some kind'a damage."

"Mother isn't going to like that. She's already crazy to get things

35

cleaned up."

"Take her away somewhere for a month or two. Maybe I'll have things shipshape by then. Why don't you all go see Cassie in Atlanta—there's a good idea," he added hopefully.

"Sorry to burst your bubble, Billy, but Cassie came home yesterday afternoon. Anyhow, there's no way Mother will ever leave things looking like this. She doesn't care how bad things are anywhere else. This storm was a personal affront to her sense of order and neatness."

I sent Billy away after extracting his promise to return later in the week with mortar and shingles to repair the roof and chimneys before it rained again. He admitted that he was too chicken to talk to Mother, so I broke the bad news myself.

"Two months! I simply won't stand for it! Surely there is another way. Why can't we hire some men from...."

"Look, Mother, Billy has already thought of more possibilities than you or I ever could. You'll just have to exercise some patience for once and wait your turn. Just think of it this way, we're lucky we can wait."

"Well," she agreed reluctantly, "I am grateful we have a roof over our heads—and, oh, I forgot to tell you! Our electricity came back on a few minutes ago. Now we can finish the food baskets. The driveway was cleared just in the nick of time!" she declared with a smile. "My, isn't it nice that everything worked out so well?"

She turned on her heels and headed for the kitchen. She had apparently dismissed the storm-ravaged yard from her mind. I stared at her retreating back and wondered how much time would pass before she placed the first phone call to Billy, nagging him to hurry things up.

That's when I remembered that Watson was still trapped in the garage.

"Damn!"

I had to lean against the corner of the house to keep from falling when the bottom fell out of my chest. My heart fluttered like the wings of a butterfly as I tried to get my breath. I sat down hard in the grass and bent over from the waist until my vision cleared. It was a moment or two before I could inhale freely once again. I had to get the Jeep out! Like it or not, a visit to the medicine man was in order.

CHAPTER SEVEN

Cassie returned some time around four. By then, Mother had several Thermos bottles full of hot cream of potato soup and my picnic basket full of homemade cornmeal muffins ready to go. I didn't have the heart to turn her down when she asked me to drive her to the homes of her elderly friends. Some of them still had no electricity, and it was almost dinnertime.

Cassie went straight to her room without speaking to either of us. I figured she had at least one more day of silence in her, maybe two. I carried the goodies to the rental car and put them in the trunk. When I climbed into the driver's seat I noticed some papers tucked under the front seat. I pulled one out and read it with amusement bordering on fury.

Cassie had been busy. She had printed up some flyers offering a reward of far too much filthy lucre for her lost puppy. Aggie was described as "loving and sweet, with a friendly disposition." She had even managed to find a photograph of the dog that seemed to meet that erroneous description.

I wondered vaguely if tornado insurance would cover "lost dog rewards." Maybe Cassie had five hundred big ones to throw around like that, but I certainly didn't.

My daughter had also used up all the gas in the rental car. I grumbled about her lack of consideration all the way to the filling station. As usual, Mother defended her actions even though she herself had fussed about Cassie's lack of thoughtfulness earlier. It was going to be a long afternoon.

It was even worse than I imagined. Every street we turned down was full of fallen trees. Crews were busy clearing the main street from the highway into town, but it was obvious it would be a while before they got to the side streets. We had to walk to almost every house on Mother's list. By the time we were down to the last Thermos, we were both pooped.

"Looks like Miss Lolly's street isn't too bad," I observed gratefully. "With a little maneuvering, I can drive you right to her front door."

"Thank goodness! I was wondering where I was going to hide you. Now you can wait in the car. You don't mind, do you, dear?"

"I'm getting pretty damn tired of paying for childhood sins at this late date," I admitted with a sneer.

"Spray painting her cat was more than a simple peccadillo, Paisley. And you know how old people are. They remember more of the past than the present. In Miss Lolly's mind, the incident with her cat happened just yesterday and not over thirty years ago."

"Well," I sighed, "I don't like her either. She smells like stale talcum powder and her hair looks like a used Brillo pad. You need any help with the basket?"

I parked the car in the driveway under the spreading limbs of a big oak tree that had been spared by the storm. The Parsons sisters had lived in this big old house all of their lives. Their papa built the house with the spoils of his thriving lumberyard back at the turn of the century. For years it was the largest, most beautiful house in Lakeland County. When Papa Parsons passed away, the house started to die, too. It was rumored that the sisters were difficult to please, and painters, roofers, and yardmen often failed to answer their calls for help. Gradually, the green expanse of lawn died while moss grew in thick green patches on the roof. The white paint on the intricate gingerbread trim began to peel and flake off. The grass that no longer flourished in the front yard poked up healthy and vigorous between gaping cracks in the driveway. In short, the Parsons Mansion had turned into a big decaying grey elephant that nothing short of a deep pocketful of money and lots of love could revive. The sisters might still have the money, but they were both dried up little spinsters and definitely bankrupt in the love department.

Mother's head and torso vanished behind the green leaves of the big oak as she climbed the steps to the front door. I lay back in the seat and watched her feet as I idly eavesdropped on her conversation.

"Hello, Miss Lolly," Mother greeted the old woman brightly. "How did you and Miss Hannah weather the storm?"

"Hummpf!"

Never at a loss for words, Mother continued, "Looks like your street was lucky. Not too much damage here."

"I suppose," the old woman admitted reluctantly. Her voice was high and thin and full of decades of sour disapproval.

"I brought you all some hot soup and corn muffins." Mother waited politely for a response, and getting none, pressed on. "I hope Miss Hannah is well?"

Suddenly Lolly Parsons turned on her talking machine.

"Yes, yes, but of course she's fine. Fit as a fiddle she is! Why do you ask?" she inquired suspiciously.

"Why, er, the storm," stammered Mother. "It sometimes puts people out of sorts. Even Paisley was..."

"Paisley Sterling! That young rascal! Is she with you!"

"She's, ah, waiting in the car," admitted Mother reluctantly.

"Well, she'd better not put a foot on my lawn! That's all I have to say! You and John really failed to do your duty with that child. Spare the rod and spoil the child. Your Paisley is a perfect example of that."

"Miss Lolly, I'll have you know that Paisley is quite a successful novelist!"

"Not in my book! Did she help you make these corn muffins?"

"Well, no."

"The soup?"

"She peeled the potatoes."

"Keep it!"

A dry, withered, old arm snaked out the door, grabbed the picnic basket off the stoop, and quickly pulled it into the house. I heard the front door slam, and saw Mother's right foot stomp once with vexation. By the time she got to the car, I was laughing out loud.

"Stop it, Paisley!" she ordered as she blotted her damp upper lip with a dainty linen handkerchief. "My, it's gotten hot!"

"You just got a mite agitated, that's all. By the way Mother, thanks for the 'successful novelist' bit."

"Why in the world did you ever have to mess with that old hag's cat?" she asked crossly as she checked her makeup in the mirror.

"Because it was there!" I answered with an evil grin.

We decided to take the leftover Thermos of soup to Andy Joiner. Mother was quite fond of our Chief of Police, and I knew he would be working overtime because of the storm. His wife, Connie, had probably sent him lunch, but it was already dinnertime.

This time, I left Mother resting in the car while I ran into the police station. It was absolute bedlam—with phones ringing off the hook and people scurrying in every direction shouting clipped orders to each other.

I hugged the Thermos to my chest and backed into a corner out of the way, searching until I finally spotted Andy standing in the middle of a group of firemen and policemen. They were crowded in front of a large wall map of Lakeland County. Andy was obviously giving out work assignments. I knew he wouldn't welcome an interruption now if I were bearing champagne and lobster tails.

I turned to leave and ran smack dab into Horatio Raleigh, knocking a large brown envelope out of his hand. We both stared down at the floor where glossy photographs of an obviously very dead gentleman were scattered.

"Oh, my!" stated Horatio.

I bent down hurriedly and picked up the pictures before Horatio could get to them. "My indeed," I observed wryly. "Since when does a tornado victim have his throat slit from ear to ear?"

"Please, Paisley! Keep your voice down."

I put my head closer to his but didn't soften my voice.

"Relax. There's so much going on in here nobody would notice if we both stood here stark naked."

Horatio raised an elegant eyebrow and looked around the room.

"I suppose you're right, my dear," he laughed.

"And Andy doesn't have time right now for anything. Why don't you come out in the car and share these photos with ghoulish little old me. You know how I love tidbits like this for my books."

"I shouldn't," he protested. "This is strictly a matter for the police."

"You look tired, Horatio. How does some of Mother's delicious cream of potato soup sound to you?"

CHAPTER EIGHT

Mother sat with Horatio on the concrete bench in front of the courthouse while he enjoyed her superlative soup and she enjoyed watching the passers-by. It was the cool of the evening—that lovely time in a summer's day just before nightfall, when the breeze picks up and the first stars begin to twinkle above a golden sunset.

Mother wasn't the only one glad to be out and about. Lots of folks had been unable to leave their homes after the storm. Now with some trees cleared from streets and driveways, they were free to stroll around town and exchange their storm experiences with friends and neighbors.

I had lingered for a moment by Mother's side and chatted with Horatio before I crossed the street again and climbed into the car to examine the photographs of the dead man who had been found on our farm.

Horatio hadn't given me permission, but he had deliberately left the envelope in the front seat of the car when he helped Mother out. I slipped the pictures from the envelope and held my breath when I saw the full horror of the gaping wounds. I thanked my lucky stars that I hadn't eaten any of Mother's soup as I choked back the sour taste in my mouth. The photographs were in living color, and Horatio had made certain from every angle that not a single gruesome detail was left out.

The dead man appeared to be a foreigner, although it was difficult to tell. His facial features were distorted, flattened almost. He had dark hair and eyes and a thin mustache over full lips. He could have been Asian, or Hispanic, or anything in between. It was hard to imagine what he had looked like when he was alive. What was easy to deduce was the cause of death. He couldn't have lived very long with his throat cut wide enough to expose his cervical vertebra.

I didn't know much about forensic science, but as I flipped from one picture to another in the waning light it seemed to me that the dead man was oddly deformed. His joints were hyperextended and his limbs—even his feet—were at odd angles.

I banged my head painfully on the steering wheel when Horatio startled me by opening the car door.

"Ouch! You scared me."

"Sorry, my dear," he said as he slipped in beside me.

"Where's Mother?"

"Mavis Madden."

"Oh."

Mavis was an erstwhile friend of Mother's who talked a mile a minute about absolutely nothing but everybody else's business. Mother tolerated her out of good manners and as an investment against becoming a target for her considerable venom.

"I'm afraid we should stem your morbid appetite, my dear," Horatio observed. "A pretty young woman like you should...."

"Thanks for the 'pretty' and the 'young,' Horatio, but I'm a mystery writer. I need to keep things authentic. For some time now I've been meaning to ask you to let me view some of your, ah, clients, especially ones who have come to a violent end. Leonard's always coming across dead bodies and sometimes I'm at a loss to describe them."

"Oh, dear, why couldn't you have found your muse in pastoral verse? That's such a lovely occupation for a Southern lady."

"For God's sake, Horatio! You don't really mean that, do you?"

Even in the deepening twilight I caught a glimpse of the amused twinkle in his eyes. We both shared a companionable chuckle as he tucked the photographs of the dead man back in the envelope.

"By the way, what was wrong with his arms and legs? Did he have some kind of congenital defect?"

"Velocity and gravity, my dear," answered Horatio dryly.

"What?"

"I think this unlucky gentleman was the object you saw falling from that airplane the other afternoon."

Horatio bade us "goodnight," and went to make another attempt to see Andy Joiner. I was more than ready to head for home, but Mother reminded me that we had never made our trip to the grocery. I mumbled and grumbled as I lobbied against it, but she won. We tore her long grocery list in half and each set off with a basket to fill. Ordinarily, I loved going to the grocery. There was something so wonderfully American about the bright and shiny display of good food in such abundance. In San Romero, even those who could afford the vastly inflated prices for imported, or even domestic foods, suffered the seasonal shortages of the most basic items. My friends and I had often complained that we were reduced to the level of primitive man. We were the Cro-Magnon females, the hunter-gatherers for the tribe, running from store to store in search of toilet paper and mayonnaise.

The colorful packages and attractive displays held no interest for me tonight. I was bone tired. I rounded the aisle of the bread section where a slovenly woman with three dirty-faced children blocked my way. I stood aside and waited while they manhandled every package of Twinkies and sweet rolls on the shelf. When the woman started moving again, I tried to go around her, but she stopped in front of the honey buns.

I wanted desperately to tell her that three kids hopped up on sugar would be the last thing I would want in a storm-damaged house without electricity, but I bit my tongue.

The woman didn't appear to be in any hurry, and I knew Mother would be waiting, so I left my cart and walked around her and the kids to get to the bread.

"My! Someone's impatient, ain't they?"

"I din't do nuttin, Mama," whined the older one of the children.

"I don't mean you, honey," said the woman pointing a finger at me. "I meant HER!"

"Excuse me?" I said turning to face her.

"You! You're being impatient!" she spat.

The woman's face was mottled with anger. Bright red patches blazed on her cheeks. The blouse she had tucked hastily into her skin-tight jeans was rumpled and dirty, and buttoned wrong. I longed to tell her that, too. I grabbed my two loaves of bread and made a move to get back to my cart.

"I'm talkin' to you!" she shouted as she blocked my way. "You're impatient, ya know it? You need to learn some patience! Ain't that right, kids?"

The three little children hovered around their mother—one holding on to her ample waist and the other two grabbing at her knees. They all looked at me with wide frightened eyes. I shook my head. I couldn't believe this was happening. Neither could they. They knew their mother was losing it.

"You're crazy," I said. "Please move."

"CRAZY? You called me crazy in front of my kids! I'm gonna have you arrested!" she screamed.

I pushed past her and pitched the bread in my grocery cart. A second later a small box of raisins hit me in the shoulder. I didn't look back. I kept moving as box after box of dried fruit sailed through the air, knocking over jars of minced garlic, pickles, olives, and other condiments in flight. The sharp smell of vinegar filled the air as I dodged in and out the aisles like a hunted animal. By the time I reached Mother at the checkout line, I was shaking.

Cassie had locked herself in her room by the time we got home.

43

After we put the groceries away, Mother excused herself and went to bed. I was too charged up to even think of sleeping. I grabbed an open bottle of Chablis out of the fridge and headed out to the patio.

Cassie had done some yard work. The walkway and half the patio were cleared of the smaller limbs and branches. I flopped down in the chaise lounge and popped the top. Relishing the fact that Mother wasn't here to see me and complain, I swigged the wine straight from the bottle. It went down great—even the little pieces of cork.

I lay back and looked up at the night sky. It was so clear I could see the broad fuzzy band of the Milky Way against the velvet blackness. Fireflies danced over my head and vied with the twinkling of the stars for my attention. It was beautiful—as long as I kept looking up and not around me at the damage the storm had done.

I mourned a while over the ruin of my moonlight garden. I could still smell the sweetness of the crushed lilies and the blooms on the dying gardenia bush. It had taken two years to plant everything and create exactly the look I wanted. It had been a fairy garden—all white and dainty. I wasn't sure I could do it again.

The tears ran down my cheeks like two little cold wet snails. I wiped and sniffed and wiped again. Then I turned myself loose and cried big. I boo-hooed and whah-hahed for at least fifteen minutes until I slowly began to feel a little better. I found myself wishing the Raisin Lady was within reach and discovered my anger. I wanted to tackle the bitch and hold her down while I slapped her puffy fat face. When I realized how foolish that was. Mother was right, yet again. The crazy lady and I were both showing the effects of post-traumatic stress. I started laughing and couldn't stop until I was exhausted enough to go to bed. I knew my heart problems were over. I was back to being me—Paisley Sterling again.

CHAPTER NINE

The birds woke me up early the next morning with their loud, incessant chirping. Since the storm, the blue jays and cardinals had been fussing and fighting over territorial rights to the few bushes and other remaining bits of greenery tall enough and strong enough to support a nest. While I sympathized with their plight, I deeply resented the rude interruption of my dreams. The tearful session with my innermost self the night before had left me relaxed and calm enough to have the first good night's sleep I'd had since the tornado hit. I felt almost as well-rested as the princess who had slept without the pea under her mattress.

I stretched my arms and legs and decided self-indulgently that it was not quite time to get up. Then I heard the barking.

"Rats!"

I quickly hopped out of bed and landed precariously on the handmade hooked rug that Mother insisted gave my room "a finished look." I fought to keep my balance as I slid wildly across the highly polished wooden floor. When I met the raised transom in front of the bathroom door, I went sprawling. My head missed the edge of the bathtub by a mere centimeter as I fell forward with enough force to shake my toothbrush off the sink and into the open toilet below.

"Damn! Drat and drat!"

I crawled over to the toilet and stared in dismay as I watched my toothbrush slowly sinking to the bottom of the bowl.

"Bother!"

Cassie had a lot to answer for if she got another dog without asking for her grandmother's permission. And she owed me another toothbrush.

I heard the barking again. And I heard laughter and bits and pieces of conversation—in Spanish of all things.

I got back to my feet and climbed into the bathtub so I could see out the window in the direction of the patio. Sure enough, Cassie was sitting on one of the wrought iron chairs holding a skinny little white dog in her lap. Unlike Aggie with her long silky fur, this mutt was short-haired and had a pointy little nose—and appeared to be affectionate. At the moment, the puppy was standing in Cassie's lap energetically licking her chin and face, a thin little rat-like tail wagging madly all the while. In the two years we had Aggie she had never wagged her tail even once. The worse thing was that Cassie seemed to be in love with the dog already.

I supposed the man sitting with Cassie was the dog's owner. I puzzled over his identity for a moment. He appeared clean, but he was very thin and poorly dressed. I wondered where my daughter had met him and why on earth he was giving her a dog.

I ran a comb through my hair and used my index finger slathered with toothpaste to "brush" my teeth before I slipped into some sweats and moccasins. I was starving, but Mother had joined the party on the patio and I didn't want to miss any of the conversation. She had to be as angry as I was that Cass had impetuously gone ahead and procured a replacement for Aggie without asking. I might have to act as referee.

But Mother surprised me. She was full of smiles and laughter. And Cassie definitely seemed to have gotten over her "mad."

"Mom! Look!" she shouted as I opened the screened door.

"I am looking," I grumbled.

The man sitting across from her jumped to his feet and bobbed his head quickly in my direction. His smile was broad and full of darkly stained teeth. He clutched a tattered straw hat in his hands. His right index finger was wrapped with a dirty bandage, but his nails were clean and clipped and he had obviously made an effort to look presentable.

"Señor Rudolfo," said Cassie as she smiled in the man's direction. "This is my mother, Señora DeLeon."

"*Encantada*, Señora," he said. His voice was warm and mellow, with a surprisingly well-educated Mexican accent. "I am so pleased to meet the lovely mother of the young señorita."

"Er, yeah," I muttered suspiciously. "*Encantada* to you, too."

Mother was seated at the wrought iron table presiding over a large tray laden with her next-to-best china and third best silver coffee pot. The little white dog had curled up comfortably in Cassie's lap and gone to sleep. Rudolfo sat back down when I took a seat across from Mother and smiled broadly at the three of us.

"Cassie," I began.

"Mr. Rudolfo has kindly offered to help us out for a while. Isn't that marvelous, Paisley?" interrupted Mother, with a gracious smile in the man's direction.

Rudolfo didn't understand her words but knew he was being discussed. His smile broadened and his head began to bob up and down again.

I tried once more. "What about the...?"

"And," continued Mother, without missing a beat, "he has some friends who might be persuaded to join him."

"I just bet he does," I sneered.

"Aren't we lucky?" she persisted. "We'll have things cleaned up and back to normal in no time at all," this with another smile in the man's direction. "Will you pass Mr. Rudolfo his coffee, please Paisley?"

"But what about the dog?" I finally managed to ask.

"That's why I asked you to pass the coffee," she explained with exaggerated patience. "Cassie can't get up or she'll disturb poor dear little Aggie, and I...."

"Aggie?" I shouted, almost spilling the coffee in Rudolfo's lap as I handed the cup to him.

The little white dog's ears twitched as she squirmed in her sleep.

"Mom, please!" hissed Cassandra. "Don't wake her up! She's exhausted."

I grabbed the cup Mother extended to me and sat down heavily in my chair.

"Where in the world did you find her?" I croaked. "And what happened to her? She looks like hell."

"You would, too, if you'd been through what she has," chastised Cassie.

"But she's been shaved to the bone!" I protested.

"Señor Rudolfo said he had no choice. When he found her, she was filthy. Her hair was wet and muddy, and so matted that he had to cut it all off." Cassie smiled down at the sleeping puppy. "I think she looks cute," she insisted.

Rudolfo held the dainty china cup awkwardly in his injured hand and continued to smile benevolently as he drank his coffee.

"Did she bite him for his troubles?" I asked nodding at Rudolfo's hand.

"No, dear" explained Mother. "Cassie says he was hurt during the tornado. I do hope he had someone look at it."

Cassie turned and spoke rapidly to her new friend for a few moments. I tried to keep up with the conversation, but the Spanish she had learned in college was much better than the idioms I had learned on the streets of San Romero. I was lost in no time.

"No," she finally said. "No money for doctors. And, get this! Doc Wallace won't see the Mexican laborers even if they have the money. He says they carry too many diseases."

I had never had much respect for Winston Wallace, but I was still amazed when I heard something else that reminded me of his abysmal stupidity. Even Mother, who still believed in the Easter Bunny, was taken aback.

"Cassie, surely you jest!" she laughed.

"Sorry, Gran. It's the truth. And Señor Rudolfo says the doctor has passed this information along to the Rowan Springs City Park. They won't let the Mexicans swim in the pool or picnic on the grounds. And several local restaurants have refused to serve them."

"But, Cassie," I argued, "that's real discrimination. They can't do that."

Rudolfo was nodding his head vigorously. He seemed to understand the gist of the conversation.

"*Sí*, Señora," he said. "*Es verdad.*"

"Believe him, Mom. He's a nice guy."

"And rich," I said sarcastically. "How much did you promise for the safe return of that scrawny little rat? Five hundred smackeroos buys a lot of smiles."

Cassie was outraged. "That's mean!" she cried. "And, yes, I did offer a reward; but he won't accept it."

"Yeah?"

"That's right, Paisley, dear," affirmed Mother. "I heard it with my own ears. I even understood a smattering of the conversation. That's when I offered to let Mr. Rudolfo and his friends come and work for us."

"You mean, you jumped on him like a duck on a June bug!" I laughed.

I was still suspicious of this short, dark stranger, but I was vastly relieved that I wouldn't have to part with five hundred dollars to get back a mutt who had already cost me that much in doctor bills.

Cassie made me take Aggie from her lap so she could give Rudolfo a ride back home. She watched me like a hawk from the car as I carried the sleepy puppy onto the porch and placed her in her basket. I turned and smiled and waved them off, ignoring the distinct growl of canine displeasure coming from behind me. As soon as Cassie was down the driveway, her beloved pet summoned up enough energy to launch herself at my ankle and take a furtive but hearty nip.

"Damn it, dog!"

And thus, she reestablished herself as the alpha dog in our pack.

CHAPTER TEN

True to his word, Rudolfo returned early the next morning with a whole posse of his buddies. I was never exactly sure of the number of men who came with him because like ants at a picnic, they were all over the place. They appeared to be absolutely tireless—working through the day without taking breaks or lunch. They brought wicked-looking machetes that they used to strip the larger fallen trees of branches, and in turn to reduce those branches into huge piles of debris that they dumped into the dry pond bed.

By late afternoon they lifted the tree off the carriage house, and Watson was free. I jumped in the driver's seat and without another thought, was down the driveway and on the road with the radio at full blast. Dolly and I serenaded the cows in every pasture all the way to Morgantown and back as I celebrated my own freedom.

To show my appreciation, I stopped and bought the men a couple of cases of cold beer and a ton of hot wings and barbeque at the convenience store just across the county line. Andy Joiner wouldn't dare arrest them for having alcohol as guests in the home of Anna Howard Sterling. It was time to party hearty.

By the time I got back, I could see the lawn again, or what was left of it, and the pond bed was full. We ate our wings and barbeque on the patio while we waited for nightfall so we could light the bonfire. Cassie passed around the first marshmallows the Mexicans had ever seen and showed them how to make s'mores. While the fire blazed merrily, we stuffed ourselves on chocolate and graham crackers and sang every Mexican song we knew.

When the huge bonfire was a smoldering pile of ashes, we waved our new friends off and trudged wearily to our beds.

Mother woke us up at dawn—even before the birds got up. Rudolfo and his pals had promised to return at seven, and Mother wanted to fix breakfast for them. Cassie and I scrambled a million eggs while Mother made biscuits and pancakes. Soon the kitchen was full of the delicious aroma of sizzling bacon and baking bread. By nine o'clock it was gathering flies—a huge soggy mess on the patio table.

"I can't believe this," pronounced Mother in a voice filled with displeasure. "Of all the inconsiderate things!"

"I can't believe it, either," I grumbled. "All that good food gone to waste. Thanks a lot for not letting us eat until they got here, Cassie. Now I wouldn't touch that crap with a ten foot pole. And I'm starving."

"We couldn't have eaten first!" protested my daughter. "It would not have been polite."

"Yeah? And just what do a bunch of illiterate wetbacks know about manners?" I responded angrily. "They didn't even call to tell us they weren't coming!"

"Mom! How could you?" cried Cassie as she burst into tears. "How could you be such a bigot! Remember, it was one of those so-called illiterate wetbacks who saved our Aggie!"

"Yeah! And thanks a bunch for that, too! Just what I always wanted, 'the return of Fang'."

Cassie jumped up and ran into the house. She slammed the screened door so hard the wind chimes detached from the porch ceiling and fell to the floor with a loud melodic crash.

"Oh, dear," murmured Mother. "Do you think that was all quite necessary, Paisley?"

I sat back in my chair and gazed morosely at our moldering breakfast buffet.

"I suppose not. But I'm mad as hell."

"Language, dear."

"Damn it, Mother, I am mad. And hungry. Pass me a biscuit—from underneath the pile. Maybe there's one or two left that the flies haven't crapped on."

"Please."

"What?" I asked distractedly. I thought I heard a car coming up the driveway. Maybe the Mexicans were coming after all.

"You forgot to say 'please.' And I've asked you repeatedly not to use foul language," she protested. "Paisley, I'm your mother and this is my home. You need to honor my wishes."

Andy Joiner's police car pulled into view and ruined the rest of my morning.

"Damn it all to hell. Look who's here, Mother. It's Deputy Dawg. Damn! Drat and drat!"

"Paisley Sterling! Have you not heard a word I've said?" declared my outraged parent.

"Hmm? What, Mother? I'm sorry. Tell me again after Andy leaves."

I grabbed the silver coffee pot and poured the tepid liquid out in the grass at the edge of the patio.

"Paisley, what on earth are you doing? You'll ruin what's left of the grass," she sputtered.

"How's the cream? Is it still okay?" I asked, still ignoring her.

I sniffed deeply of the cream pitcher, and poked viciously with my index finger at the soft sagging stick on the butter dish.

"Paisley! That's quite enough!"

"You're right. I'll get some fresh butter and cream, too."

I balanced the pitchers and butter dish in my arms and hurried towards the kitchen. I smiled as I heard Mother utter one of my "vile epitaphs" under her breath. I had won this round. My mood was improving by the minute.

I dumped the souring cream in the sink and grabbed a clean pitcher from the china cabinet. I deliberately chose an old one with a chip in the handle. Mother would hate that. And when I put fresh butter on the dish, I left a piece of the wrapper on the stick. She wouldn't say anything in front of Andy, but she would be brooding over those two minor details the whole time he was here. I bounced back out to the patio in total good humor.

God got me almost immediately. Andy Joiner was his instrument.

"Morning, Andy," I sang out gaily. "Fresh hot coffee? The eggs and bacon are rotten, but the biscuits and jam are still better here than any where else in Lakeland County, even if the flies have been...."

"Paisley, shut up!" shouted Mother, astounding both me and Andy.

"Well, sure. If you say so. Although I...."

"Paisley," she continued in a tightly controlled voice, "Andy has just presented me—us—the inhabitants of Meadowdale Farm, with an injunction against the direct hiring of non-citizens to perform any labor whatsoever on our property."

"What the hell?" I protested.

"Look, Paisley, Miz Sterling—this has nothing to do with you all personally," said Andy, as he shifted uncomfortably from one big foot to the other.

"I should hope not!" declared Mother.

"What does it have to do with, Andy?" I asked softly. "Is it just a coincidence that we sat here for two hours watching fifty pounds of food go bad while we waited for a bunch of guys who can't help us anymore—and you show up with this paper? What's going on?"

"Look, Paisley," he began. "Mind if I sit down?"

"Help yourself," I said, plopping down in a chair opposite him. "And help yourself to some coffee, and biscuits. The ones on top are the freshest," I added wickedly.

Mother and I went over the legal papers while Andy fixed his coffee. I watched out of the corner of my eye as he picked three big biscuits from the top of the pile. He ate them quickly, washing them down with a second cup of coffee.

"Thanks," he sighed with satisfaction. "I didn't have time for breakfast this morning and I was a mite famished."

"Have some more then," I said pushing the biscuit plate closer. "And some bacon. Make yourself a sandwich."

"Thanks, Paisley. I really appreciate your not holding a grudge," he said with a winning smile.

I felt a guilty little twinge in the pit of my stomach. "Let me fix some fresh bacon. Won't take me but a minute."

"There's no bacon left, Paisley. We cooked it all," observed Mother dryly.

"Thanks, just the same, ladies. I don't really need anything else. It'll be lunchtime soon and Connie's bringing something to the office for me.

"Who is behind this nonsense, Andy?" insisted Mother waving the injunction like a banner. "Jimmy Hershey's been a friend for fifty years. I can't believe he signed this ridiculous piece of paper. What's going on?"

Andy shook his head slowly.

"I'm not really sure what's going on. Seems to me like it would be a good idea to let those guys help out. Everybody else in town is swamped, and I know the Mexicans need the money. Most of the tobacco crop was wiped out by the storm, and they don't have anything else to do right now. They don't make much money in the best of times, and what they do make most of 'em send it back regular to their families. Two months without work could make a big difference, and it'll be at least that long before plantin' time. But I guess their contractor won't let 'em do any outside work."

Andy looked acutely uncomfortable. That was a long speech for him and I was sure he felt like he'd said too much. I probably should have let it go at that, but he had said something that piqued my interest.

"Contractor? I thought these men were independents who went wherever there was a need for laborers."

"I'm not just exactly sure how it works," said Andy, "but from what I've gathered, it's a lot more organized than that. This bunch here definitely has a labor contractor. He brings 'em in from Mexico, sets 'em up with a work permit, finds 'em a job and a place to live, and sends 'em back home when their work permits expire."

Mother was quick as a bunny. "The labor contractor must be the person who got Jimmy Hershey to sign the injunction," she guessed.

Andy turned a bright telltale red from his neck to his ears. "I'm sorry, Miz Sterling. I'm just the bearer of bad tidings. I'm not at liberty to say any more. I've said enough already," he added under his breath.

He stood up and brushed the biscuit crumbs from his starched uniform shirt.

"Gotta be going. Thanks again for the breakfast. It really hit the spot."

CHAPTER ELEVEN

Mother and I spent an hour cleaning up the breakfast mess and throwing spoiled food away. Aggie was still so tired she remained in her basket even when she heard me scraping plates into the garbage can. That was usually the clarion call that brought her from one end of the farm to another. It seemed strange when she didn't move a muscle.

"Do you think we should take Aggie to the vet for a once over?" I asked Mother.

"I thought you didn't care, dear," she said with a knowing smile.

"I don't! Not about her, anyway. But if she's going to keep biting me and sleeping with Cassie...."

"I think she's fine, Paisley. She's just exhausted and frightened like we were after the storm. And she was a long way from home. That must have been a terrifying experience for such a little animal."

She reached down and caressed the sleeping puppy.

"I must say, I'm quite happy to have her back again. And I think you are, too, dear."

"Hummfp."

I swept the last of the crumbs off the patio and took stock of the work that remained to be done in the yard. The larger fallen trees had been stripped of their branches and rolled into the orchard where they lay waiting to be cut into logs. The giant holes where trees were uprooted remained to be filled. Most of the lawn would have to be tilled and replanted, and my moon garden was still a mess.

Three more days with the Mexicans would have set us to rights. And now that I knew the poor guys needed the work and the money, it seemed even more unfair that we couldn't use them. Maybe there was still something we could do about it. I was never so foolish as to underestimate Mother's considerable charms. Perhaps now was the time for her to use them on Judge Hershey, but first I had to pay Rudolfo and his friends for the work they had already done. And for that I needed Cassie.

I knocked on her door and politely asked to be admitted.

"Go away!" she shouted angrily.

"Please, Cassie," I begged. "I'll tell you why Andy was here."

"I couldn't care less."

"I made him eat fly turds. I'm sure you want to hear about that."

I thought I heard muffled laughter.

"You're a terrible person, Paisley Sterling DeLeon. You know that, don't you?" she said as she opened the door and then climbed back on her bed.

"I know," I sighed, looking around at the disarray of clothes and open suitcases cluttering her pretty room.

I sat down on the pink and lavender striped chaise, pushing aside dirty socks to make room. Now was not the time to criticize her for being messy. Instead, I agreed with her assessment of me.

"It's a curse, but someone around here has to be the monster. Mother is too elegant and proper, and you're too angelic and beautiful. Guess I'm elected."

"I'm not angelic," denied my daughter, sticking out her tongue to prove it.

"Then maybe I'm not such a terrible person?"

"You are terrible sometimes, Mom. And you hate Aggie. And worst of all, you're prejudiced and bigoted against Latinos!"

I laughed heartily for a full minute until I saw from her reaction that she was truly serious about her accusations.

"Cassandra, how can you say such things?" I asked incredulously.

"Because they're true," she mumbled into her lace-trimmed pillow

"I married your father, didn't I," I asked softly. "I had his child and lived happily in his home for eight wonderful years. Is that the behavior of a person who dislikes Latinos? Your grandparents and aunts were Latinos...."

"And we never have anything to do with them, do we!" she retorted accusingly.

"Cassie, you know that was their decision. They thought it best to cut any ties. It was for our own safety. Because we still don't know why your father disappeared."

Cassie rose up and looked at me, tears spilling down her cheeks and her dark eyes filled with pain and longing. I never knew until that moment just how much she missed the rest of her family.

"Oh, darling!"

I crawled up next to her in bed and held her while she cried softly on my shoulder. "Don't misunderstand me, Mom," she hiccoughed finally. "I'm not that unhappy, really I'm not. It's just that sometimes I feel like half of me is missing."

"I know, pumpkin," I soothed. "Sometimes I feel the same way."

She bounced up on her knees and hugged me.

"I'm sorry, Mom. I'm such a self-centered creep. I forgot that you have to miss Daddy, too."

"Wow," I said with the tiniest of snuffles. "What a pair we are! You're a creep and I'm a monster. Do we have any redeeming value?"

"You bet we do!" she said as she gave me a rib-squeezing bear hug. "And I love you very much."

"Even if your dog and I don't get along very well?"

"Even then. And besides, it really doesn't matter that much anymore because she'll be coming with me."

"Excuse me, did I miss something here? Are you going somewhere, Cassie?"

She untangled her arms from around me and sat up. "Come on, Mom. You knew I would be moving out and making a life of my own after college. Admit it. I've warned you often enough."

"Yes," I sighed. "I knew you would be leaving home sooner or later. But somehow I hoped it would be a later than sooner—maybe in the fall. Couldn't you spend the summer with us, at least?"

"Celestine needs me now."

"Celestine? Who the hell is...you mean the girl who owns the coffee bar downtown on Main Street?"

"Yep! I start work first thing Monday morning," she announced with a huge grin.

"What?" I shouted with dismay. "You're going to work in a coffee shop?"

"Just until I save up enough money to open a book store," she answered defensively.

"I simply cannot believe this," I cried. "Is this why I sent you for all that expensive Emory education? At the very least, I thought you would be going out in the world to beat your head against a few corporate brick walls first."

"Mom, I watched all my friends mailing off resumes and interviewing for fancy yuppie jobs in Atlanta's glass towers, and I knew I just couldn't live like that."

She smiled and gave me another hug. This time I sat like a lump and didn't respond. I was too stunned.

"Thanks for my education," she continued persuasively. "My mind is full of wonderful facts, but it is my mind. And one thing an education—the proper kind of education—does is teach you how to think for yourself. I did just that, for quite a long time, and this is what I want to do."

"But Rowan Springs is about as country as you can get," I protested, "and you're a city mouse."

56

"So are you, Mom. And look how much happier you are here than you were in New York three years ago. I can see the difference in your face. You look ten years younger. Horatio says we really do look like sisters."

"Never mind flattering me. I still think you should go and seek your fortune like the old fairy tales say."

"And come to the same conclusion twenty years later like you did? Why not now before all the lumps and disappointments? This is my laughing place, Mom. This is where I'm the happiest me. Let me stay and I promise you won't be disappointed. There's a lot I can do to set this old town on its ear."

"Okay, sweetie," I sighed. "I can't really say I'm sorry you won't be hundreds of miles away. I just thought you would need to be out on your own."

"I'll be on my own. I'm getting the apartment above Celestine's as part of my compensation. I'm the morning manager," she added with pride.

"Wow, and it took a 3.8 GPA to get that job, I bet."

"Celestine had a 4.0."

CHAPTER TWELVE

Cassie insisted on driving Watson to the trailer park where Rudolfo lived. She used both her knowledge of the direction to take and the argument that when she moved out she would no longer have the use of the car to convince me.

"Maybe we can find an inexpensive little...."

"Mom, forget it. For twenty-two years you have taken care of my every need and desire. Now it's time I took care of myself. Besides, I'll be living downtown and won't need a car. The grocery stores will be within walking distance, and for anything else, I have my bike."

"What if you should happen to want to visit your poor old relatives?"

"I'll give you a call," she laughed. "But remember, I'll be working six days a week. There won't be much time for visits."

"I predict that your grandmother and I will soon develop an insatiable thirst for that strange exotic coffee Celestine sells."

We discussed the merits of Raspberry Truffle Jubilee as opposed to Maxwell House instant until we turned off the main highway. Cassie aimed Watson down a dirt track that led to several rows of dilapidated and rusting trailers that were mercifully hidden from the road by some really tall and beautiful cedars.

The rain had washed deep gullies in the red dirt, but the road was dry now and very dusty. We kicked up a small dirt storm as we drove on into the trailer park.

Overflowing garbage cans abuzz with large black-green flies stood at the entrance to each row of trailers, and the air was ripe with the odor of rotten food. Latin music from several competing radio stations blared at us from the open windows of every trailer we passed. Flimsy plastic fans tried valiantly to move the air in and out of the small windows, but I could only imagine the sweltering heat inside the trailers. Angry shouts followed the swirling dust cloud we kicked up with our passing, and for once, I was glad I couldn't understand their meaning.

"I guess they don't have air conditioning," I observed dryly.

"They don't have much of anything, Mom."

"What's it look like inside these sardine cans?" I asked.

"I don't know. Rudolfo wouldn't even let me come this far when I brought him home, but he did point out his trailer. It's the one on the end."

We pulled up next to the one she indicated and parked Watson. We waited for a minute or two until the dust settled so we could get out without choking to death. Rudolfo's trailer was the only one with all the windows closed. When we tried it, we found the door tightly shut and locked as well.

"Nobody's home," I announced unnecessarily.

"Wonder where he is," said Cassie, peering in the dust-covered window.

"Gone back where he come from, that's where. And good riddance, I say!"

Cassie and I turned startled heads in the direction of a large man wearing a red and white flowered shirt and the biggest pair of blue jeans I had ever seen. The jeans were tucked inside beautifully tooled leather cowboy boots and belted at his considerable waist with silver *conchos* the size of small saucers.

"What in the blue-eyed world do you two ladies think you're doin' out here?"

"We have some business with Señor Rudolfo," I said, as politely as I could muster.

"*Seenor* Rudolf don't have no business I don't know about. And I don't know nuthin' about anything he might have to do with the likes of you, Ma'am," he added with a sarcastic sneer.

"He performed some services the other day for which we would like to pay him," I insisted. When the words were out, I realized how much I sounded like Mother—and what a mistake that was.

A sleazy smirk distorted the big man's weathered face. His eyes were light brown, almost yellow, and narrow like a serpent's. It was hard to believe that a mouth as small as his could take in enough sustenance to keep his heavy body fueled.

"And I wonder just what kind of *servicing* he did for you ladies? I'll be glad to give Rudolf your money," he added slyly, "And perform any more *services*...."

"I just bet you would," interrupted Cassie, angrily. "I thought you said he was gone."

"Maybe he is, and maybe he ain't. Damn flies!" he shouted slapping at his face. "I keep telling these pigs they gotta bury their leavins. Animals, that's what they are, nuthin' but animals."

"Are you the manager of this delightful place?" I asked.

The music was barely audible now, and I knew our little discussion was the object of intense interest for the silent observers behind the thin metal walls of the trailers all around us.

"And just who wants to know?" he demanded, with the same awareness of an audience.

"Paisley DeLeon. I'm Anna Howard Sterling's daughter, and this is my daughter, Cassandra."

"Well, how de freakin' do," he snorted. "Nice to meet the little lady that got one of my best men in trouble with the law."

"Wha...what do you mean?" stammered Cassie.

"Rudolph Ramírez. Thanks to you and your meddlin' old bitch of a grandmother, Ramírez got deported this morning—along with three other men who didn't pay no attention to the rules."

"You fat tub of guts!" I shouted angrily. "How dare you...."

Cassie grabbed my arm and began pulling me toward the car.

"Let me go, Cassie," I panted. "That fat pig needs to be told a thing or two."

The big man turned and watched with great interest as Cassie pushed me in the car and slammed the door. As we backed out of the drive, he deliberately and carefully mouthed two words in my direction, "You're dead!"

By the time we got back to the highway, my heart had quit racing, but I was drenched with sweat and still shaking with anger.

"Mom, are you all right?" asked Cassie, her voice filled with concern.

"Damn, damn, and double damn!"

"Yeah, you're fine," she laughed. "Want something to drink? I'm dying for a soda, myself."

"Aren't you furious, Cassie?" I sputtered. "Why aren't you furious?"

"Because it won't help matters, and besides, I'm sure you'll think of a way to pay him back in spades for calling Gran names."

"I already have!"

I wiped the sweat from my face with my shirtsleeve and turned to face her.

"It's been a long time since you and I went on a prowl together," I observed in a conspiratorial voice.

"Oh, no!" she laughed. "I'm not sneaking out after midnight and tiptoeing over rooftops with you ever again."

"Don't never say ever," I chuckled, putting my own spin on the old cliché. "Come on, Cassie. It'll be fun. Just like old times."

"I'm not saying yes, but I am curious," she admitted. "Just what do you have in mind?"

No matter how hard I tried, I couldn't convince my reluctant daughter to sneak back to the trailer park after midnight and do a little snooping. She professed a complete lack of interest, until, out of desperation, I mentioned the dead body that was found on our property. Not for a moment did I believe the corpse had anything to do with the sticky situation our Mexican friends found themselves in, but I was shameless enough to pretend if it would help change my daughter's mind. Unfortunately, it got a little out of hand.

"Wow! Were the buzzards eating him up?"

"Ugh! I'd rather not go into that if you don't mind. But I did see Horatio's photos and they were pretty gruesome."

"Photographs? Does Horatio still have them or did he give the only copies to Chief Joiner?"

"I don't know, Cassie. But I doubt if he'd let you see them either way. He already thinks I'm a ghoul. I know he would disapprove of your...."

"But, Mom," she protested, "this is turning out to be a real investigation—a Leonard Paisley-style investigation. Especially," she added pointedly, "if there are any nighttime activities involved. A corpse on our very own farm! Just imagine!"

"Sorry you're moving out, pumpkin?"

"In a way," she replied wistfully. "And not just because of the dead body."

"I should hope not!"

"Yeah," she teased, "I'll miss cable television."

"Stinker!"

Mother was standing on the patio tapping her foot with impatience when we drove up.

"Oh, gosh! I told your grandmother we would be home for lunch."

"We're not that late," laughed Cassie.

"Depends on what she cooked. Soufflé or quiche, and we're dead as that corpse you so crazy about."

We were lucky. Mother had fixed a lovely fruit salad with a delicate yogurt and honey dressing. I dispatched a ton of kiwi, papaya, and mango, while Cassie told her about our trip to the trailer park. She diplomatically omitted the name calling on both sides, but Mother got the message that we had inadvertently stepped on some toes.

"I wonder," she said. "Do you think Mr. Rudolfo knew he wasn't supposed to take on any outside work? I mean," she continued, "surely someone explained the terms of the contract to him. He must have understood what his work permit would and would not allow before he entered this country."

"Umm, great salad, Mother," I sighed with contentment.

"What do you think, Cassandra? Your mother is obviously too much of a glutton to consider anything else but her stomach."

"There's a time and place for everything," I mumbled around a deliciously sweet chunk of fresh guava.

"Maybe he wanted to break his contract. Maybe he just wanted to go back home," Cassie hypothesized.

I patted my lips carefully with a linen napkin and sat back in my chair.

"Ah, that was delicious, Mother. That's one more thing you'll miss, sweetie," I observed with a wink at Cass. I realized much too late that I had just let the cat out of the bag.

By the time we had explained to her grandmother why Cassie was moving out—why she felt the need to disgrace her ancestors as well as the living, and therefore more important members of her family by working in a coffee bar—it was mid-afternoon.

"I give up, my dear," Mother said finally. "If you simply feel no ambitious yearnings to make something more of yourself, no call to the finer things, then by all means serve your little coffees."

I was exhausted, but Mother didn't fool me. She was the toughest and most resilient of the three of us. I could tell she was not finished but gathering strength for the *coup de grace*, when suddenly Cassie amazed me.

"Of course, you realize I'll be living in the apartment upstairs. You know the one, Gran. Your friend Mary Margaret Devere tried to buy the lease last year, didn't she?"

Mother sat very still. She watched Cassie carefully without taking a breath until she realized her granddaughter was perfectly serious.

"You'll be living in the apartment Granstaff Armstong-Jones designed?"

"The very one," Cassie said with a smug little smile. "And I was wondering...oh, but, you're probably too busy. Never mind, I'll just pop out to Walmart on my bicycle and grab whatever's on sale."

Mother still hadn't taken a breath, but her eyes sparkled with barely suppressed excitement.

"Of course, I could ask Mom," continued Cassie, "but she has no more sense of style than...."

"I'll be delighted to help, my dear," Mother allowed in one explosive breath. "I had no idea you were so fortunate as to live in that divine old apartment."

She lowered her voice to a whisper, "Mary Margaret will be livid when she finds out. Perhaps we can we ask her to tea some afternoon?"

"By all means, Gran," laughed Cassie. "But let's make it coffee, shall we?"

CHAPTER THIRTEEN

A year ago I learned a painful lesson: there was no keeping a proposed midnight outing from my mother. Cassie and I quietly made some tentative plans, then laid them out for Mother's consideration as we all cleaned up the kitchen.

"It won't work," Mother informed us decisively. "From start to finish, it's a disaster. You'll be seen, get caught, put in jail, and wind up embarrassing me again. I simply cannot allow it."

My hackles went up so far they tickled my ears. "Excuse me," I sputtered. "I don't think...."

"You didn't think at all. That's the problem, dear," she observed calmly.

Cassie jumped in to mediate. "Okay, Mom, simmer down a minute. Let Gran tell us how she would pull it off."

She turned to her grandmother and blessed her with a beautiful "may I please have another piece of pie" smile. "Go ahead, Gran. Tell us what you would do."

Mother took off her lace-trimmed apron and put down the linen towel she was using to dry her silver coffee pot. We followed her out to the screened porch and watched while she took her time arranging herself in her favorite chaise. Cassie sat on the floor by her feet and I pulled up a chair as we waited impatiently for her to speak.

"Firstly," she said, ticking off the details on her fingers, "I'd forget the car."

"How in the world...?"

"Please be patient and show some respect, Paisley. For heaven's sake, your daughter is behaving in a more mature manner than you are."

I ground my teeth together and managed not to utter something that would make me feel better but infuriate her. After all, she had an uncanny way of knowing exactly what to do in the most unusual of circumstances, and we might as well take advantage of it.

"You already told me that the road was dry. And I saw Watson when you drove up this afternoon. The poor thing was covered with dust."

"But, at night, Gran? Will it matter?"

"Under a full moon it will," she pointed out sagely.

"Ohhh," Cassie and I muttered in unison.

"That's right, my children. According to the latest issue of *The Farmer's Almanac*, there is a full moon tonight. And to make matters worse, the forecast is for clear skies. Could you possibly postpone your plans for later in the week? I don't think there's really any urgency, is there?"

I thought for a moment while Cassie fidgeted. I knew she wanted to go tonight. So did I, but I didn't have a really good reason."

"I suppose," Mother continued, "that you are thinking it's Friday night and most of the men in the trailer park will go out somewhere to relax. Therefore, you will run a smaller chance of being discovered."

"Yeah, that's right! You're right, Mother," I agreed enthusiastically.

She was way ahead of me, and she was still cooking.

"Did you know that a branch of the Green River borders the land where the trailer park is located?"

"Are you sure, Gran?" Cassie asked skeptically. "It's so sterile and arid looking. It's hard to believe there's water anywhere around that God forsaken place."

Mother lifted her chin and pronounced, "I may be mistaken about a great many things, but not about the topography of Lakeland County. Cassie, bring me the map, please. It's in the library on the...."

"I know," laughed Cassie as she got up in one graceful, athletic motion. "It's on the map table."

We studied the map for a few minutes without speaking. Mother was right. The Green River emptied into Bass Bay, and from there, a small branch headed west. The trailer park sat up on a bluff above the river.

"I can't recall exactly how high the cliffs are, but I would guess at least thirty or forty feet above the river."

"You've been to the trailer park, Mother? Whatever for?"

"Not the trailer park, dear. Years ago we young people used to go out there for picnics. Jimmy Hershey's family owned the land...."

"You're kidding me," I interrupted. "Judge Hershey owns that cesspool?"

"Please, Paisley, you're manners are showing," she chided. "I said, if you will recall, that the Hershey family *owned* the land. That was years ago. I have no idea who owns it now. I do recall some really beautiful cedar trees. We used to swim in the river and climb up the cliffs to picnic under those trees. Your father cut quite the dashing figure, Paisley, dear. He and Jimmy used to show off by taking turns jumping off the bluffs."

She smiled fondly in remembrance. "Your father always won. He had no fear, that man. Jimmy never quite dared jump from the top, but he was so generous in his admiration of your father. Ah," she sighed, "we did have such good times. I'm afraid young people nowadays don't enjoy themselves the way we did. They don't realize they have all of their lives to work and should take some time to smell the roses."

"Okay, Gran," said Cassie with a knowing grin. "Let's not go there, if you don't mind."

"The point being, my dears, that if you want to approach the area without being seen, you must go by way of the river. And for that, I'm afraid you need a boat and a lot more time to plan than you have now. That is if you want to succeed, of course," she warned.

Mother took a quick peek at the dainty diamond watch on her wrist and looked up in alarm. "My goodness, I had no idea it was so late. Horatio will be here any minute and I haven't a clue as to what I'm going to wear."

Cassie jumped up with a smile on her face. "I help you decide," she offered. "I love looking in your closet." She went in the house, turning on lights on her way to her grandmother's room.

"Where to, Mother?" I asked. "Wha'cha' gonna do?"

In spite of her tardiness, she took the time to stop and turn on her heels to give me a speech lesson. "Paisley, you're far too old and entrenched in your habits for me to dream of being able to...."

"So give up on me, already," I sighed as I settled myself comfortably in the chaise she had vacated.

"You used to have such a wonderful command of the English language before you became *that person*."

"Leonard Paisley?"

"Yes, dear. The very same. He's rough, dear, and uncouth. Don't you think it's time you put him on the shelf and became someone a little more...?"

"Socially acceptable?"

"Exactly! Someone who wears lovely clothes and has delightfully interesting friends—poets and artists, famous lawyers and doctors."

"Not pimps and drug dealers."

"Definitely not!"

I lied quite freely, and without any remorse whatsoever. "I'll give it a thought."

"Thank you, dear, that's all I ask," she said with a smile. "What do you think of my blue chiffon?"

"Lovely," I answered absently as I considered a world without Leonard. I shuddered and gave up the dreadful thought immediately. Leonard was my meal ticket, and quite a successful one, too. My agent had made me promise to keep the Leonard series alive for at least a dozen books, and hopefully twice that many more. Since I had come out of the closet last year as Leonard's creator, sales had risen instead of plummeted as she had feared. Women mystery writers were becoming quite the thing in literary circles. We were giving the men a run for their money. I might come up with a new protagonist in the future, but meanwhile, Leonard and I were partners in crime, even if my language and wardrobe suffered because of it.

Horatio was running a bit late, and Mother managed to be ready when he arrived, but they didn't take time for their usual cocktail so Cassie didn't get to ask him about our resident corpse. I even forgot to ask Mother in a proper manner where they were going.

"Did she tell you?" I asked Cassie.

"Just dinner and cards," she said quietly.

"What's up, pumpkin?"

"Why do we need more time to make plans?" she pouted. "It's only a little after seven. We have all night. If we don't go now, I might not get to go at all."

I grabbed a Perrier and a hunk of Gouda from the fridge and joined her at the kitchen table.

"Gran doesn't like it when you don't use the cheese knife," she said pointedly.

"Bother the cheese knife. Let her cut the cheese."

"Oh, Mom," laughed my daughter. "You're terrible."

"Well, I'm teed off. Can you imagine? She wants me to do away with Leonard—so my conversation will improve, of all things!"

"You're not going to," asked Cassie alarmed.

"Hell, no! Leonard is indestructible, anyway. Couldn't kill him off if I tried."

"I bet Leonard would go on our adventure tonight—no matter what," she observed wistfully.

"What would he do for a boat? And how would he get it to the river. And where would he...?" I didn't remind her that only a few hours ago I had to persuade her to go with me.

"You're making this way too complicated, Mom, and you're thinking like Gran. Think like Leonard for a moment, and see what you come up with."

I nibbled on my Gouda and took a swig of Perrier while I cogitated.

"No boat?" I guessed.

"Precisely!" she grinned happily.

"Then how?"

"Grandad and Jimmy Hershey didn't have a boat when they went out there for picnics in the good old days. Look at the map," Cassie said, pulling it over in front of me. "Bass Bay is practically within spittin' distance of the bluffs. It's a warm night. We could strip to our skivvies, swim around the bend, and climb that little old cliff before anybody knows wha'cha' doin'. "

"Careful. You're starting to sound vulgar and uncouth."

"It's the company I keep," she laughed.

CHAPTER FOURTEEN

For once we didn't have to worry about what to do with Aggie. She was still sleeping. Cassie didn't seem to be at all concerned about the fact that her puppy was completely devoid of energy.

"It's her hair," she explained as we drove down the driveway. "She mortified—simply humiliated beyond belief. When her beautiful hair starts to grow out she'll be herself again."

"Oh, goody. I can hardly wait."

"Be kind for a few more days, Mom. She'll be gone soon."

"And so will you," I observed mournfully.

"So let's have fun tonight instead of playing the guilt game, okay?"

"You're right! You're absolutely right," I sighed. "Think we'll have time for a midnight snack at the Pelican before we head for home?"

"Hooray! I wouldn't miss a chance to eat greasy eggs and salty country ham with that bunch of sweaty old reprobates for a million dollars."

The Pelican was the only eatery within a hundred miles that stayed open past midnight. They specialized in serving cholesterol-laden meals to truckers and drunks who had to sober up before going home. If you found a fly in your soup you got charged extra, and the big-haired waitresses had more attitude than Godzilla. It was the sort of place my mother would rather die than step one dainty Ferragamo-shod foot in, even if it were for the last crust of bread on earth. I loved it, and so did Cassie.

This time I drove. Cassie wasn't as familiar with the area around the lakes, but it was my stomping ground. I loved meandering through the woods along the shore. I found it to be both restful and invigorating at the same time. I didn't get writer's block, ever, but sometimes I had trouble figuring Leonard's way out of a sticky spot. Whenever that happened, I would hop in Watson, whistle for the dog, and head for the lakes.

Weather permitting, I would walk with Aggie through the woods until she was exhausted. I enjoyed watching her sniff the trails left by creatures as unknown to her as Martians were to me. After our walk, I would sit on a picnic table and watch the sun set over the water while she dozed in my lap. These peaceful outings never failed to resolve Leonard's predicaments. And they were, practically speaking, the only occasions when the dog and I enjoyed each other's company.

I had been to Bass Bay many times but never at night. It was magical. A huge silver-white moon gilded the tips of gentle waves until they burst into a delicate spray of diamonds against the rocky shore. The soft breeze lifting the branches of trees at the water's edge carried just the faintest hint of honeysuckle and Carolina jasmine.

I parked Watson off the road under a big weeping willow. From ten feet away, even the outline of the big Jeep was lost in the shadows.

Cassie and I got out and closed the doors as quietly as we could. A whippoorwill stopped in mid-song when he heard the soft clicks, but then resumed his baleful melody. The rocks under our feet crunched as we walked, and I had to quell an urge to tiptoe.

"Why do I feel like whispering?" whispered Cass.

"It's so still," I whispered back.

We both nearly jumped out of our skins when a huge fish flung itself at the moon and fell back into the water with a resounding splash.

"Wow, I'd hate to come up against that sucker in the dark. Cassie, maybe we do need a boat after all. You took a biology course. Are there any freshwater sharks?"

"You're being a goofball, Mom. Quit fooling around and head for the other end of the beach."

"This is no beach. This is Rock City. Can you imagine lying out here on a towel to sunbathe? You'd have to be an Indian fakir."

Cassie stopped in her tracks and turned to face me. In the moonlight the classic planes of her face seemed to be carved from alabaster. She was Diana, the huntress—goddess of the moon. I was startled by her beauty.

"Are you finking out on me?" whispered the goddess, angrily. "'Cause if you are, I'm going on alone. This was your idea, but now I'm the only one who seems to be interested. What's the deal, Mom?"

"I'm sorry, Cassie. I just got cold feet for a minute. Maybe this isn't such a good idea after all. What if Hopalong Fatty is up there on the bluffs waiting for us with a shotgun?"

"I thought so!" she sputtered with her hands on her hips. "You always get these harebrained schemes and talk me into going along, then you chicken out and start worrying about my getting hurt. Well, I got news for you: you can't have it both ways."

"Maybe you should just wait here for me," I suggested weakly.

"Are you crazy? I'd go nuts wondering what was going on. Besides, you were right in the first place. You need me. I've been there more times than you have."

"Once more," I scoffed.

"Yeah? Well, I also know more about Rudolfo, and Fabián, and Joaquín. I bet you don't even remember what they look like?"

"Well, no," I admitted.

"And," she raised her voice a trifle as she came in for the kill, "thanks to four years of college, I speak better Spanish than you do."

"I...."

"Ready?"

I grinned at my daughter—tall and beautiful in the moonlight.

"Ready."

"Then let's get on with it. We don't have all night."

We made our way around the edge of the bay to the other side of the rocky beach. I tread carefully, knowing that a twisted ankle would render me *hors de combat.* I was quite certain that my ruthless child would leave me and go it alone.

From the other side of the little bay we could see the rocky outcropping of the bluffs looming large across the water.

"Wow, they look higher than thirty feet to me. Not that I'm suggesting anything," I hastened to add.

"We'd better take our shoes. It looks like a rough climb. Tie them around your neck by the laces, Mom. And tuck your flashlight into the front of your bathing suit. It's waterproof. No use wasting energy trying to hold it above the water."

Cassie unbuttoned her jeans and hopped on one foot and then the other to pull them off. I had to sit on the sharp rocks to perform the same task.

"At least it's not cold. And aren't you glad Gran kept these antique swimsuits?"

I laughed. I was wearing the suit I had worn on my college swim team.

We folded our clothes in a neat little pile at the water's edge and put a rock on top in case the wind picked up. Cassie boldly led the way into the dark water. I closed my mind against the sound of the splash we had heard earlier and followed in her wake. The water was cool, but not cold, and before long I found myself enjoying our swim.

"Hey," I sputtered. "This is swell! We should do this more often. Wonder why more people don't come here for a nocturnal swim?"

Cassie stopped paddling and tread water in front of me while she answered.

"I guess because the lake is off limits at night except for fishermen with special permits and people with houseboats."

"What? How do you know that? Are you sure?"

"Says so on the sign at the entrance from the main highway."

"Why didn't you say something?"

"And miss this? Not on your life!"

She turned and resumed her silent breaststroke. I paddled noisily up to her side.

"Is there a fine or something? I mean what could happen to us?"

"Incarceration and stiff penalty—I forget exactly what," she muttered. "Forget it, Mom. And hush. Sound travels over water."

I dropped back and swam as silently as I could in her shadow. It wasn't long before my toes touched the bottom. We were almost at the other side of the bay. I floated on my back and looked up at the sandstone cliffs rising high above the water's edge. They were indeed considerably taller than thirty feet—maybe even taller than forty. My father had to have been some kind of daredevil if he found leaping from that height amusing.

Cassie pulled herself up on a rock ledge and reached out to help me up. We sat for a minute to let the water roll off our bodies, then put our tennis shoes on.

"I'll go first," she whispered. "You follow me. Put your hands and feet where I put mine."

I did just as she ordered, wondering just when she had taken charge. We crawled up the cliff face slowly and carefully. The sandstone was dry and friable, and several times my heart lurched when a piece broke off under the weight of a foot or the grasp of a hand. Cassie's progress sent little showers of sand raining down on my hair and face, but she never made a misstep, and we were soon pulling ourselves up over the top.

We lay on our stomachs and looked back down at the dark water below.

"Wow!" I whispered proudly. "Look at what we did!"

Cassie giggled with delight. "Fun, wasn't it?"

"Yeah, it really was," I agreed, somewhat surprised. "But getting back down is going to be a bitch."

"We can always go down the way Grandad Sterling did," she chuckled.

"That'll be the day!"

We saw the tall cedars in the distance and made our way toward their distinctive outline against the night sky. We had each chosen an old black one-piece bathing suit and now our arms and legs stood out white against the darkness.

"You think we should rub some mud on? You know, for camou-flage?" I suggested.

"Ugghh!" was Cassie's only response.

I reached down and grabbed some dirt. I tried to rub it on my legs but only succeeded in getting a pebble in my shoe.

"Ouch! Stop a minute, Cassie," I called softly. "I have a rock in my shoe."

"I'll wait for you under the trees," she whispered.

"Wait, Cassie...don't...."

But she had already been swallowed up by the darkness at the edge of the woods.

CHAPTER FIFTEEN

In the time it took to blink, Cassie was gone and I was all alone. I hobbled as fast as I could in the direction she took without taking the time to remove what now felt like a boulder in my right shoe. I don't know who I was the most afraid for, my daring daughter, or myself.

"Cassie," I whispered fearfully, "where are you?"

I made my way into the shadows beneath the cedars. Leaning against the trunk of one tree, I paused to shake out my shoe as I squinted against the darkness. Cassie was nowhere to be seen.

"Damna...."

Her hand came out of the darkness and muffled the rest of my curse against my lips.

"Shhhh," she whispered softly in my ear. "He's over there taking a pee."

I looked in the direction of her extended finger and saw the bulky outline of the man we had met earlier in the day. He was casually relieving himself against the side of one of the trailers. He belched loudly as he zipped up and staggered drunkenly back around to the front. We heard the door slam and saw a light go on inside.

"Good!" said Cassie. "He's tucked in for the night. He must have tied one on pretty early."

"Either that, or he's a cheap drunk."

"Where to, Mom?" asked Cassie, deferring to me for the first time.

"Gee, I thought you'd never ask."

"Don't be silly," she laughed. "I'm just better at the action stuff than you are. Now it's brain time, and that means it's your turn."

"How about starting at Rudolfo's trailer? It's the only one we can be sure is empty."

We circled the trailers from behind, trying to avoid as much as possible the area of the garbage cans and the stench that surrounded them. For a moment I puzzled over something that bothered me. Then I finally realized that not a sound came from any of the trailers, and the only light other than Fatty's single bulb was from the moon above.

Nobody was home! I wanted to tell Cassie, but we had arrived at Rudolfo's trailer. I decided to wait until we were safely inside before risking any more conversation.

Since Cassie had already tried to open the front door this morning without success, we had agreed that the back window was our best hope of gaining entrance. She reached up to open the screen, but the wire netting was so rusted that it came away in her hands.

"Oops," she whispered, as she pushed it under the trailer. "That solves that problem. Okay Mom," she said, bending over, "climb up."

This was the part of our plan that I dreaded the most. I had seen poodles at the circus do this hundreds of times, but they were much more agile than I.

"Cassie," I began, "I just don't think...."

"Hurry, Mom! Someone's coming!"

I was up on her back and through the window in two seconds flat. I reached out and pulled her inside in less time than that. I hugged the floor, praying that we hadn't been seen until she poked me in the back and giggled.

"Gotcha!"

"Cassie! You wicked child! You should be ashamed," I sputtered.

"Well, sorry, but you seemed to need a little encouragement."

"Geez, this place stinks." I said changing the subject so I wouldn't stay mad. "You think we can cover the window with something so we can turn on the flashlight? Smells like something curled up and died in here. I'd just as soon not step on whatever it is in the dark."

Cassie bumped around and came up with an indiscriminate article of clothing which she draped carefully over the window. We turned on our flashlights and surveyed our surroundings.

"I thought he left," whispered Cass.

"Fatty said so, but it sure doesn't look like he packed first."

The inside of the trailer was a mess. Dirty clothes were strewn all over the cracked linoleum floor. Three stained twin bed mattresses were laid end to end down the length of the narrow trailer. A couple of filthy pillows were scattered about, but I could see no evidence of sheets or other bedclothes. In one corner, a small wooden table with only three legs leaned precariously against a rickety chair for support. The kitchen counter was full of dirty dishes and more were soaking in the small sink. The greyish water was afloat with chicken bones, pizza crust, and cigarette butts. The stench was almost overpowering.

The fake wood paneling on the walls was bare except for a calendar with pictures of pretty dark-haired girls in provocative poses and a crude hand-lettered sign reminding the inhabitants that no prostitutes were allowed on the premises.

"Wow," I sighed. "Home sweet home."

"Awful, isn't it," agreed Cassie.

"See anything that might tell us something about what's going on here?"

"Looks like somebody else might have beat us to it," she observed looking at the scattered articles on the floor.

"I think you're right." I kicked aside a dirty shirt, and cringed as I saw a huge cockroach scurry across the floor.

"But," I continued hopefully, "we might find something they overlooked, if we're lucky."

"Or smarter," suggested Cass. "Remember, these guys don't have a safety deposit box or a checking account. They wire money home when they can, but in the meanwhile, they have to have a safe place to hide it. If Rudolfo left in too much of a hurry to pack his clothes, he might have left his stash—and maybe a forwarding address behind as well."

"Gee, Cassie, your Uncle Leonard would be proud. What other assumptions can you make?"

"You think these mattresses have fleas or something? I'd like to sit down while I think."

"Better not," I cautioned. "Too much bare skin exposed in that swimsuit."

Cassie pushed one of the mattresses aside with her foot and carefully examined the chipped and scarred edges of the baseboard.

"It's too risky for them to carry their goodies while they're working. They'd have to have a hiding place close to home."

"That could be anywhere," I complained, "even outside."

In spite of my abbreviated costume I was beginning to work up a serious sweat inside the stuffy little aluminum box. I couldn't imagine how horrible life must have been for the men who spent night after night inside this hot trailer, then worked out in the fields under the broiling sun all day long.

"I wouldn't hide anything outside," continued Cassie with her deductions. "I would want it close by so I could hold it and look at it whenever I wanted. And I would like to have it close at hand when I was sleeping so I could get to it quickly if I had to make a getaway during the night."

"You think that's what happened? Rudolfo made a run for it, and Fatso just said he was deported to cover up the fact that he got away?"

"I don't know, Mom. Do you think this linoleum will lift up if I pull hard enough?"

"I have to pee."

Cassie looked at me incredulously.

"Why didn't you go before we left the house?"

I smiled, remembering the hundreds of times when she was small and I had asked her the same question.

"Do I dare use the bathroom?"

"It's through that plastic curtain—if you have the guts," she told me. "I peeked in there a minute ago. It makes the rest of this place look like the Taj Mahal."

I pushed the curtain aside with my flashlight and watched in disgust as several huge water bugs ducked back into hiding. Cassie was right. The tiny room was a pigsty. The sink and narrow shower stall were covered with dark mildew stains, and brown tepid water dripped in a steady rhythm from the rusting faucets. The area reeked of urine.

The toilet seat was hanging by one bolt, but I didn't care. There was no way I would ever dare sit down. Necessity forced me to quell the desire to run for my life as I pulled down my suit and held on to the towel rack while I squatted over the bowl.

I could hear Cassie knocking furniture about in her search and I opened my mouth to caution her against making noise when the towel rack came apart under my weight and fell to the floor with a resounding clatter.

She pushed the curtain to one side and we stared at one another in dismay.

"You think anyone heard that?" I whispered hoarsely.

"Anyone and everyone!" she hissed. "Including the inhabitants of Cedar Hill Cemetery."

"Don't be mean, Cassie. It's not like I meant to do it!"

I pulled up my suit and inadvertently kicked the cheap metal towel rack once again.

"Mom, for Pete's sake!"

I turned the flashlight on the floor to keep from hitting the rack again and risk further annoying my daughter.

"Well, will you look at this," I muttered in surprise.

Cassie pulled the curtain aside one more time.

"My God, Mom! You found his stash!"

CHAPTER SIXTEEN

$100 bills—rolled tightly into crisp little green and white cylinders poked out the end of the metal towel rack. Before I could stop her, Cassie knelt down on the nasty floor and began to gently extricate the money.

"There must be over a thousand dollars here!" she exclaimed.

"Much more than that. Look, there's still some caught in the holder on the wall."

We gathered up the money until our hands were full. Cassie began stuffing bills in the front of her bathing suit. I followed her example.

"What's this?" she said as she turned the bar around and poked tentatively at the other end. "This isn't money."

She stuck her index finger in the metal hole.

"Damn! I can't reach it."

"Bring it. We'll get whatever it is out when we get home. Mother has some long-necked tweezers."

"Looks like I'll have to, Mom. My finger's stuck."

"WHAT!"

"Shhhh! I hear somebody coming."

"Yeah, right! You already pulled that one on me once, remember? I can't believe you did something so stupid...."

The flimsy trailer door shook with the blows of a heavy fist.

"Who's in there?" shouted a man's voice. "I know you're in there! Open the door."

The thin walls of the trailer quivered as the mighty blows resumed.

"My God, Mom," cried Cassie. "What'll we do?"

"Make a run for it," I whispered urgently. "Maybe he'll forget there's another way out."

I grabbed the towel rack affixed to Cassie's finger and gave it an experimental tug.

"Ouch!"

"Be careful with that thing. You don't want to lose your pointer," I cautioned unnecessarily. "I'll go first this time so I can help you."

We hurried to the back of the trailer and pulled the rag off the window. I took a cautious peek outside but didn't see another soul. The blows continued to rain on the door. It was only a matter of minutes before it caved in under the tremendous punishment. Without thinking once of clever poodles, I climbed out the window and dropped fearlessly to the ground below.

Cassie was stuck. No matter which way she turned she couldn't hold on to the window frame so she could climb out. For a briefly insane moment I considered running around to the front door and acting as a decoy so my daughter could escape. She stopped me just in time.

"I'm coming out head first, Mom," she whispered. "Catch me!"

I managed to grab her around the middle as she tumbled out the window. We both fell backwards and rolled over end to end like dung beetles in the dust.

"Ommph!"

"Cassie? Are you okay?"

For an answer she grabbed my hand to pull me up, and off we ran. She held the metal bar close to her body to avoid hitting first the trailers and then tree branches as we skirted the enclave and made our way back to the cedar forest.

Under cover of the spreading branches, we stopped to get our breath and listen.

"Did he catch on?"

"Unless he's an idiot," I panted.

"I don't hear anything."

"Me neither, but I don't want to wait until we do. Let's get going. Can you climb back down the cliff with that thing hanging off your hand?"

"I'll have to, won't I?" she answered. "But this time you go first in case I fall."

"Oh, God, Cassie," I begged. "Please be careful."

"Like I wouldn't if you didn't tell me to," she snorted. "That always makes me so mad when you…."

"He's coming!"

I wasn't sure if I heard anything or not, but I was certain we would get caught if we stood there arguing like ninnies. We ran side by side back down the path to the cliffs.

Cassie's eyes and reflexes were twenty years younger than mine. She managed to catch me before I ran full tilt over the precipice. I flopped over on my stomach and backed down over the ledge searching for a toehold with my foot. I heard Cassie's metal appendage clank on a rock. She was right behind me.

"Go, Mom, go!" she called softly and urgently. "I don't want to kick you in the face."

I scrambled down the rocky cliff as fast as I could, but I wasn't fast enough.

A bright light flashed in my face and suddenly I was blinded—frozen on the spot like a bug pinned under a microscope.

"Stop right there, bitch!" warned a man's angry voice. "I have a gun and it's pointed right at your head. If you don't come back up here right now, I'll blow you away."

"I...I can't see," I called back. "Turn the light off. You're blinding me."

"Do you think I'm stupid?" he sneered.

"No, no, I can't see, honestly. Just turn the light off, and I'll climb back up."

The man grunted and grudgingly moved the light slowly away from my face. I held my breath, praying that he wouldn't turn the light in Cassie's direction, and made noises like I was climbing. When my eyes adjusted to the dark I could see Cassie's outline above me. She was poised right underneath the overhang at the top. He still hadn't seen her, and it was up to me to make sure that he never did. I made my decision in a split second.

"Arghh!" I cried out theatrically. "I'm slipping! Help! Help!" And I stepped backwards into the darkness.

It seemed to me that I fell slowly, fully aware of everything that was happening. The man above followed my progress with his flashlight beam until I was out of range. I heard the loud explosion of his gun and decided I was dying because I had not hit the water yet.

I was going straight to hell without passing "Go," just like Mother always warned I would. A vague feeling of remorse for the use of the foul language that apparently was my undoing crossed my mind. I found myself wishing I had committed some other sins that were a lot more fun. Then I hit the surface of the water. I hit hard. My body shot down to the rocky bottom of the bay like a torpedo. The water wasn't very deep and my feet and then my knees doubled up painfully beneath me. The water stung the raw places where the rocks scraped the skin from my legs and brought me back to my senses. I had to get some air in my lungs, but I had to do it quietly. I was supposed to be dead, after all.

I swam under water as far as I could before I surfaced. I was ten or fifteen feet from where I fell in. Even though my lungs burned, I forced my mouth closed and breathed the air I so desperately needed through my nose.

I granted myself the luxury of floating for a moment and looked back up to the top of the cliff. The man was still making a futile effort to shine his light towards the black waters of the bay. It wasn't long before he realized it was hopeless. The light changed directions and then bobbed away from the edge and gradually out of sight.

I swam quietly back to the bottom of the cliff and waited silently until I heard the occasional clink of metal against rock.

"Cassie, I'm here," I called softly.

"Mom, oh, Mom," she snuffled. "I thought...."

And she was down beside me in the water and holding on for dear life.

I laughed and cried with her for a minute or two, then held her at arm's length.

"Let's hope Fatty thinks I'm dead, too. And just pray we have enough time to get back to Watson before he decides to drive down to the lakeshore to see if my body turns up. I imagine by now he's realized what an embarrassment my poor little corpse could be."

Cassie found it impossible to swim with the metal rack on her finger. She finally turned over on her back and let me pull her lifesaver style. When we reached the shore, she went to pick up our clothes, and I headed for the car at a dead run. I had the engine on and was ready to go by the time she climbed inside.

"Hand me that Atlanta Braves cap from the back seat, Cassie. And put on Gran's big straw hat. If anybody comes along looking for us maybe they won't recognize a man and a woman necking."

"Necking?"

"Yeah," I laughed. "Scoot over close to me and put your arm around my shoulder. That ought to fool them."

"Wow, Mom, you're really something! I don't think I've ever seen you so charged."

"Near death experiences tend to have that effect on me," I acknowledged with a grin. "And I'm starving! Are you still up for some hot salty grease?"

"What about this thing on my hand?" she asked.

"Order the home fries, it'll slide off in no time," I promised.

80

CHAPTER SEVENTEEN

Because the Pelican was only a short distance from the lake, it was a favorite spot for fisherman to take their hungry families after a disappointing day at the lonesome end of a fishing pole. I had to admit, some of the best catfish I've ever eaten was served to me by the Pelican's star waitress.

Wanda Blake was a distant cousin of the owner and the mother of at least one of his six children. That son left town several years ago and made his mother proud by achieving somewhat of a reputation as the stud de jour in several higher class porn movies. Over the years Hector, A.K.A. Dirk Blade, had sent Wanda enough money to purchase the modest cottage he grew up in and do nothing for the rest of her days but watch daytime television. While he found it hard to believe she preferred to work, I didn't. Wanda was a total extrovert. She would shrivel up and die if she stayed home by herself.

The parking area in front of the restaurant was full of cars with out-of-state plates and local pickup trucks with boat trailers attached. I drove around to the back and stationed Watson in a dark corner—well away from the tall mercury lamp that painted the night with its ghostly green glow.

"Gosh, Mom. Why are we hiding back here? You don't think Fatty is still on our trail, do you?"

She got out without even waiting for my answer. "Remember," she continued, "he was so drunk he could hardly stand not so very long ago. I'm surprised he was able to waddle down to the cliffs. I bet he collapsed when he got back to his trailer and forgot the whole thing."

I climbed stiffly out of the car and peered in the side view mirror to see if there was something I could do to make myself more presentable. I was startled to see my reflection looking back, white and scared in the ghoulish light.

"Oh, my," I whispered.

"What's that, Mom?" asked Cassie as she turned and leaned against the fender to slip on her jeans.

"Oh, my, is right, Mom! Your poor shins! What happened?"

Cassie quickly zipped up her pants and knelt at my side. I looked down and saw what she meant. The skin on the front of my legs and the tops of my feet had been rubbed raw by the rocks on the bottom of Bass Bay. Little rivulets of blood had congealed in irregular lines from knees to ankles causing my pale legs to resemble factory reject peppermint sticks.

"Yukkk!" pronounced my daughter.

"Is that opinion medical or cosmetic?"

"Mom, you really ought to go home and take care of this. You might even need a tetanus shot."

"I need something to eat," I insisted. "Help me put on these jeans. I'll worry about my legs later. My tummy is my main problem right now."

"I'll ask Wanda if we can sit in the kitchen," worried Cassie. "You don't look too good."

"Gee, thanks a lot! I may not be young and beautiful enough to look good after jumping off a sixty-foot cliff...."

"Forty."

"Whatever. And landing in five feet of water."

"Fifteen."

"Whatever! But I'm not over the hill, yet!"

Cassie brushed the hair back from my forehead with the fingers of her free hand and gave me an awkward little hug.

"You look great, Mom. But let's sit in the kitchen anyway, okay."

We opened the back door to the bright lights and noisy conversation of the busy restaurant. Cassie waited for a moment until she caught Wanda's eye and called her over.

Somehow she convinced her to let us pass unnoticed through the swinging door of the dining room into the kitchen. The burly cook turned to order us out and got a good look at Cassie. His broad face broke into a huge welcoming grin, and he waved his meat cleaver in a fond salute. Wanda led us around behind the stainless steel counters and big iron stoves to a quiet worktable in the corner where we would be out of the way.

Wanda didn't even blink when she took in our disheveled appearance. Her only response to the metal towel rack on Cassie's finger was to hand her a small plastic bag of ice.

"Keep this on that finger for a minute, hun. Soon's the swelling goes down it'll fall right off. What can I get you folks tonight?"

Cassie and I ordered the works: country ham, fried eggs, grits, hash browns, gravy, sausage, bacon, and biscuits. While we waited for our food, I began to feel the adrenaline drain away. My legs started hurting and my emotions took an abrupt nosedive. When Wanda startled me by slapping the huge platters of food down on the table, I burst into tears.

"Oh, for goodness sakes? What's wrong, hun? Did you want 'em scrambled?" she asked.

"Just bring her some hot tea, please, Wanda," sighed Cassie. "And I guess you'd better take that feast away. Maybe she could have a poached egg and some dry toast instead?"

Cassie dug unashamedly into her food and let me sob. She knew I had to cry myself out.

"Okay, Mom," she said finally as she wiped egg yolk off her cheek, "It just now hit you that we got shot at, right?"

"Yes," I hiccoughed.

"And you're blaming yourself again because you took your little chick into harm's way?"

"Something like that," I sighed remorsefully.

"If I were a friend—Pam for instance—would you be crying, or would you be dancing with the excitement and thrill of it all?"

"Well...."

"I'll tell you," she interrupted. "You'd be jumping up and down with glee that we got away with it, and," she lowered her voice, "found at least part of what we went looking for."

"But, you're my baby," I protested tearfully. "I'm supposed to protect you with my last breath."

"Mom, you're the most wonderful parent anyone ever had. One of the things I like best about us is that sometimes you forget you're a mom. When you treat me like an equal, then I know I'm the kind of person you would chose for a friend. That makes me intensely proud. I had a terrific time tonight. I wouldn't have missed it for the world. If you had gone out there without me I would have been furious, and terribly hurt. And you might be an unwelcome guest in Fatty's trailer."

"How come?"

"Because if I hadn't been there, you would have climbed back up that cliff instead of jumping to protect me. Now can I have a piece of pie?"

"May I have a piece of pie," I corrected with a tentative little smile.

"Yes, you may," laughed my daughter.

"I love you, Cassie."

"I...hey, the ice worked! The rack came off my finger."

She plopped the towel bar down on the table.

"Now, let's see if I can...."

"For heaven's sake, don't stick another finger...."

Cassie was about to give me that withering look reserved for mothers who make the mistake of saying the obvious, when Wanda leaned over the table.

"Some jerk's out front demanding to know if a woman with curly red hair came in the restaurant," she whispered with a conspiratorial wink. "Nobody saw you two come in so's they all said no. I thought I'd best warn you because he may try to look in the kitchen."

"Thanks, Wanda!" said Cassie, as she hopped up and grabbed the towel rack.

I fished a crumpled twenty out of my jeans pocket and handed it to her.

"Will this cover everything and leave enough for you?"

"More than these yokels ever tip me, hun. Now scat!"

Cassie and I followed Wanda to the back of the kitchen and hurried through the door she opened for us. We found ourselves in the parking lot about ten feet from Watson. Wanda blew us a kiss and closed the door. We stood side by side in the shadows and listened.

"What are we waiting for?" whispered Cassie impatiently.

I, too, longed to run for the safety of the car, but caution kept me from acting on impulse. Cassie started to push me out of the doorway when we both heard the soft crunching of gravel as a truck drove slowly around from the front. We flattened ourselves against the wall and held our breath as the truck circled the other cars in the lot.

"That's Fatty's truck," whispered Cassie. "I saw it earlier at the trailer park."

"I know, but I don't think that's him driving."

"Why not? Who else would it be?"

"I don't know, but Fatty knows our names and what Watson looks like, remember? He wouldn't have to describe me."

We watched as the truck drove slowly back to the front entrance, then pulled out on the highway. The driver put the pedal to the metal and was soon out of sight.

"Whew! Thank God for Wanda. Now we can relax."

"We've got to get home quickly, Cassie."

"Why the big hurry?"

"Just in case I'm wrong and that was Fatty. Thanks to my big mouth, he not only knows our names, he knows where we live. By now Mother is probably back at the farm. And she's all alone."

"Aggie's there."

"Big whoop."

CHAPTER EIGHTEEN

We were home in less than fifteen minutes. I took the freeway instead of the local road so I could exceed the speed limit without worrying about broadsiding meandering cows, chickens, or goats. The farmers who live in Lakeland County are notorious for eschewing fences in favor of open pastures, and they shared watering holes for their livestock. It was a neighborly concept, but made traveling at night a tad interesting.

The house was dark. I couldn't tell if Mother had gotten home and gone to bed, or had not yet arrived. And there was no sign of Fatty, or anyone else.

"What'll we do?" asked Cassie. "Do you want me to go in a check on Gran, or stay out here and wait with you?"

"Go check on her," I decided abruptly.

"I hate to leave you alone in case Fatty comes roaring up the driveway with guns drawn."

"I'll be fine. Just make sure Mother is okay, then come back and let me know."

Cassie opened the car door and hopped out. As soon as I saw that she was safely in the house I drove around the circular drive and parked Watson behind the few crepe myrtles and rhododendrons that had escaped the storm.

I got out of the car and waited in the bushes for Cassie to reappear. It didn't take long. She came running around from the front of the house to surprise me after I had stared nervously at the back door for a full five minutes.

"What's the deal, Cassie?" I whispered impatiently.

"Gran's not home, yet."

"And?"

"I climbed out my bedroom window in case she came home while I was inside the house. I also stuffed our beds with pillows to make it look like we were sleeping. Neat, huh?"

"And all this was in aid of what?" I asked crossly.

Even in the moonlight I could see the excitement ebb from her face. I immediately wished I could take the words back.

"I'm sorry, Cassie. I'm tired and irritable. I didn't mean to sound snotty, but what did you have in mind? Not staying out here all night, I hope?"

"You're the one who was all hot to trot for this adventure," she retorted. "I was perfectly willing to spend my last weekend on the farm in peace and quiet. A nice glass of wine and some of that Dutch cheese—maybe a good book—certainly not one of Leonard's, by the way...."

I grabbed her arm and pulled her down behind the crepe myrtle.

"Somebody's coming!"

"That's getting pretty old, Mom. Crying wolf is...."

"I should have parked down by the raspberry patch," I moaned. "Anyone who comes up the drive and goes around the circle will see us! How stupid can I get?"

"False alarm," laughed Cassie. "Whoever it was just backed out and turned around."

"Did you see the car?"

"Nope, only the lights."

Cassie stood and stretched.

"Can we go in now? You're too tired to be any fun, and I'm ready for a warm shower and my pajamas. And," she threatened, "if you don't do something about your legs, I'll phone Winston Wallace, M.D., and ask him to make a house call."

"I suppose you're right," I sighed. "If that was Fatty at the Pelican he would have been here waiting for us when we got home. We probably should have gone to the police station and had one of Andy's men accompany us."

"Oh, sure," scoffed my loving daughter, "and tell him we just trespassed on private property, committed B&E, and made off with over a thousand dollars. By the way, Mom, what are we going to do with our ill-gotten gains?"

"I forgot about the money. Thanks for reminding me. I would have washed it down the drain with my bath. Do you still have all of yours?"

"Yeah," she answered.

She stuck her hand down the front of her swimsuit and wiggled around for a moment.

"Uff! Here it is," she said as she handed me the tight little curls of money. "I think that's all."

I held the money in one hand and fished around in my jeans pocket for my house key with the other.

"I hate to ask you, Cassie, but do you mind...?"

"Putting Watson away? Of course not, Mom, just leave me some hot water. I'll be there in a sec."

My legs were sore and stiff, yet wobbly at the same time. I trudged up the walk with the gait of a hundred year-old woman. I turned the light on in the kitchen and made my way painfully through the house.

When I opened the bedroom door, my wonderful bed loaded with down pillows and soft satiny pink sheets beckoned with a siren's call. I replaced the pillows Cassie had used to fake my sleeping body and straightened the covers. Then somehow I found the will to force myself to turn away and enter the bathroom.

When I tried to undress, I discovered that the fabric of my jeans had stuck to the raw abrasions on my legs. The only way I could think of to free myself without causing more damage was a good soak.

I filled the tub and slipped cautiously down into the warm water. I bit my lip against the stinging pain, then gradually sat back and relaxed as it eased. I positioned a towel underneath my neck and settled even deeper into the warm water. It felt heavenly. My eyelids drooped and I let myself doze as I enjoyed the bliss of the moment.

I woke up when the water got cold and the wet jeans clutched my thighs in a clammy embrace. I sat up quickly and grimaced as pain shot through the muscles in my stiff neck and shoulders.

"Damn! I bet Cassie has used the rest of the hot water by now."

I turned on the faucet and grinned with relief as the unexpected warmth flowed over my fingers. I let the cold water out and shucked off my jeans and swimsuit while the tub refilled.

The sight of my injured legs filled me with dismay, but I knew from experience they probably looked worse than they really were. I had been sidewalk rollerskating champion of my neighborhood when I was ten. I spent most of that year with concrete burns that were far worse than this.

I washed every raw spot carefully with antibacterial soap and rinsed off with clean hot water. There was still plenty left after Cassie's shower, and I decided I had been asleep longer than I realized. It took Mother's enormous hot water heater at least forty minutes to refill and heat up.

I patted myself down with a soft towel and applied first aid cream liberally to each leg. A pair of old flannel pajamas from the bottom drawer of my chest felt wonderful against my sensitive skin and would protect my sheets. Having incurred the wrath of Fatty was one thing, making my mother angry by ruining her precious bed linens was something entirely different.

I sat down at my dresser and was attempting to comb the frizzes out of my hair when someone knocked.

"Come on in, Cassie."

"It's me," said Mother, as she opened the door. "May I come in anyway?"

"Of course," I answered looking around nervously. My jeans were still in the bathroom along with my swimsuit and soggy tennis shoes, but I had dumped the money in a careless little pile on my bed.

"Here, Mother," I offered as I stood up hastily. "Sit here so you won't muss that lovely dress."

As I plopped down on my bed, I reached behind my back to push the bills under a pillow. I hoped that Cassie had taken the time to tuck her dirty clothes out of the way. Mother was a better detective than Leonard would ever be, and I wasn't ready for her to find out where we had been tonight, not yet anyway. I needed a good night's sleep before I tackled that little confession.

"You and Horatio have a good time hobbing and knobbing with the *hoi polloi*?"

"Naturally," she smiled. "And we won the grand prize, thanks to Horatio's fearless bidding in the last round."

"And that would be?"

"Two tickets to the Mid-Summer Night's Ball at the country club. Horatio had already bought ours. You wouldn't have a use for them, would you?" she asked with raised eyebrows.

I leaned back against the pillows and sighed theatrically. "Give it a rest, Mother. You cannot make me over in your image, not now, not ever. Think of it as a sow's ear, silk purse kind of thing."

"Nonsense, my dear. All you need is the right incentive. Someday a Prince Charming...."

"Let's not go there, if you don't mind. It's late and I don't want to go to bed angry."

"Very well," she sighed. "Anyway, I was planning all along to give them to Cassandra. Perhaps she knows someone she would like to go with. It will make a nice little reintroduction to the social life of Rowan Springs."

"Give me a break!"

Mother ignored me and brushed away a nonexistent wrinkle in her skirt.

"Where is Cassie?" she asked.

"She said she was going to take a shower, then go straight to bed. She has to finish packing tomorrow morning. I promised to help her move early in the afternoon."

"Oh, my, I am going to miss her. And it won't seem the same without dear little Aggie, either."

"Yeah," I grinned. "Ain't it a pity?"

Mother stood and backed up to the bed so I could unzip her dress. "I'm off to sleep, dear. I'll check on Cassie and see if she's still awake. I can't wait to tell her of our good fortune. I know she'll love going to the ball."

She stood in the doorway, smiling. "Maybe we can take a trip to Wieuca City to shop for her party dress. Won't that be fun?"

"I can hardly wait."

"Sarcasm is so unbecoming, Paisley. And by the way, you could use some sprucing up, too, my dear. One simply cannot go through life wearing blue jeans."

"One can give it one's best shot, though, Mother. If one simply hangs tough. Sleep tight."

When I heard the distant sound of her bedroom door closing, I got up and rescued the money from under my pillow. I looked around for a quick and convenient place to hide it for the night. Tomorrow I would go to the bank and stick it in the lockbox. It was, after all, not mine to keep. I was sure that Rudolfo or one of the men who shared his digs would be coming back for it. I finally settled on my jewelry box for lack of a better hiding place. It was way too obvious, but it was only for tonight. I counted the little rolls as I tucked them under my pearls. Rudolfo had amassed a small fortune. There were twenty-seven fresh new $100 bills in the bunch.

I yawned deeply and stretched some of the kinks out of my stiff muscles. The warm bath had done wonders for my body and my psyche. I felt almost human again.

I crossed over to close the bedroom door and was surprised to see Aggie waiting timidly on the threshold.

"Wow, you have had a change of personality. What's the matter, beast, amnesia, or schizophrenia?"

She cocked her skinny little head and uttered the tiniest of sounds. It was a cross between a sad little cry and pitiful whine. Her big brown eyes held a world of "please" in them.

"All right," I relented. "Come on." I ushered her inside and closed the door. "After all, this is your last night on the farm."

I helped her up on the bed and looked her sternly in the eye. "That's the only reason I'm giving in, you understand. This doesn't change a thing in our relationship. You're the dog and I'm the person. You sleep at the foot of the bed and I get the down pillow."

I brushed my teeth and hung my wet jeans over a towel rack where I hoped they would dry overnight.

When I got back to my bed, Aggie was comfortably ensconced in the middle of my favorite pillow. Her soft little doggie snores left me no alternative. She was skinny and tired, but her bite was still worse than her bark. I pulled the covers down on the other side of the bed and climbed in carefully so I wouldn't disturb her sleep.

CHAPTER NINETEEN

When I awoke the next morning, Aggie's warm little butt was wedged comfortably under my left armpit. She was still snoring, and I had to use the bathroom. I lay there for a few minutes trying to decide if I could move quickly enough to avoid disturbing her and thereby keep from getting bitten. Finally, nature forced the issue and I made a move to jump out of bed. Unfortunately, I forgot to figure into the equation the abuse I had imposed upon my forty-three-year-old muscles the night before. My agile mind hopped up, but my abused body dragged behind. Aggie woke up with a vicious growl and took a quick nip out of my lagging derriere.

"Damn! Damn and damn! You little piece of crap dog! As soon as I pee, I'm taking you to Cassie's room and placing you in her custody until the move. And good riddance!"

My legs looked much better. I slathered on some more first aid cream and slipped into a house robe.

Aggie didn't have to be invited out of my room for the second time. That surprised me a little, but I supposed it was the mention of her beloved mistress's name that propelled her down the hall and across the house to the other wing.

Cassie's door was still closed and there was no answer when I knocked.

"You're going in anyway, dog. You've lost your right to liberty and the pursuit of happiness."

I opened the door and gingerly pushed Aggie inside with my foot. She ran around me and darted back out again. I turned to follow and caught sight of Cassie's bed. The rounded hump of pillows under the cover might have fooled some, but I could never have mistaken the lumpy outline for my daughter's slender figure.

"Cassie?" I called as I stepped into the room and crossed over to her bed. I pulled back the bedspread and saw two pillows placed end to end. They sat on top of a summer blanket and smooth sheets tucked snugly under the sides of the mattress. The bed had not been slept in.

"What the hell did you do, Cassie? Stay up all night on watch?"

I put the pillows back in their normal position at the top of the bed and rearranged the covers. Still unconcerned, I busied about filling one of the packing boxes with the books still remaining on her shelf.

In a few minutes Aggie came back to the door and barked. The sound surprised me so much I dropped Bartlett's *Familiar Quotations,* ripping the paper jacket.

"Fine time you picked to come out of your funk, dog."

I sighed and gave up on the books. Aggie obviously would keep on making a nuisance of herself if I didn't let her out and feed her. Cassie was a big girl now. If she stayed up all night, she would just have to pay the consequences.

Mother was sitting at the kitchen table buttering a flaky homemade croissant. The kitchen was fragrant with the scent of bread baking in the oven and freshly ground coffee beans.

"Umm, I'm starving!"

"Good morning to you too, Paisley, dear," chided Mother.

"I'm sorry, Mother," I grinned. "But I really am starving."

"I seriously doubt that, my child. But I am glad to see that little Aggie has her appetite back."

"Yeah! She made an *hors d'oeuvre* of my butt this morning," I complained. "But you're right. She does appear to be more like her old self—rotten and stinkin'."

I poured some hot water over a tea bag and grabbed two croissants off the platter warming on the stove.

"Where's Cassie?" I asked as I sat down. "She have breakfast already?"

Mother dabbed at a few errant crumbs with a dainty linen napkin and looked at me quizzically. "No. I assumed she was still sleeping. Didn't you just come from her bedroom?"

I took the croissant out of my mouth and put it slowly down on my plate. My heart skipped a beat as her words etched themselves on my brain. I turned and faced her squarely.

"She wasn't there. Her bed hasn't been slept in."

"Nonsense, dear," answered Mother with a reassuring smile. "I saw her in bed myself when I peeked in her room last night. She must have...."

"No! That wasn't her," I cried. "Those were pillows she piled up to look like she was sleeping. She did the same thing to my bed before she climbed out the window."

Mother's face turned pale but her lips tightened in a firm, uncompromising line.

"I think you need to fill in some blanks, Paisley. And quickly."

I jumped up from the table and looked out the kitchen window. Thanks to the storm, I could see all the way to the carriage house, but the garage doors were on the other side. I couldn't tell if Watson was still there.

"Come with me. I'll fill you in on the way."

We hurried across the gravel drive looking like two awkward storks with our housecoats flapping in the morning breeze.

I heard the tired beeping of the seatbelt warning before we rounded the corner. Cassie had parked the car and turned off the engine, but she hadn't had time to close the door.

"Oh, my God!" breathed Mother. "What happened?"

"Somebody's snatched Cassie, that's what," I whispered hoarsely.

The words squeezed painfully through the sudden stricture in my throat. A huge empty pit opened somewhere beneath my diaphragm and my heart fell all the way to the darkness at the bottom.

When I opened my eyes, the first thing I saw was Doctor Winston Wallace.

"Um, wha...what the hell are you doing here?" I mumbled angrily as I pushed myself up in bed. "And what am I doing in bed? What's going on?"

"Relax, dear lady," said Wallace, pulling his chair closer. "Your Mother called me. You lost consciousness about thirty minutes ago."

"A half hour! And just how long have you been here alone in my bedroom staring at me?"

Wallace turned a bright shade of crimson and officiously straightened the lapels on his starched white clinic jacket. He face was thinner than I remembered and so was his hair. But he sported the same artificially acquired tan, and the big gold Rolex still circled one bony wrist.

"I assure you, dear lady, I have not been alone with you until a few moments ago. Your mother received a phone call and excused herself just before you opened your eyes."

"Oh, sorry," I offered as a grudging apology. "So what's wrong with me?"

When the words left my mouth, the memory of Cassie's disappearance came flooding back. I groaned and clutched my chest to still the sudden rapid beat of my heart.

Alarmed, Wallace jumped up and grabbed my wrist in an attempt to take my pulse. I jerked away from him and tried to get out of bed.

"Paisley," said Mother sharply as she entered the room. "Stop behaving like a child and let Dr. Wallace examine you. Cassie and I have been quite worried."

Startled by the mention of Cassie's name I flopped back against the pillows. "Cassie? She's...?"

"She's quite concerned about you. She just called to say she'll be home as soon as she can. She has some business of her own to take care of—something you can't help her with. She said not to worry."

Mother's face was a study in marble. I could tell nothing from her expression, but she gave the slightest nod and she darted her eyes in Wallace's direction.

"By the way, she also said to remind you to be sure and let her Aunt Amelia have her new address."

A warm slow wave of relief flooded through my body as I realized that Cassie was all right. I still didn't know what had happened to her, but she had sent me a message of reassurance, and that was good enough for me. I even managed to give Wallace a shaky little smile.

"Okay, Doc," I said as I stuck out my arm, "take as much pulse as you need."

"I'll leave you two alone," said Mother, "if that's all right with you, dear. I *would* like to get dressed before the clock strikes noon."

Winston Wallace opened his leather bag of goodies and took out his little doctor toys. He took my blood pressure, listened to my heart, looked down my throat, up my nose, and in my ears.

"So what's the deal, Doc?"

"Have you been having any unusual symptoms lately?" he asked in a stern clinical voice—one that immediately brought back the cold fear of my concern. I quietly told him about the episodes of breathlessness and the palpations.

"I meant to see a doctor, but there just never seemed to be time. What's wrong with me?"

He sat back in the chair and peered over tented fingers. The pose seemed choreographed, as if he had practiced for hours in front of a mirror.

"Have you ever had an EKG?" he asked.

"No. I don't think so, anyway. The last complete exam I had was in New York about two years ago and everything was hunky dory. I should have had one last year, but Dr. Baxter died, and you...."

"Yes, I know," he smiled crookedly. "We've had our little contre-temps. There is another physician in Rowan Springs now—foreigner, an Indian doctor named Dhanvantari, if you'd care to see him."

He leaned forward and looked at me earnestly. "But you should give me a second chance, Paisley. I have changed. And a large part of that was your doing. After you exposed my drug habit I went into re-hab, and now I'm completely clean. I tried to straighten out my marriage, but it was too late. My wife left me six months ago."

His narrow little eyes squenched up as if he were going to cry, but it was hard to tell what Winston was feeling. His facial expressions were just a tad off, as if he wasn't quite sure how he was supposed to feel. I reached out and gave him an awkward pat on the arm just in case.

"I am sorry, Winston."

"Are you, dear lady?" he asked. "Of course, you know how I feel. My great loss, I mean—and the loneliness. I heard you had quite a romantic fling with Bert Atkins before he disappeared. You must be lonely, too."

I began to regret my offering of sympathy, but I was feeling so much better about Cassie I let him get away with his intrusion into my private life.

"Yeah, well. So you think I have a heart condition?" I asked with an effort to keep my voice steady.

"No, no, nothing that serious," he said with a reassuring smile. "I'm quite certain that all of your symptoms are due to stress. They're classic signs of hyperventilation and post-traumatic reaction. Of course, it doesn't hurt to play it safe, so perhaps you should make an appointment sometime soon for that EKG. Meanwhile, I'll give you a prescription for a mild sedative which will keep you on an even keel."

"I don't like taking pills," I said, making a childish face.

"I don't know many of my patients who do," he laughed. It sounded almost natural.

"Are you sure there's nothing seriously wrong with me?"

I was too superstitious to accept the double good fortune of having my frightening symptoms amount to nothing and finding out that Cassie was okay at the same time.

"Let's check your heart one more time," he smiled. This time it was genuine.

He placed the cold stethoscope between my breasts and listened intently.

"Nothing wrong there. Please turn around, if you don't mind, and slip your pajama shirt down in the back."

I did as he asked, and breathed deeply on his command.

"So what...?"

"Shhh."

I waited impatiently while he listened.

"Turn, please. No, leave your shirt down."

I did as he asked, but I was beginning to feel uncomfortable. If there was nothing wrong with me but an overactive nervous system, why, I wondered, was he spending so much time on my chest.

"I hope you took the precaution of protecting your skin when you were living in the tropics. You're quite fair, you know, Paisley. With that lovely red hair and light green eyes, you're a prime candidate for skin cancer."

"Watch it, Doc," I laughed uncomfortably. "If I didn't know better I might think you were flirting with me."

He stuck the stethoscope down under my left breast, and leaned closer to me.

"And if I were, would you like it? Would you like this?" he whispered as he brushed his palm against my nipple.

I jerked back and pulled his hand out of my shirt. "What the hell?"

"Come on, Paisley," he smiled salaciously. "You're a beautiful woman. You've been alone too long. You have needs—the strong physical needs of a woman in her sexual prime. I couldn't give you a better prescription for what ails you than me."

"You?" I gasped.

"Why not? I'm free, you're free—and you're obviously attracted to me."

It was a very short distance from the end of my patience to his throat. I grabbed his stethoscope with both hands and pulled it tightly against his Adam's apple.

"You creepy little worm. I'd rather have leprosy than you!"

"Please!" he gasped, his eyes protruding and his face turning red.

"In a minute—when I let you go—you're going to grab your little doctor bag and be out of here in half that time. And you can spend the next few days wondering if I'm going to report you to the State Medical Board. It's 'two strikes and you're out,' isn't it? This little charade would pretty much finish you."

I pushed him back as hard as I could and laughed while he fumbled around with his belongings. His coat billowed like a starched white sail behind him as he ran out of my room. I heard the back door slam in the distance and grinned.

I felt better than I had in weeks.

CHAPTER TWENTY

Mother came back and tapped lightly on my door while I was getting dressed.

"Winston left in quite a hurry. Did he have an emergency?"

"I guess you could say that," I laughed, enjoying the sound of wicked delight in my voice.

Mother stood in the doorway for a moment watching me, then walked over to the front window. For a moment she gazed sadly out at the trees—raw of limbs and leaves—and the twisted lawn furniture. Her voice was quiet and very serious when she spoke again.

"Paisley, I understand that you and Cassandra have a language common only to the two of you. Perhaps you take it for granted that I am privy to the understanding of it; however, I assure you I am quite in the dark about this whole affair and I would very much appreciate being apprised of the situation." She smiled gently, chidingly, and continued, "I have been very worried about you both for the last few hours. I think it only fair that you let me in on what's happening."

She sat gracefully in my grandmother's dainty rose-covered brocade chair and crossed her legs at the ankles. She looked elegant and poised in a pewter linen pantsuit and white silk blouse. The Sterling family pearls gleamed lustrously at the base of her slender neck. She was a lady through and through, and she made me feel like a heel. Typically, I reacted like a spoiled brat.

"That really was a mouthful, Mother. Why can't you just say, 'what the hell's going on?' and save us both a lot of time?"

Her dark eyes filled with tears, and the guilt that only a mother can engender sliced stiletto deep into my heart.

"Okay, okay! I'm sorry," I said with a deep sigh. I had lost again.

I sat down on the bottom of my bed and angrily pulled on my socks. "I really am sorry, Mother. This has been a hell of a morning, and even though I am relieved that we heard from Cassie, I'm still jumpy. Please repeat her exact words and I'll explain."

Mother dabbed at her eyes with a lace-edged handkerchief and sniffed ever so delicately while she pretended to recall the telephone conversation. I took advantage of the pause to rummage through the bottom of my closet for some shoes.

"Have you seen my old moccasins?" I turned to ask.

"Please don't interrupt me, dear. I'm thinking."

I crawled around on the floor of the closet tipping over boxes and turning up dust bunnies to no avail. "Damn, damn, and drat!"

"I think I have it, dear," she called.

"My shoes?"

"No, Cassie's exact words."

I crawled out of the closet and sat on the hooked rug by the bed to give Mother my full attention. It was obviously what she was wanted all along.

"She said to tell you that she was fine and would come home as soon as she could. That part I understood completely."

"How did she sound? Was her voice strained? Was she stressed?"

"May we please leave that for later?"

I gritted my teeth in annoyance, but gave her a nod so she would continue.

"Then she said to tell you to please give her Aunt Amelia her new address. That's what sounded so odd to me. I thought I knew all of Raphael's family, but for the life of me I cannot recall an Aunt Amelia. And there's no one on our side of the family named Amelia."

"Of course not," I grinned. "She's talking about Amelia Earhart."

Mother sat back in the chair and stared at me in astonishment, the guilt game forgotten.

"How in the world do you know that?"

"Bartlett's. She had *Familiar Quotations* on her bookshelf. It was open to a statement about courage attributed to Earhart. I had mentioned it to Cassie once before. She must have looked it up recently. I don't remember the exact words, but it's something about courage being the price for freedom."

"My goodness! What a clever girl!"

"She is that, isn't she?" I said with a fond smile. "And you don't know the half of it. The address part is even better. She's protecting us by keeping her whereabouts a secret like Rafe's family did."

"And how do you feel about that, Paisley, dear?"

"What do you mean?"

"Aren't you going to say one of your nasty words and go charging off half-cocked to find our precious child?"

"Way to go, Mother!" I shouted happily.

I never did find my beloved old Cole-Haans, and therefore I was out of sorts right from the beginning of our trip to town. After a lot of arguing back and forth, I finally convinced Mother not to report Cassie's disappearance to Andy Joiner, but we both decided we needed Horatio's sage advice.

I was relieved to find the visitor's parking lot at the funeral home empty. It was a rare event. Funerals are one of the premier social events in Rowan Springs, particularly when Horatio was in charge, and there usually was one at least every second day.

I pulled around to the back entrance and parked next to the door. Two limo drivers were taking advantage of the lull in business by washing and polishing Horatio's fleet of shiny black hearses. They waved and tipped their hats to Mother and went on about their business.

"Umm," I muttered under my breath, "looks like you're fairly well known in these here parts, Ma'am."

"Don't be foolish, Paisley! I hardly ever come here."

A thin bleached blond with skin the color and texture of an old saddlebag came out of the funeral home just as we got to the door. She was carrying a makeup case and a bag overflowing with brushes and a hair dryer.

"Hi, Miz Sterling," she shouted with enthusiasm. "Nice to see you again so soon. This your daughter Priscilla?"

Her grin was wide enough to show us more than we wanted to know about her lack of dental hygiene and excessive use of tobacco. I tried to slip through the open door without acknowledging her remarks, but Mother, ever the lady, placed a restraining hand on my arm.

"Paisley, this is Ruby Dawn Coleman."

The admonishing look in her eye gave me no choice but to smile and make an attempt to be pleasant to the woman.

"Hello." I might have said more, but Ruby Dawn didn't give me a chance.

"Mr. Raleigh says you write books, honey. I been wantin' to meet you for the longest time. My boyfriend says I ought'a write a book about all the things I've seen in my line of business."

"Oh, really? And just what is that?" I asked politely.

"I do hair and makeup for them." She leaned in closer and whispered loudly, "you know, the dead. I get to work on all kinds of folks, young, old—lots of teenagers who need extra special makeup. You know, from goin' thorough windshields an' all. Yes, sir, I could write a book. Maybe we could have a drink sometime, huh? Discreet like a' course, this bein' a dry county and all, and you could give me some pointers. Could ya, huh, honey?"

With every word she kept advancing on me. I backed up—my retreat ultimately halted by the door. Her last question enveloped me in a miasma of drug store perfume, stale tobacco smoke, and bad breath. I wanted to run for my life. The thought of having to spend any amount time with this dreadful woman frightened me into silence.

Mother came to my rescue. "I'm sure my daughter will be more than delighted to send you some books on writing, dear. However, she has signed a legal contract not to work with budding authors in case she might inadvertently borrow one of their ideas. We must protect our fledgling artists. You do understand, don't you?"

Mother's voice was soothing and persuasive. As she spoke, she expertly guided Ruby out of the doorway and toward the parking lot, allowing me to escape into the airconditioned sanctum inside.

It had been a while since I had been in Horatio's lair. His older sister had been in sole charge of the decor until her own demise three years ago. From the looks of things, Horatio had made some improvements.

Dema Raleigh's taste ran to large oil paintings of hunting scenes with dead animals and heavy mahogany furniture reminiscent of English manor houses. She had never married, although there were rumors of a torrid affair with a British officer during her wartime service in London. Toward the end of her life she was confined to a nursing home catering to Alzheimer's patients. Once a nurse confided to Mother that Miss Dema Raleigh was known to shout, "Tally ho!" whenever her rectal temperature was taken.

"That young woman is a walking, talking, country music song," laughed Mother as she came through the door. "You might want to reconsider and invest some time conversing with her, dear. She has seen quite a lot."

"So did Ma Barker, Ted Bundy, and Charles Manson."

"That's quite enough, Paisley. I get the point. Sometimes you can be quite tiresome, dear."

"Yeah, well, you know what? Today is not my favorite day. My darling daughter has disappeared, I had a fainting spell, my mother's physician groped me, and now a makeup artist for the deceased wants to become my new best friend."

I stomped angrily down the corridor toward Horatio's office. The thick foam soles of my new sneakers caught on the thick pile of the new carpet causing me to trip twice before I reached the fancy hand-carved door to Horatio's office. Dema had ordered the door from the Philippines shortly before she became ill. It was one of the few touches that Horatio had retained.

I knocked, and waited impatiently to be invited inside. I couldn't believe my extended lack of good fortune when none other than Andy Joiner opened the door.

"Paisley! What are you doing here?" he asked in a voice heavy with suspicion.

It was not like Andy to be heavy-handed, or rude. I was too surprised to think of anything that wouldn't give us away. Once again, Mother's Southern lady manners saved the day.

"Andy, dear. How nice to see you. How are Connie and the girls?"

CHAPTER TWENTY-ONE

Andy, red-faced and obviously angry, murmured something unintelligible that contained the phrases, "...in bed with a cold...fine, I guess...and getting ready for kindergarten graduation," and practically ran for the exit. Bemused, Mother and I stood there for a moment, then heeded Horatio's polite request to enter his office.

"How are you today, Paisley, dear?" he asked as he came around his desk to greet my mother warmly. He clasped her hands and tenderly kissed the one on top, then showed Mother to a comfortable armchair and motioned for me to sit across from his desk. When he had taken a seat in the leather chair that had been his father's, he turned back to Mother.

"I hope you're well, Anna, my dear? I was quite concerned when you called to say you were coming. Your voice sounded a bit strained."

"Ah, Horatio," smiled Mother, "as perceptive as ever. You have every reason to be concerned. I'll let Paisley fill you in on the sordid details, but it comes down to the dreadful fact that our Cassandra has been kidnapped. And," she continued as she stopped him from picking up the telephone, "While we know from her own admission that she is in no immediate danger, we are understandably ill at ease. Nevertheless, Paisley and I have decided to heed her wishes and not contact the police."

"Paisley?" he said with a stern lift of his elegant eyebrows, "Begin, please. And I warn you beforehand not to succumb to temptation and leave out details that might be self-incriminating."

I grinned and shook my head. He knew me so well. I took a deep breath and told them everything, including some of the "self-incriminating details" that I had kept from Mother.

The telling of the tale took about fifteen minutes. Horatio interrupted several times to ask questions that I failed to see the importance of at the time. I indulged him anyway. I was not eager to be on his naughty list because it became obvious as I talked that I had zoomed to the top of Mother's—where I could remain, possibly, for life.

When I finished, she let me have it.

"I cannot believe," she said with tears in her eyes, "that you would take your beloved daughter on such an impetuous and dangerous escapade."

Horatio took a pipe out of his pocket and fished around in the humidor for his favorite tobacco. Mother's tears didn't move me that much. I had seen too many over the years, but when I saw Horatio's hand tremble ever so slightly as he filled his pipe, I was filled with instant remorse.

"You're right!" I admitted guiltily. "I should never have taken her with me—no matter how hard she begged me."

Horatio offered a small but reassuring smile. "I know how persuasive Cassandra can be, Paisley. You mustn't be too hard on yourself. I'm sure you feel pretty rotten about the whole thing."

"Right again," I sniffed loudly. "And deep down inside," I confessed, "I have this dreadful fear that I might not ever see her again—just like Rafe."

I choked back tears and made a mighty effort to pull myself together.

"You got some tea, maybe?" I hiccoughed at length. "I'll brew it."

"How about luncheon instead?" asked Horatio consolingly.

"Oh, I don't think I could...."

"Nonsense, Paisley. Some stout southern cuisine under your belt is just what the doctor, no, make that the mortician, ordered. How about you, Anna, my dear? What say we take our errant child to the Pelican for lunch?"

In spite of Mother's protestations we headed out for "that dreadful greasy spoon." Horatio explained that he wanted to talk to Wanda Blake. She was the one person who could describe the man who came to the restaurant looking for us last night. For some reason, Horatio tended to agree with me that it was someone other than Fatty. It didn't occur to me to ask him why until we pulled into the Pelican's parking lot.

"Because," he explained, "I'm fairly certain that the man you referred to as 'Fatty' was dead before you and Cassie fled from the trailer park."

No matter how hard I pried, he refused to say anything more as we entered the Pelican.

"Damn!" I whispered, while we were waiting to be seated. "You're being so unfair, Horatio."

"Ah," he smiled enigmatically, "the young. Always wanting instant answers, instant gratification, and instant 'on' buttons for everything. When you get to be my age, my dear, you will see that a proper period of anticipation...." He paused to smile at the gum-chewing waitress who came to seat us.

"Three, please, young lady, for your non-smoking section."

The girl rolled her eyes and pointed at the far corner of the crowded dining room.

"In this place there ain't no such animal, Mister. But that corner over there breathes a bit better than most 'cause of the fan overhead. Take it or leave it. But make it snappy, I ain't got all day. Wanda's out sick and nobody else around here knows their butt from a hole in the ground."

"In that case," smiled Horatio as he pressed a five dollar bill in her hand, "please excuse us. My young friend suffers from allergies and smoke can be quite detrimental to her health."

Mother practically broke into a run as she gratefully escaped what she considered to be a luncheon fate worse than death. I, on the other hand, was now starving. I never did finish my breakfast and the smell of food cooking in good old-fashioned salty grease had awakened my appetite.

"Wait, Horatio," I panted as I caught up to them in the parking lot. "Can't we get something...?"

"Hurry, Paisley. No time to be considering our stomachs. We must seek out Miss Blake without a moment's hesitation."

I stared longingly at the Pelican in the rearview mirror until we were out of sight. I, quite frankly, didn't see what the big hurry was all about.

"Frankly, I don't see the big hurry. Can't you wait until I grab something to go?"

Mother didn't respond, but I saw her lips tighten with disapproval. She always found fault with my appetite. Horatio took care of that with a few carefully chosen words.

"The big hurry, Paisley, is to try and save a life."

"Wha...wha...whose life?" I stammered. "You don't mean Cassie? Do you?"

"No, not at the moment. I agree with Anna's assessment. Cassie was much too quick to call and let you know she was all right for her to be in any immediate danger, and she's obviously not under any restraint or she would not have been free to call in the first place. Her hidden message that she is protecting you by not letting you know where she was sounded exactly like the youthful idealistic Cassie we all are familiar with. It's your waitress friend that I am concerned about."

"Wanda? Why her? What does she have to do with anything?"

"She saw your pursuer. And possibly Fatty's killer," he stated.

"Hold on a minute there," I demanded. "Now you have plenty of time to tell me why you think Fatty is dead."

"Sorry, my dear," he said as he pulled the nose of his silver-grey Bentley into the narrow gravel drive leading to Wanda Blake's neat little cottage. "We're here."

Mother decided to stay in the car. I climbed out and paused for a moment to admire Wanda's home. She had planted flowers everywhere. Pots of geraniums and petunias stood in every nook and cranny of the pretty little front porch, while hanging baskets filled with colorful blooms graced the eaves. The cottage sported a fresh coat of white paint, and bright green shutters framed the front windows. It was very attractive. It was the kind of house I might have chosen for myself, if I lived alone.

Horatio tapped politely on the front door with its shiny brass knocker while I peered curiously in the window. Ruffled organdy curtains kept me from seeing clearly, but when a woman scurried across the back of the house, I saw her silhouette momentarily framed against the sunlight streaming in through a patio door.

"She's in there, Horatio," I whispered. "I saw her. Why do you think she won't come to the door?"

"Because she has the good sense to be frightened," he answered quietly.

"Look, Horatio, you've got to stop being so mysterious and explain...."

"Paisley," he interrupted urgently, "she knows you. Go around to the back while I keep knocking, and find a way to let her know it's you. If she lets you in, please tell her who I am and open the door. I'll explain everything to the both of you once I'm inside the house."

"And Mother? She'll be miffed if you leave her out."

"I'll handle your mother. Now hurry. We have no time to waste."

I climbed over the railing on the side of the porch—almost knocking off a pot of lavender petunias in the process. Horatio shook his head impatiently and motioned for me to be more careful. Thus admonished, I cautiously picked my way around the side of the house, stooping low as I passed the windows and trying to be as quiet as possible.

The backyard was small, but sweetly landscaped with tall boxwood hedges, climbing roses, and day lilies. A trellis overflowing with the bright green leaves and red berries of scarlet runner vines framed the small flagstone patio that in turn bordered a charming water garden. In the center of the little pond stood a beautifully wrought bronze statuette. I promised myself that later I would get close enough to confirm my suspicion that the lovely naked lady bore a more than passing resemblance to Wanda.

I heard a sound in the window above me and saw the metal Venetian blinds sway as someone peered out. I hugged the foundation and crawled around the corner to the back of the house. The patio doors were right there—not two feet away. A sheer net curtain hung from top to bottom, but the reflection of the sunlight on the glass kept me from seeing inside.

Everything was buttoned up tightly, and an air-conditioning unit hummed loudly on the other side of the doors. I wasn't sure Wanda could even hear me, but following Horatio's instructions, I knocked on the door and called out.

"It's me, Ms. Blake, Paisley Sterling. I'm Cassie's mother. Remember me from last night?"

I paused for a moment trying to think of anything that might make her open the door. "I need your help. Cassie's been kidnapped, and I...."

The door opened swiftly. The curtains parted and a forearm made strong from years of carrying trays loaded with heavy dishes pulled me inside.

"The hell, you say!" she whispered loudly. "They put the snatch on that sweet kid? Son of a bitch!"

Wanda pushed me into the dark interior of her house. The blinds were drawn and every door was shut. What must have been a bright, sunny, and very cheerful place had become dim and filled with shadows.

I started toward the front of the house to let Horatio inside, but Wanda had other ideas.

"What are you doing?" she whispered anxiously. "You crazy or somethin'?"

"It's all right," I assured her. "That's Horatio Raleigh at the front door. He's a friend of mine. He's trying to help us—all of us."

Wanda grabbed my sleeve and pulled me back into the shadows.

"I heard a car pull up in the driveway!" she cautioned.

"I know, I know," I whispered. "That was Horatio's car. My mother is here, too. Anna Sterling, Cassie's grandmother."

"I mean just now, you twit!" she spat. "Somebody just now pulled up to the house. You think I don't know what that sounds like after living here for thirty years? I don't need no alarm. I know every little piece of gravel out there. It's my nightingale floor, just like those Chinese emperors had in their palaces."

"Jeez! Who...?"

"Get away from the windows, damn it!" she warned. "The man who called me last night said to get out of town, or he'd kill me. From the mean sound of his voice, ain't no way he'd let a little locked door stop him—if he thought I was in here."

She pulled nervously on her lower lip and urged me further into the shadow of a large armoire that stood against the dining room wall. I was framing a careful question about the threatening phone call when she asked one instead.

"How did you know where to come looking for me?"

"A waitress at the Pelican told us you had called in sick, that you were at home. She was nice enough to give us directions."

"Tall, heavy-set, chews gum like a maniac?"

I nodded my head in assent.

"Reba! Bitch! Stupid bitch! Man, I really owe her for that. I just hope I live long enough to pay her back."

"Wanda, this is silly. We can't hide here forever. If Horatio is still outside he'll take care of us."

"That tall, skinny, old man? Hah! He couldn't help a flea find a dog."

"Horatio has had, eh, certain training that gives me reason to trust him in any situation. Besides, he always carries a gun under the front seat of his car."

"Well, he's gonna need a cannon because I just heard two more cars pull up. We've got major company!"

Against Wanda's protestations, I tiptoed over to the front window. The blinds were closed tightly, but by leaning close to the window frame I could see part of the driveway and front walk. And I heard voices.

"Did you order pizza?" I asked her incredulously. "And Wing-dings?"

"Of course, not! I ain't no idiot."

"Well, there's two pizza delivery boys, a kid with a large order of Wing-dings, and a bakery van out front," I said with a nervous laugh. "You got any money?"

CHAPTER TWENTY-TWO

I opened the front door cautiously, while Wanda rummaged through her purse for enough money to pay for our unsolicited bounty. Delivery boys were lined up knee-deep on the porch but there was no sign of my mother, Horatio, or his Bentley.

"Damn! Where did he...?"

"'Scuse me, ma'am," called a scrawny, pimply-faced, teenager from the back of the line. "I have a message for you from a Mr. Raleigh. It's written on the pizza box."

I left Wanda to pay the others and pushed past them to get to the pizza boy. I grabbed the box and tore it open. The smell of hot pepperoni and Italian sausage was more than I could bear. I picked up a slice and took a huge bite.

"Hey! You gotta pay for it first," the boy complained, as he pulled the box out of my hands.

"Give back it to me," I mumbled crossly over melted mozzarella. "The lady on the front porch will pay you."

"Gee, lady, I've delivered lots of pizzas but I ain't never seen nobody that hungry." He thrust the pizza in my hands with a disgusted look on his face, and took the steps two at a time to reach Wanda.

She was arguing with the baker over the price of the three dozen doughnuts and two chocolate cakes. "That's way out of line, kid! I'm in the food service business. You can't put one over on me. How much are you trying to stiff me for?"

Safe in the knowledge that no one would try to get at either me or Wanda with this circus going on, I sat down on the bottom step and stuffed another slice of pizza in my mouth.

The inside top of the box was covered with melted cheese and tomato sauce. I scrapped some off with my index finger and ate it. It took three bites before I was able to decipher the crudely lettered message from Horatio:

Hope you enjoy lunch. Cut through the back yard and

meet us on the other side. Tell Wanda to pack for a
week.

Horatio

By the time I finished another slice of pizza, Wanda had paid everyone and was standing in the doorway waiting for me.

"Get a suitcase and throw some things in it—enough for a week," I
said. "And hurry! We may not have much time."

She grinned. "Don't worry about that. The padded doughnut bill
was for the driver. He's supposed to wait out front in the bakery van
for fifteen more minutes. I guess your friend thought of that, too, huh?"

I nodded. My mouth was full again.

"Your Horatio must be a pretty smart cookie," she acknowledged.
"Here, have some hot wings while I get ready."

Wanda was packed and dressed in less time than it took me to finish the wings and the other half of the pizza. She took the box and
stuffed it in the kitchen garbage can on our way out. I held her heavy
duffle bag while she locked the back door.

"You have a cat or dog? Fish? Anything you need to take care of?"

"Nope. Hector always had somethin' when he was growin' up. I
changed so many litter boxes and water tanks during those years; I
swore I'd never have to get rid of anybody's else's crap again."

We made our way carefully around Wanda's little water garden
and through the arched trellis to the back of her yard. I was dismayed
to see a tall chain link fence underneath the cascade of climbing wild
roses, but Wanda headed straight for the corner and a gate that was almost hidden by the abundant growth. She lifted the latch and pushed
hard, tearing the vines apart so we could get out. Wanda held the gate
open while I squeezed through, then she followed. We each grabbed a
strap of the satchel and hefted it down the driveway of the house on the
other side to the street where Horatio's Bentley was waiting for us.

Horatio popped the trunk as we approached the car. Wanda and I
lifted the heavy duffle bag up, pushed it inside, and slammed the trunk
shut.

"Whew! I'd hate to see how heavy the bag would be if you packed
for a month! What did you bring, the family silver?"

"Ha," she laughed. "Very funny! As if any of us Blakes ever had
anything worth passing along to the next generation except bad debts."

We climbed into the back seat laughing.

"Well! I'm delighted you two are having such a lovely time,"
complained Mother. "I have been worried sick. You might have given
us some sort of signal, dear."

I opened my mouth to begin the argument of the day, but Horatio came to my rescue. "Anna, they really had no chance to offer a signal, and besides that, I don't think they knew where we were."

"That's right!" I affirmed stoutly. "We didn't know. By the way, where were you? I was scared half to death when I looked outside and saw you were gone."

Horatio started the engine and pulled the Bentley away from the curb. He looked cautiously around and headed slowly down the street before he answered. "I left as soon as I ascertained that Wanda was afraid to open the front door and let me inside. We needed a diversion, something to call attention to the cottage and make it impossible for anyone to approach without being noticed. That's when Anna got the idea of calling all the delivery people."

This time Mother's laugh was genuine. "Actually the idea was Paisley's."

"Mine? How so?" I was astonished.

"You and Velvet—but I'm sure it was your idea—used to call all the stores in town that made deliveries and place orders to the homes of schoolmates you were on the outs with. Naturally, neither your father nor I were aware of the pranks you were playing until much later. When we found out, we made you both contribute your allowances toward making up the money your lack of consideration had cost the merchants. I'm surprised you don't remember it, dear. It made quite an impression on you at the time."

"Well," I sighed, sinking back into the expensive softness of the Bentley's seat, "I'm just glad you remembered. It was a great ploy. And a fairly good lunch, too. Thanks a lot, you two, for saving our butts."

"Paisley, must you always be so common in your speech?"

Wanda had been quietly resting in her corner, but Mother's complaint made her chuckle.

"What's so funny, Wanda?" I wanted to know.

"Us mothers is all alike. As soon as the danger is over, we're out lookin' to keep our little chicks in line at the feeder." She smiled in Mother's direction. "I'm real sorry, Miz Sterling. I guess you think that sounds common, too."

"No, Wanda, dear," she said with an answering smile. "And you're quite correct. Keeping Paisley in line has always been something of a challenge."

I snorted loudly and snuggled deeper into the seat while they discussed me as if I were a piece of furniture that needed to be refinished.

"...and Hector...you should have seen...I never...."

I closed my eyes and let the soft hum of the big car's engine lull me to sleep. Right before I drifted off, I heard Wanda offer up her philosophy of life.

"It's like I always say," she said with a hearty laugh. "Sometimes you're the windshield and sometimes you're the bug."

I woke up from my catnap when Horatio pulled up to the back door of the funeral home. He had determined that Wanda should stay in the small apartment above his office for the time being. Horatio was fairly certain the man who called and threatened to kill her would never think to look in a mortuary for his quarry.

"Very few people even know the suite is there, my dear. And I'm sure some of those who once knew have forgotten it exists. You should be quite safe there for as long as you care to stay."

Wanda fidgeted in her seat, shifting nervously from one buttock to the other, seemingly unaware that her hands were fluttering like frightened birds.

"I...I don't know about this, Mr. Raleigh. I got a job, a house, and a life. I can't just hare off to your apartment and move in like some kinda...."

"My dear," interrupted Horatio. "You're in this pickle because of something that my young friend and her daughter stumbled into. I'm just now beginning to realize that it may be far more serious than any of us realize. We must take all the necessary precautions until we know what we're dealing with. Please humor me in this."

"Okay," Wanda said slowly, "but only as long as I have to. I ain't used to sleeping in somebody else's bed." She turned beet red and hurried on to say, "I mean, I don't sleep around. Damn! Oh, I'm sorry Miz Sterling. I don't know what I mean anymore," she finished miserably.

"That's quite all right, my dear," said Mother soothingly. "Never you mind about anything for a while. Just think of this as a vacation. I'll stop by every day and visit, and I'm sure Paisley will keep you company on occasion as well."

"But what about her daughter? Ain't it true about Cassie's bein' kidnapped?"

Horatio turned around and faced Wanda. "Yes, it is. And naturally we're concerned, but Cassie has called and assured us that she is fine. You, on the other hand, are in need of immediate protection. Now," he said with a smile, "will you please an old man and do as he requests?"

I had never seen Horatio's upstairs apartment. It was unexpectedly attractive, and no one would ever guess it was above an embalming room. The small bedroom and adjoining bath were separated from the pretty little sitting area by curtained French doors. The colors were light and bright: soft blues and yellows, and Wanda was immediately entranced.

"It's so pretty. Are you sure...?"

Mother interrupted by taking Wanda by the arm and showing her a fully-equipped little kitchenette which was cleverly hidden behind sliding pocket doors.

"There are some essentials in the refrigerator—eggs, butter, that sort of thing. Paisley and I can run to the grocery for you if you'll make a list."

"Thanks, Miz Sterling," said Wanda as she swiped at a tear. "You all are being so nice to me."

"Like I said before, my dear, you are quite the innocent bystander in this affair."

I had remained silent the whole time, leaving it to Horatio and Mother to make Wanda at ease in her new temporary quarters, but the terrible truth was that I had been trying to think of a nice way to grill her about the man who had threatened to kill her last night. We still didn't have a clue about his identity.

"So...Wanda," I ventured, "How about some nice barbequed chicken, or do you prefer beef? I can run down to Cloudt's and be back in about thirty minutes. You could probably go with me if you put on a scarf and some dark glasses. We could talk a little on the way about this guy that's...."

Horatio squashed my idea immediately. "I hardly think that's a good idea, Paisley. Let's not take any foolish chances with her welfare. If you want to talk to Wanda, then I suggest you do it here."

"Could I take a warm bath and have a little nap first?" she begged. "Honestly, I was so scared last night I didn't close my eyes a wink, and I never did get to wash the kitchen smell out of my hair." She gave me a tired smile. "It'll just be a couple of hours. My mind's a lot clearer when I'm not so tired. Maybe I'll be able to remember more details."

"Of course, Wanda." I was thoroughly ashamed of myself. "Take all the time you need. I'll make a barbeque run for all of us. Maybe we could meet back here around seven tonight and have dinner." I turned to Mother and Horatio. "I'll take Mother's rental car, if that's okay. I'd like to go home first to check the answering machine. Maybe Cassie has called again."

"If she has called," said Mother, "please let me know. I can't help but worry about her."

I turned to go out the door.

"Oh, and check on Aggie, too, dear. She'll probably need to take a walk."

I immediately stumbled and stubbed my toe on the doorframe. "Damn dog!"

CHAPTER TWENTY-THREE

Mother was right as usual—Aggie was whining for a romp in the orchard. I walked with her down through the sad and sorry sight of the stumps of the fruit trees that had brought such pleasure into the lives of so many Sterlings over the years. It was still hard for me to look at the devastation the tornado had wrought without crying. And I was worried about Cassie. There had been no new phone calls from her.

My daughter and I were at a new place in our lives—that juncture when I have to prepare to say goodbye. These are the years when she will start a career, and then a family that I will see only at holiday time. I'll be the grandmother in the "Over the river and through the woods to grandmother's house we go," song. I'll hug them briefly, then have to let them go again. They'll love me—a lot, I hope, because I plan to be the world's greatest grandmother—but it will never be the same. I'll miss that "down the hall in the next room" feeling of closeness I have now. I'll miss the minutia of everyday life with my daughter. I'll be a red ring around a certain date on the calendar in her kitchen. She'll look forward to coming home, then be happy to return to her own house to unpack and get back to her life once more. I'll be the one waiting and dreaming for the next circled date to come around.

And right now, I had no choice but to let her handle things her own way. She told Mother that quite clearly. I could worry all I wanted—gnash my teeth to splinters, but I had to wait until I was summoned.

I sat on the stump of a chestnut tree and cried my heart out.

Aggie is not good for much, but she is sweet when you're blue. Since I don't get the blues that often, the dog is useless—if not downright dangerous most of the time; but when I'm sad, she seems to sense it and tries to comfort me.

She nuzzled her wet little black nose up under my hair and licked away the tears on my chin. I laughed, wiped away doggie spit, and playfully ruffled the new growth of feathery fur on her chest. She growled immediately and danced away after a bumblebee.

I walked slowly back to the house, admiring Billy's brickwork on the repaired chimneys and the new shingles on the roof. At least, I thought, Grandmother's house will be looking good.

Aggie hopped up on my bed and plopped on her/my pillow for another few hours of her perpetual doggie nap while I went to freshen up a bit before my drive down to Cloudt's. Even after my nap in Horatio's car I was still tired. It had been a long and eventful day and I was sorry I offered to get dinner. I could very easily have forgone the barbeque and crawled up next to Aggie to gather some more shut eye. I sighed and ran my fingers through my hair, then dabbed on some fresh lip gloss.

I was about to lock the back door when I remembered the stash hidden in my jewelry box. Until we were able to give the money back to Rudolfo, I was responsible for his loot. The money should be in the bank.

As soon as I touched the jewelry box I knew that someone had been there before me. For starters, it had been moved slightly from its accustomed spot on the corner of my dresser. My hands were sweaty as I raised the lid and looked inside. I was more solvent than I used to be, but replacing twenty-seven hundred bucks would still be a pain. The money was there! But it was on top of my pearls, and I distinctly remembered tucking the rolls underneath. And besides that, there were ten little cylinders missing.

I sank down on the bed, ignoring Aggie's protesting growls, and tried to sort it all out. The door had been locked when I got here, and I had not seen any signs of forced entry. Nothing else looked disturbed. Whoever had taken the money had known where to look and had a key to the house. It had to be Cassie. And either she had been alone or whoever she was with had not forced her to take all of the money, or any of my own personal goodies. In other words, that other person was most likely not of a criminal bent.

I sighed with relief and decided to leave the money where it was in case Cassie needed some more, then just for the fun of it, I bounced happily once or twice on the bed to disturb Aggie. She gave me a hateful look, passed a small explosion of doggie gas, and snuggled down deeper into my pillow.

I was still laughing as I locked the door and started down the walk to the car. I was almost halfway there when I heard the telephone ringing. By the time I struggled to open the door again and got to the hallway, it was too late. Cassie had just said goodbye to the answering machine and was hanging up. I grabbed the receiver and dialed *69, the call-back number, but got only the recorded message telling me the call-back service could not respond. Cassie had called from a private number.

"Damn!" I pushed the button to play back the recording and sat down in the Windsor chair to listen.

"Hi, Mom. First of all—I'm fine. But I need you to come as soon as you hear this message. Like I said, I'm okay, so please, no mad, furious driving, but don't stop for gas." Then her voice dropped down to a whisper. "You won't believe what I've discovered!" She resumed her normal tone and told me where to find her. "I'm staying where my friend with the funny little car lived last year. I love you, Mom. Bye."

I smiled slowly. Cassie's friend had an ancient and rusty orange Karmen Ghia. He had parked it under a garage apartment where he'd lived for three months last summer. The apartment was behind the Parsons house. Cassie was hiding out with my old nemesis, Miss Lolly.

The look Aggie gave me when I left for the second and final time was one of total disgust and contempt. Her naps were sacred and not to be disturbed by anyone, especially me.

I decided it was a good thing that I was driving Mother's rental car. She often paid her elderly friends a courtesy call. It wouldn't look out of place for her car to be in the Parsons' driveway, whereas the whole town knew Miss Lolly had hated me for more than thirty years—ever since I spray painted a white stripe down the back of her black cat, Mr. Whiskers. And both the sisters, Hannah and Lolly, loved Cassie. When her friend Ethan had stayed in their apartment, she had bonded with the old ladies. She still went to see them every time she came home from school for tea and some of their famous nut bread.

I parked the car at the end of the drive and got out. The back of the house appeared tightly shuttered and locked, but I heard Cassie whisper loudly as I started towards the garage.

"Mom! This way."

I turned around and saw her peeking through a crack in the back door. Her beautiful face was a sight for sore eyes. I told her so while I hugged her madly.

"I told Gran I was okay. What's the big deal?" she said as she pulled away from my arms. "Don't you trust me?"

"Cassie, for Pete's sake! Have a heart. You disappear in the dead of night, then call with a mysterious message and expect me to be fine and dandy with it? And it's not about trust at all, it's about fearing for the worst."

She started laughing. "Can you possibly think of a few more cliches? I hope Leonard doesn't start talking like that."

"You're changing the subject. Besides, Leonard can take care of himself."

"So can I, Mom. So can I."

I sighed and gave up. This was just one more argument that I would never win.

"What's this unbelievable thing you discovered?" I asked instead.

Cassie bent her head close to mine. "Miss Hannah's dead body," she whispered.

"My God! Cassie, you can't be serious. And that's a pretty damn stupid joke."

"Shhhh!" she cautioned. "I don't want to wake Miss Lolly. Did you know her sister was nearly ninety?" Miss Lolly told me told me about their pact. You see, whoever died first promised to freeze the other."

"Wha...whatever for?" I stammered. "Some religious thing? I thought they were Presbyterians—levelheaded and all."

"They are...Presbyterians, that is. No, they decided it would be impossible for the remaining sister to live on one of their meager Social Security checks. If it were to appear that they both were still alive, the two checks would keep coming."

Cassie led me down a long dark hall and through the butler's pantry into a big old-fashioned kitchen. She switched on the single light bulb which hung on a long black cord dangling from the center of the high white ceiling. It moved slightly when she closed the door casting fleeting shadows down the length of the sparsely furnished room.

"They thought they could get away with it," Cassie continued. "No one ever ventured inside the house except old Doc Baxter, and he died last year. It was a great scheme, and it probably would have worked if the electricity hadn't gone out."

"The tornado!"

"Exactly, Mom. The tornado took out the power on this street for two days. When the electricity came back on, the old freezer compressor failed. Miss Hannah started to defrost, and Miss Lolly had what she calls a conniption."

"What happened? Did the old broad start to stink?"

"Mom!"

"Come on, Cassie. We're talking about a geriatric Popsicle. That's pretty shocking all by itself."

Cassie motioned for me to follow her to the back of the kitchen. She stopped in front of an ancient white freezer like the one my Grandmother Howard used to have on her back porch. It was rectangular, about six feet long and four feet high. It looked like it had the capacity to hold ten little old ladies.

"Help me push up the top, Mom. It's pretty rusty."

Together we opened the freezer and propped up the lid, then we stood side by side and stared at the faint outline of Miss Hannah Parsons beneath the frosty surface of a block of ice three feet deep and the width and breadth of the freezer. There were three inches or more of melted ice water on each side.

"I saw an old movie once," I said in a quiet voice. "It was called *The Thing from Outer Space*. An alien spacecraft crashes in the Antarctic and this creature stumbles out in the melted ice only to collapse and be frozen over by the ice cap. The scientists at the weather station cut him out in one big block of ice...."

Cassie sighed dramatically. "And it starred Bert Douglas...."

"That's Kurt Douglas, smarty pants. Besides, it was James Arness."

"Does everything have to remind you of some stupid old movie?"

"Cassie, this is very shocking. There's an old lady in there, and she's frozen solid. I'm trying to relate it to something familiar so I won't run screaming into the night. By the way, how did you discover her body?"

"I was hungry."

"WHAT?"

"Hungry," she insisted patiently. "Rudolfo had gone to bed...."

"RUDOLFO?"

Cassie eased the top back down on the freezer. She took me by the hand and led me over to a cheap white enameled kitchen table and sat me down. She sat across from me and took both my cold hands in hers.

"Stay with me, Mom. We have to make some decisions, and I need you to keep up."

"But, Rudolfo...?" I insisted.

"Rudolfo is an agent with the Departamento Justicia del Distrito Federale de México."

"You're kidding!"

She grinned a big old Cassie grin. "No, I'm not. He's with some section that deals with international affairs. He and a Texas Ranger came here on a tip that the man they've been chasing over half the southern United States is in Kentucky posing as a migrant worker."

I sat back with my mouth agape as I marveled at how easily that little man had fooled me.

"And you'll never guess who the Texas Ranger is," she laughed delightedly. "Fatty, from the trailer park!"

"Holy cow!"

"Exactly! They've been working together on this case for almost two years. He wouldn't tell me much more, for my own good, he said; but he warned me to be...."

"Cassie," I interrupted, "Fatty is dead."

Her smiled faded as the rosy color left her cheeks. "Dead? As in—

DEAD?"

"Yes. I don't know much more. Horatio never got a chance to explain...."

"Horatio?"

"When Gran and I went to see him this morning we met Andy Joiner as he was coming out of Horatio's office. Apparently he had just brought the body to the mortuary."

"I guess that's why Rudolfo was sure his cover had been blown," she said softly.

"What else did he tell you? And why did he tell you anything at all? Seems highly unprofessional to me to unload a thing like this on an innocent young woman you hardly know."

Cassie jumped to Rudolfo's defense. "How else was he going to get me to help him? He surprised me last night when I drove into the carriage house. He was hiding inside and scared me half to death. He said his life was in danger and begged me to help him find some place to stay. I offered our attic...."

"Really, Cassie!"

"...but he said that was too obvious since you and Gran had hired him to work for you. Besides, he didn't want to put you in danger."

"So instead, he kidnaps you," I scoffed angrily.

"So instead, he makes it look like I was kidnapped," she explained with exaggerated patience. "That's why I left Watson's door open."

"And just how did he convince you he was on the up and up?"

"He showed me his badge."

"It could have come from a Cracker Jack box," I snorted. "How could you...?"

"And a letter from the FBI giving him permission to carry a gun in this country. And," Cassie continued as she held up her hand to stop me from further protests, "another letter from the Attorney General expressing the desire to help him in his investigation in any way he could."

"So you went with him."

"Yes. We cut back through the field to the airport. He had an old farm truck waiting by the runway. I puzzled over a safe place to hide him all the time we were walking. Then I remembered the garage apartment behind Miss Lolly's and the way she was so eager to help me last summer. She really is a dear old thing."

"And she agreed?"

Cassie frowned. "No, at first she seemed very reluctant. I suppose now I know why. It was only because it was it was so late and we had nowhere else to go that I kept insisting. Finally she gave in, but she said I had to stay in the house with her because it was improper for me to stay alone with a man. Rudolfo parked the truck in the garage and went upstairs. Miss Lolly took me inside, showed me to a bedroom, and said goodnight. Everything would have been okay except I got hungry," she admitted ruefully. "I sneaked back downstairs and tried to find something to eat. There's hardly anything in the fridge, so I opened the freezer thinking maybe they had frozen some of that terrific nut bread, and found Miss Hannah instead. I screamed and Miss Lolly came running. She broke down, poor thing, and confessed after crying a bucket or two. She's been under a terrible strain trying to hide her sister's death."

"She's a nut!"

"No, Mom, really she's not. She was just desperate. You might have done the same thing under the circumstances."

I gave my daughter a wicked grin. "I must admit that the thought of your Aunt Velvet on ice does sound enticing."

"So, now what do we do?" she answered, ignoring my barb.

"We?"

"Yes, Mom. We have to help her. She's all alone in the world, and she hasn't got a clue as to what to do."

"First things first. Where's Rudofo?"

"He left after all the hullabaloo in the kitchen. He said he would find a quieter place to hide out. He'll get back in touch. He promised."

"Well, that's just great! He kidnaps you and then drops you like a hot potato; and now we have to help this silly old bag..."

"MOM!"

"Sorry, Cassie, but there's too many things going on here. And I promised to bring supper for Wanda and...."

"Wanda?"

"Long story. Take me to Miss Lolly. Let's get this show on the road."

CHAPTER TWENTY-FOUR

At first Miss Lolly wouldn't even look at me, but after ten minutes of cajoling and pleading, Cassie managed to get her to sit down and help us make some decisions. I suggested that we call Bruce Hawkins. He was Mother's lawyer and I knew we could trust him to help Lolly Parsons with this mess. But she was from the old school where it was family history that counted. She wanted to call Judge Hershey because her father had helped send him through law school.

Finally, Cassie convinced her that might cause some kind of conflict of interest down the road, and besides, she argued, "Miss Lolly, you really need your own lawyer."

I told her to worry about payment later. Right now she needed an advocate to keep her out of the loony bin.

Cassie helped her back to her room while I went downstairs to make some phone calls. Bruce answered right away. He listened intently as I gave a cursory explanation of the situation, and promised to come immediately. He also offered to call his aunt. She was a bit younger than the Parsons sisters but had gone to the same finishing school for young ladies. He was sure she would want to help, and would probably even offer to stay with Miss Lolly until things were sorted out. That was the best news I had heard all night because I had things to do and places to go. And I was tired of being called a sassy young whippersnapper by a woman older than my Mother's antique cherry coffee table.

My second telephone call was to Horatio. I wanted to warn him that he would have to find a really big coffin, or think of a way to defrost Miss Hannah. There was no answer at the funeral home. I tried calling home in case he and Mother had gone there, but received the same lack of response.

"Where is everybody?" I wondered crossly.

I helped Cassie make supper for her old friend, then sat at the kitchen table and waited for Bruce while she took the tray of soup and cheese toast upstairs for Miss Lolly.

I had never been inside this big old house before, and I longed to explore. Only the good manners that Mother says I'm missing kept me from doing so. I satisfied myself with poking around the museum of domesticity the Parsons sisters called a kitchen. I admired the shiny white tile counter tops and the tiny little hexagon floor tiles—there must have been a million of them. The butler's pantry was filled with some wonderful old china. There were serving pieces I had never seen before—probably for roast grouse, or goose mousse, or whatever the Parsons family used to eat in their heyday. Conspicuously absent was any sterling silver—no cutlery and no trays or teapots. I imagined they had been sold long ago. I began to feel sorry for the two little old ladies who had lived beyond the years when they had means.

After a while, I got bored with the kitchen and was about to make good my mother's poor opinion of me by snooping around the rest of the downstairs when I heard a car pull up in the driveway. Bruce Hawkins was waiting impatiently at the back door by the time I found my way through the darkened house.

"The ceilings are about fourteen feet high, and most of these old houses don't have light switches in every room," Bruce explained as we fumbled our way back to the kitchen in the dark. "I love these old homes. Mona and I tried to buy one in Atherton, but it was tied up in a trust. I suppose this one is, too."

"Well, you'll probably get a chance to find out, if Miss Lolly likes you, that is. She hates me. She'd sooner go to jail than ask for my help."

"So who told her I was coming?" he asked.

"Cassie, my daughter. She's upstairs with Miss Lolly now. Can you help her out of this mess, Bruce?"

"She can't stand the sight of you, but you are so concerned about her welfare that you're willing to foot all her legal bills. How's that add up?" He looked at me carefully over his little half glasses as he sat down at the table.

I had forgotten what a good-looking man Bruce Hawkins was. He'd lost a tad more hair, but his eyes were still a beautiful deep blue and his smile was warm and open. I knew he was as honest and upright as he looked. Miss Lolly could trust him all the way to the bank—if she would give him the chance.

"I'd hate to see anyone put away in Sunny Acres just because they happen to choose an unusual way of keeping their head above water," I explained. I failed to add that I felt somewhat guilty because I fully intended to use the imagery of a body in a freezer for Leonard's next book. And there was also the need to atone for my long ago sins against that fabled feline, Mr. Whiskers.

"Sunny Acres and not jail? What makes you think that?" asked Bruce.

"She froze her sister, for Pete's sake."

"Hummn, I see your point," he said slowly. "Judge Hershey may decide to hold a sanity hearing. Or he might turn the case over to the County Attorney."

"I'm sure he'll do the right thing. Mother says he's very fair."

"A year ago I would have agreed with her one hundred percent, but just between you and me—and I mean that," he added sternly, "since he's hired that shifty-eyed assistant of his, the old man's let things slide." Bruce looked me straight in the eye. "I wouldn't be talking out of school, except it may impact what happens to your friend upstairs."

"What assistant?"

"A fellow named Newton. Came highly recommended from a law firm in California. Has a lot of big city ideas. Every time someone disagrees with him he says they're 'archaic and insular'."

"Looks like you've been called that one too many times," I laughed.

He smiled. "I like being archaic and insular if it means living peacefully among friends and neighbors and working things out to suit what's best for everybody—not just going by the book all the time." He stretched his long arms above his head and looked around the kitchen. "Where's the freezer?" he asked. "I have to see this with my own eyes. And let me say right from the start that I'll forgo any legal fees on this one, Paisley. If you are willing to help Miss Lolly, then so am I."

Bruce managed to look fairly nonchalant when he saw Miss Hannah in her frozen bed, but I could tell from the twinkle in his eyes he was dying to run home and relate the story to his wife. He examined the freezer for a few minutes, then got out a yellow legal pad from his briefcase and made a list of things to do.

I tried to call Horatio again, but there was still no answer at the funeral home. Mother didn't answer either. Bruce offered to call Andy Joiner and explain everything. He thought he could keep the matter quiet if the powers that be would cooperate. He also had a suggestion.

"If Miss Lolly agrees to go to a nursing home I think I can persuade Hershey not to hold a sanity hearing. He'll probably want to appoint someone as her legal guardian. If you don't want your daughter to do it, I'll be glad to stand in."

"That's up to Cassie," I said. "But I can tell you this—Miss Lolly will really hate leaving this old house. She's never lived anywhere else. It's going to break her heart."

"Sorry, Paisley, but I don't think she'll have a choice. If there is a sanity hearing she'll mostly likely be committed."

"I know," I sighed. "It's just sad, that's all."

Bruce stood up and stretched again. "Aunt Matilda should be here any minute. She'll take care of Miss Lolly until we can decide what to do."

"Great! I should have been somewhere else two hours ago. Cassie, too. We're late for dinner. I was supposed to bring the food," I added ruefully.

"Before I go upstairs, Paisley, I like to ask you something," said Bruce as though he weren't quite sure. "I heard that some of the Mexican laborers came out to your Mother's place to work and you all kicked them out because they got unruly. Is that true?"

"Of course, not!" I denied heatedly. "To a man, they were polite and extremely hard working! And we really needed them for a few more days. We were just about to get things back to normal when Andy Joiner served us with an injunction prohibiting them for working on the farm."

"Do you remember who signed it?"

"Sure. It was Hershey, himself."

Bruce shook his head slowly. "I'd bet my bottom dollar it wasn't him. Newton has been pretty free with the old man's signature stamp." He looked up from his briefcase and blushed with the next question. "Do...er, women usually come across the border with those guys?"

I must have looked a little surprised. He hurried to explain.

"Several Mexican babies have been adopted by parents in western Kentucky. Oddly enough, almost all of the adoptions have been processed through the courthouse here in Rowan Springs. I was just curious as to where the babies are coming from, that's all. I've been told the infants are anywhere from a few days to a few hours old. That seems kind of young to me, especially if the babies are really coming all the way from Mexico."

"Well, I don't know a thing about any women. Cassie might know, though. She talked to the men a lot more than I did. And she, ah...spent some time with their foreman. Ask her when you go upstairs. And send her back down, if you don't mind. We've got to get going."

CHAPTER TWENTY-FIVE

Cassie refused to leave Miss Lolly's side until Matilda Hawkins arrived and the two women spent enough time together to get reacquainted. Miss Lolly's mood lightened somewhat as the tension of keeping her terrible secret faded away and she even seemed to enjoy the company. She smiled as she waved goodbye to Cassie, though I still didn't warrant so much as a glance.

"She'll forgive you one day, Mom," Cassie assured me.

"She should live so long," I muttered.

"Don't be mean," chided my kindly daughter. "Miss Lolly's had a hard time."

"It's her own fault," I protested. "She didn't have to stay cooped up in that old mausoleum. She could have had a life if she hadn't been so selfish."

Cassie stayed quiet, deep in thought, as we drove back down Main Street toward the funeral home. She didn't even look up until I remembered something and slammed on the brakes in the middle of Chestnut Street.

"Damn!"

"What's wrong, Mom."

"Dinner! I was supposed to go to Cloudt's and get barbeque."

"Well, it's too late now. It's almost eight. Cloudt's will be closed by the time we get there. Why not just pick up some burgers at the Dairy Queen?"

"Horatio would never eat anything as vulgar as a hamburger."

"Horatio loves hamburgers! You're such a snob, Mom."

"Snob? Me a snob? You must be kidding!" I protested vehemently. "Some kind of snob I am—dressed in jeans, a tee shirt, and loafers, hah!"

"Exactly! You proved my point," she laughed.

"Oh, yeah! How's that?"

"From top to bottom," Cassie replied, looking me up and down. "Ralph Lauren, Calvin Klein, and Cole-Haan."

"Hummpf! I wear these clothes because they're comfortable. And my other moccasins were falling apart. I suspect Mother threw them out. Besides, these were on sale. You know I never buy anything that's not on sale."

"Just get the burgers, Mom. And don't forget extra ketchup for the fries."

When we finally got our order from the Dairy Queen, it was eight-thirty. I consoled myself with the idea that Horatio would probably be grateful for anything by the time we showed up with dinner.

The funeral home appeared deserted as we drove up. Only the three long black hearses, their hoods shining like beetle carapaces in the moonlight, waited silently in the parking lot. Horatio's Bentley was conspicuously absent.

"Looks like nobody's home," observed Cassie with a nervous little laugh. "It's a little spooky."

"Nonsense! Bother and nonsense," I muttered: a mantra against the dark. "Wanda is upstairs for sure because Horatio made her promise not to leave. We just can't see the parlor light from back here." I got out and hefted the bag of drinks. "Can you carry the food by yourself, or do we need to make two trips?"

"I don't know about you, Mom, but I'm not coming back down here in the dark for anything. I'll carry it all now, even if I get a hernia."

Cassie balanced the two big sacks of food over each slender hip and walked carefully towards the entrance. I placed both hands underneath the drinks and tried to ignore the icy cold of the sloshing liquids as I braced the paper bag against my chest.

The situation was ripe for disaster. I could see us dropping greasy food and sticky drinks all over Horatio's new carpet. Mother would be furious.

"Maybe we'd better go in thorough the ambulance entrance, Cassie. Horatio has just redecorated. I'd really hate to spill any of this plebeian banquet in the foyer and ruin something."

"The ambulance entrance? Isn't that where the dead bodies go?" she squeaked.

"There's probably nobody there tonight," I assured her.

"But you said Fatty...."

"Well, maybe Fatty...?"

"No thanks, Mom," she insisted firmly. "I'll be careful."

"I'll have to go in the back way, Cassie. This bag is wet, and it's starting to leak."

"See you upstairs, then," she said over her shoulder as she hurriedly disappeared—leaving me standing alone in the moonlight.

The paper bag was not only wet and leaking, it was also beginning to come apart. I would have to leave some of the drinks downstairs and make a second trip. And I had to hurry because the dam was about to break. I fumbled with the handle and pushed the door to the ambulance entrance open with my hip.

Just as I got inside, the drink cup on the top of the stack lost its little plastic cover. Cassie's cherry coke and half a cup of crushed ice sloshed out on my tee shirt and down my bra.

"Drat! Drat, and double drat."

The morgue was almost completely dark. The only light in the room came from the parking lot, and after it filtered through the frosted glass in the doors it didn't illuminate much. I waited for a moment to let my eyes adjust, but the cold drinks against my soaking tee shirt got to be more than I could stand. I did a blind shuffle to the left and then to the right until I stubbed my toe against the leg of a heavy steel table.

"Ouch!"

I set down my wet burden on the cold metal surface and rubbed my injured foot against the back of my other leg. I turned around trying to get my bearings, but in the dark it was no use. I had been in this room only once before and I couldn't remember where the light switches were. It was like being in Miss Lolly's house all over again.

I felt along the edge of the table hoping to come to a wall with a door or a light. Instead my groping hand came upon another's whose fingers were cold and stiff. I screamed and ran blindly forward, bumping into another metal table and knocking an assortment of metal objects clattering and banging to the floor. I switched directions and immediately fell over a metal wastebasket. I was struggling to get my foot out of the basket when the lights came on. I blinked and rubbed my eyes before I saw Cassie at the door gaping at me and the havoc I had caused.

"For goodness sake, Mom. What's going on?"

"A body!" I gasped. "There's a body back there on that table." I covered my face with my hands and tried to get a grip on my nerves. "I touched the hand!"

Cassie looked at me in horror. Her face was as white as my tee shirt used to be.

"Whose body is it? Fatty's?"

"I...I guess so." I turned to look back down the length of the room at the table where I had left the drinks. "We'll have to collect the drinks."

"Not me!" gasped Cassie. "I'll drink water. Leave them there. Let's get out of here!"

"Cassie, I can't leave that mess for Horatio to find. Mother will never let me forget it. Besides, I spilled most of your drink on me and the rest on the floor." I looked back down the aisle at the mess puddling on the linoleum. "I'll have to clean it up."

"Please hurry, Mom. This place gives me the creeps."

I held out my hand. My fingers were steady and I wasn't shaking anymore. "Pass me some of those paper towels by the sink. I'll take care of the mess. Just stand by the door and make sure the lights don't go off. I've had enough of the dark for one night."

I took the paper towels and walked deliberately back to the table where I had left the drinks. On my way, I straightened the other furniture and picked up the metal instruments and the tray I had knocked over. I was feeling better now and took the time to look around the rest of the room. The body I had touched in the dark seemed to be the only one in the morgue. Just one more example of my unfailing good luck.

"I guess it was Fatty," I called back to Cassie. "I don't see any more of Horatio's clients. Funny, the body doesn't look all that big."

I edged my way around the table, careful to avoid touching any part of the white sheet. I shuddered when I remembered the cold fingers against my own warm flesh. And I remembered, too, how small and thin they were.

"Cassie?"

"Mom, will you please hurry up!"

"Cassie, this can't be Fatty. The hand is too small." I looked more closely at the way the sheet draped over the still figure on table. "And so is the body."

"Then it's somebody else! So what! Clean up that mess and let's get out of here. I'm not hungry anymore, but Wanda might be."

A terrible thought began to form in the darkest recesses of my mind—the place where some of the ideas for Leonard's stories came from. "Cassie, did you see Wanda when you took the food upstairs?"

"No. But I didn't have a chance to look around. I rushed back down here to catch the bull in the china shop. She could have been sleeping, or been in the bathroom."

"No," I said quietly. "She's right here."

Wanda Blade looked as frightened in death as she had earlier in the afternoon when I had tried to enter her house. Her pupils were fixed, and her mouth was frozen in a silent, eternal scream. She was naked under the white cover and her marble white body was surprisingly slim and youthful. Wanda had indeed been the model for the lovely little statue in her garden. I was sure of it now.

Cassie suddenly appeared at my elbow. She clutched my arm tightly as we stared at the body. "What happened to her," she whispered hoarsely.

"I don't know." I dropped the sheet and covered Wanda's anguished face. "I didn't see any marks on her."

"Oh, Mom, what are we going to do?"

I gingerly moved the drinks off the table and wiped up the spill on the floor. My mind was working overtime but producing nothing. And my hands were shaking again. It took me a moment to realize why I was so scared.

"Cassie," I whispered, "head straight to Horatio's office as quickly as you can. I'll be right behind you."

She stared at me, her eyes as wide with fright as Wanda's. My own fear increased exponentially.

"Move it!"

She turned and ran, bumping into things and stumbling as she fought to keep her balance. I was close behind her as we climbed the five steps up to the main floor and ran down the carpeted hallway to Horatio's office. Cassie threw herself against the heavy mahogany door and jerked the handle.

"It's locked!"

"What?" I cried in dismay.

"Locked, locked, locked!" she whispered loudly. "What will we do? You think whoever killed Wanda may still be here, don't you, Mom?"

"Maybe, maybe," I gasped. It had just occurred to me that we had each entered the funeral home through doors that would normally be locked at this time of night.

"Mom! We have to get to the car."

"No!" I argued. "If the murderer's still here that's exactly what he would expect us to do. We have to think of something else. Follow me and try to be as quiet as you can."

"Good grief! Do you think I'm stupid or…?"

"Cassie! Just do it."

We crept down the hallway like two shadows. An image of Bud Abbott and Lou Costello in an old black and white film came to mind. I giggled nervously. Cassie pinched me.

"Ow!"

"Shhhh!"

We were almost at the end of the hall when we heard a door open and close. I froze and Cassie clung to my back like a barnacle.

"What door was that?" she whispered.

"I don't know," I whispered back. "We need to get to a window so we can see outside."

"There's one in the stairwell. Hurry!" urged Cassie as she brushed past me and took the stairs two at a time.

The window in the stairwell was large and oval and beautifully crafted in rippled stained glass.

"How in the hell are we supposed to see through this stuff?" I groaned.

"I thought I saw something when I first got here—someone running maybe, but it could have been a dog," she whispered as she wiped the glass with her sleeve.

"Damn! Now we don't know if it safe to leave or not."

"I say let's make a run for it, Mom. I want to go home."

"Too bad you can't click your heels together and make a wish." I sat down on the steps. The night was catching up with me. My head ached and my legs felt like they were made of foam rubber. "What if someone is waiting in the parking lot for us to come out?"

"We're fast. We can get in the car before they grab us."

"You, maybe. I don't think I could outrun a turtle right now."

"We can't just sit here and wait for the axe to fall, Mom. What if the opening door was just a ruse to make us think he left? Or even worse, what if he wasn't leaving but coming back inside."

I hadn't thought of that. Cassie was right: we had to make a run for it. There is no place like home.

We ran.

CHAPTER TWENTY-SIX

Cassie flew down the stairs on winged feet. I stumbled after her on rubbery legs and fell down the last three steps to sprawl head first on Horatio's new carpet.

"Ompff!"

"Hurry, Mom!" Cassie cried as she flung open the door to the parking lot and ran smack dab into her grandmother.

They both screamed and Cassie fell backwards into the foyer on her butt. I couldn't see what happened to Mother because the overhead lights came on abruptly, blinding me.

When I could open my eyes again, I saw Horatio standing on the bottom of the winding staircase with his hand on the light panel and his mouth open in astonishment.

"My, my!" he said as he surveyed the two of us lying on the floor. "That's something you don't see very often."

"Horatio," cried Cassie. "Thank God, it's you!"

Mother pushed her way back into the foyer. Small tendrils of white hair had escaped from her elegant French twist, her pearls were askew, and there was a telltale white spot of dust and gravel on the back of her linen pantsuit. She stepped gingerly over her granddaughter and sank down onto one of the brocade loveseats.

"Oh, my!" she said as she tried to tuck her hair back in place.

"Gran! Are you all right?" gasped Cass. "I'm sorry I knocked you down." She struggled to her knees and crawled over to her grandmother's side. "Did I hurt you?" she asked, brushing ineffectively at the dirt on her slacks.

"Anna, my dear, are you hurt?" cried Horatio anxiously as her hurried to her side. I lay on the floor and watched as they tended to my mother like she was the Queen of Sheba.

My chin was stinging and my knee burned like crazy where I had skidded across the carpet.

"What about me?" I grumped angrily. "What am I? Dog meat?"

Cassie came over to help me up. "Oh, Mom! Your chin is bleeding."

"Don't get any blood on Horatio's new carpet, dear," cautioned Mother.

I jerked the tail of my tee shirt out of my jeans and angrily put it up to my chin.

"Horatio, I there's something we need to tell...," I began.

"And I, you," he interrupted. "We have quite a little mystery on our hands."

"You don't know the half of it," said Cassie. "Wait till Mom shows you...."

"Plenty of time for show and tell, my dears. First we must help your grandmother upstairs. She's had quite a tumble. She needs to sit down and get her bearings."

"But...."

"Paisley, I left a couple of bottles of wine and a six pack of beer in the car. I thought perhaps our guest would enjoy some brew. Would you and Cassie mind?"

"But Wanda's...," started Cassie.

"Been waiting long enough," finished Horatio impatiently. "So be as quick as you can. We'll see you upstairs in a minute."

Cassie and I looked at each other and shrugged our shoulders simultaneously. She inspected my chin.

"No biggie, Mom. Just a carpet burn. How's your knee?"

"Same thing, I guess. Mostly I'm just tired to the bone. This has been some night, and something tells me it's not half over yet."

"I think you're right," she called over her shoulder as she cautiously opened the door. I limped over and waited while she inspected the parking lot.

"I don't see anything," she said. "I think it's safe. Just prop the door open so we don't get locked out. Better still, wait here for me and I'll bring the booze."

"Can you carry it all by yourself?"

"I've carried twice this much—millions of times," she laughed, then stopped suddenly. She turned back and looked at me. Her face was pale in the moonlight. "I mean when some of the guys had frat parties and I helped them get ready," she added lamely.

"Never mind the cover up," I told her. "Right now I could care less if you were a raging alcoholic with a heroin habit."

"You don't mean that, Mom," she chided as she closed the door of the Bentley.

"I don't," I admitted ruefully. "I'm just pooped."

"A glass of wine and a burger will fix you right up," she said with a smile.

"I just dread telling Horatio he has an unexpected guest in his work room," I sighed as I took the beer from her. "And I think I'll hoist a glass in honor of the deceased. She was a nice lady."

"You know, Mom," sighed Cassie, her voice unusually solemn, "we should probably take care of Wanda ourselves, if we want to keep Horatio out of trouble, that is."

"You mean, get rid of her body? How? And why, pray tell?" She didn't answer right way, so I filled in the gaps as my mind whirled around her words. "Besides, Horatio is a big boy—probably the biggest boy we know, in terms of being smart and clever. Surely he can figure out what to do about Wanda."

"Yeah, but he'll do it the right and proper way, and that just might be his undoing."

"You mean, playing hide and seek with dead bodies won't do his business or his personal reputation any favors?"

"Something like that."

"Oh, geez, Cassie! I don't think I can do it alone. Just remembering how cold her and stiff her fingers..."

"You won't have to do it alone, Mom. I can do my bit."

"Over my dead, er...no!"

"Who else then? Andy? Gran? Aggie?"

Cassie backed the car into the driveway by the ambulance entrance while I got Wanda ready for transport. I managed to wrap a couple of extra sheets around her without touching her skin, but mine was crawling when I finished.

"We've got to hurry," I whispered loudly when Cassie opened the double doors. "They think we just went out to the car for the drinks. Horatio will come looking for us in a minute."

Together, we managed to carry our burden to the car and slide her into the back seat. It wasn't easy. Wanda was a lot heavier than she looked in life or in death.

I closed the doors to the ambulance bay and Cassie got back behind the wheel.

"You're driving? I think not! There must be an extra felony charge for the getaway driver. Move over."

"Don't be a goose, Mom, and close the car door."

"I imagine her house would be the best place to leave her, don't you think? If there's no outward signs of violence, we can take her home and make it look like she died a natural death—until we find our what's going on, then we can tell the authorities everything we know."

"And if she has a big old bullet hole in her middle?" asked Cassie.

"Then we leave her in her house and let everyone think she was shot there."

"What do we use for blood? We left all the ketchup with the burgers."

"Very funny, Poirot!"

"Another one of your stupid movies?"

Wanda's little cottage was all alone and empty. It was after ten o'clock and most good citizens were in bed. We hadn't seen a soul, and I was practically positive no one had seen us. Even the parking lot of The Pelican had appeared almost deserted as we drove past.

"I guess someone at the restaurant will call the police tomorrow when they don't hear from Wanda. She won't have to be alone for long."

"Good grief, Mom."

"Sorry."

Cassie backed silently down the dead woman's driveway. Only the quick crunch of gravel heralded our arrival. I bit my lip when the memory of Wanda's comments about her nightingale floor flashed through my mind. She hadn't known when she made that remark that she would soon be as dead as those ancient emperors.

Cassie and I got out of the car quickly. She grabbed Wanda's ankles and I held onto the dead woman's shoulders. We carried her around to the back of the cottage, stumbling and lurching with the effort.

"She hid the key under a flower pot," I whispered.

"Don't need it, the door's open."

"What the hell? I saw her lock it, Cassie." The hairs on the back of my neck were at full attention.

We stood awkwardly, holding the corpse, trying not to drop Wanda and run for the safety of the car.

"We can't stand here all night holding a dead body. We'll have to chance it," I whispered. "Turn her around. I'll go in first. If someone grabs me, you run for help."

We maneuvered our burden clumsily around on the narrow steps. Once again, I was reminded of Abbott and Costello. It took my last reserves of discipline not to giggle.

"The coast is clear," I called softly, as I peered intently around the darkened kitchen. "Come on in."

I was exhausted and sweating profusely by the time we deposited Wanda carefully on her lipstick-red satin bedspread. A small bulb in the adjoining bath was the only light we had to go by. Cassie opened a drawer in the dresser searching for a nightgown. We decided along the way that we shouldn't leave her naked. It seemed disrespectful, somehow.

"Aha!" she whispered as she held up a long nylon gown covered with big red and pink and green flowers. "How's this?"

"A bit gaudy, but it'll do."

We carefully unwrapped the morgue sheets from the body, averting our eyes from Wanda's nakedness as much as possible, but relieved nonetheless, to see no outward signs of violence.

Cassie slipped the gown over Wanda's head and then stuck her arms through the shoulder straps. We both tugged and pulled at the slippery fabric until we got it down over her hips and past her knees to her bare feet."

"There!" gasped Cassie. "Should we put her under the covers, or what?"

"Damn! I don't know," I answered biting my lip.

"Let's go, Mom! Let's get out of here. I'm coming down with a bad case of the heebie-geebies."

I looked up to see my daughter's body trembling in the faint light, suddenly realizing the insanity of our actions.

"Oh, my God! Of course, honey." I grabbed Cassie's cold hand with one of mine and the sheets with the other, and pulled her toward the kitchen. We were almost out the door when I noticed the pizza box with Horatio's note on the inside—it was no longer in the garbage can but sitting open on the kitchen table. At least we knew how Wanda's whereabouts had been discovered.

CHAPTER TWENTY-SEVEN

We climbed the stairs slowly as I favored my knee. Cassie altered her gait and politely kept me company.

"Wanda was a very nice person," she sighed. "I hope...."

"Well, where is she?" called Horatio from the top of the stairs.

So we sat in the pretty blue and yellow parlor and told Mother and Horatio what we had discovered earlier in the evening, and what we had done about it.

"What arrogance! To leave her body naked in my morgue!"

I agreed. "And we were even afraid that the killer might have stayed around to watch someone find her."

"Oh, dear! Horatio, do you think he's still here?" asked Mother. "Perhaps we should call...."

"No, Anna. The last person we should call is Chief Joiner. We'd have too much to explain ourselves. The first thing he would want to know is why Wanda's not still here. That's a question we would have a hard time answering." He pulled thoughtfully on his small white goatee.

"We're already under somewhat of a cloud, Paisley, dear. Horatio's right. We have to keep any more questions of...well, a suspicious nature from being asked."

"Cloud? What kind of a cloud, Mother?" I grabbed a cold hamburger out of the sack. I needed some protein.

Horatio poured us each a glass of wine before I could open a beer. When he sat back down he told us where he and Mother had been.

"The emergency room is so dreary," added Mother. "It's too bad the poor man had to die there."

"Poor Rudolfo," moaned Cassie. "He was afraid, really afraid that he was getting too close."

"Too close to what, Cassie?" I asked gently.

"I don't know, Mom," she snuffled. "He was just afraid, that's all. He wouldn't tell me much, just that he was looking for someone really evil."

"Did he or any of the other Mexicans happen to mention anything about women being brought here with them to work?" I asked as I remembered Bruce's query.

"Mr. Hawkins asked me that same question. He seemed a bit embarrassed. I guess he was thinking about prostitutes, and was too polite to say so."

"What did you tell him? Did Rudolfo say anything about prostitutes?" I insisted.

"Not to me," said Cass shaking her head. "But then *he* was far too polite. To him, I was *la donita*, the young lady of the house—delicate sensibilities, and all that nonsense."

"Well, somebody certainly isn't worried about sensibilities, or they wouldn't have left a string of bodies behind," said Horatio, his voice heavy with unaccustomed sarcasm.

"String?" Mother asked.

"I have to believe that Rudolfo was murdered by the same person who killed that man Andy Joiner brought here this morning. Their throats were cut in almost exactly the same manner. And," he added excitedly as he suddenly put two and two together, "the man who was found at the edge of the airport runway had the same vicious wounds. He must be victim number one!"

"Then, that makes four," I observed over a mouthful of bread and meat.

"Why, Mom? Wanda's throat wasn't cut. You said there wasn't a mark on her."

"Maybe not, but I think your mother's right, Cassie," agreed Horatio. "I can't say exactly why, but something about leaving her here under our noses smacks of the same vicious intent."

"My, I'm feeling a little faint," said Mother in a tight little voice. "Do you think we could open the window just a crack. Some fresh air might help."

Cassie jumped up to do her grandmother's bidding. I dabbed a kitchen towel in some cool water and handed it to her.

"Well, it's no big mystery how the murderer got in," observed Cassie from across the room. "One of the window panes is broken."

I heard the crunching of broken glass as Horatio walked over to inspect the window. He raised it all the way and stuck his head outside. "There's a ladder in the garage," he mused. "I had a painter here this week for some touch-up work on the eaves. His wife became ill and he left some of his equipment in his hurry to get home. It wouldn't have been difficult to find the ladder. The garage is always open. My bet is that's how he got in, and we know he exited from one of the back doors."

"But why leave them both unlocked?" asked Cass.

"To put us off the track?" I guessed.

"Perhaps," said Horatio in a distant voice. He seemed deep in thought.

I finished my hamburger and reached for the fries. They were cold and lifeless, like Wanda's fingers. I shuddered, but I was still hungry. "Does anybody else want Wanda's burger?"

"Mom!"

"Well, she surely won't want it."

"Eat it, Paisley, dear, and shut up!"

"Gran!"

"Really, Cassandra! Can't you finish your sentences? You do, after all have a college education."

Cassie blushed to her roots and dropped like a rock—an injured, dramatic rock—into the armchair.

"Anna, dear," asked Horatio as he took her hand in his, "Are you quite all right?"

"I've never been better," she snapped. "But you all have forgotten one small detail."

"What's that, my dear?" asked Horatio soothingly.

"Wanda's body, of course! A murderer that arrogant will surely have no qualms about informing the police anonymously that an unexplained dead person can be found in the Raleigh Funeral Home. I quite expect to hear them pounding on Horatio's door at any moment."

"Your mother is quite right, you know," pointed out Horatio. "We mustn't waste any more time. We need to straighten up here and go home like nothing has happened."

Cassie looked as exhausted as I felt but she squared her shoulders and went to look for Wanda's clothes in the bedroom.

"They're not there," she announced from the doorway.

"Come on, Cassie," I protested. "We don't have time to fool around."

"Get real, Mom! I'm not kidding. All of Wanda's clothes are gone."

"How about her duffle bag? She brought a big duffle bag from the house. I helped her carry it."

"Nope! No duffle bag, no toothbrush, no nothing."

"Oh, jeez!"

"Language, Paisley," admonished Mother automatically.

I bit my tongue and stood to clean up the mess of paper cups and used ketchup packets. The debris was mostly mine. I was beginning to wish I hadn't eaten. I felt decidedly queasy somewhere beneath my belt.

I bent over to police the floor—to make sure that no errant French fries had fallen between the cracks. I tried to stifle it, but a loud and comfortable burp escaped my lips.

"Paisley Sterling!"

"I know, Mother, I know.... Hey! Look at this!" I knelt down, wincing as my weight rested on my sore knee, and fished a dark little dome-shaped object from under the sofa.

Horatio came over to look as I held it up in my palm.

"A cigar end," he mused, "and not from just any cigar. This is an expensive, and I might add, quite illegal, Cuban cigar. Difficult to come by in this neck of the woods. I should know, I've tried." He looked somewhat chagrined. "I'm quite fond of them myself."

"Then this is yours," I laughed. "You must come up here to hide and fire up your contraband stogies."

"Sorry to disagree with your deductions, my dear, but I haven't enjoyed one of those in quite a few years. And I'm certain I've never smoked a cigar of any kind in these quarters." He plucked the piece of cigar and held it up to the light. "This might be the only clue to our murderer."

"There's one more," I said, and told him about the pizza box on Wanda's kitchen counter.

"Still," he mused. "It did take some deduction to arrive at the funeral home."

"Not so much," disagreed Cassie. "You are probably the only 'Horatio' in these here parts."

"Then the obvious assumption is that the murderer knows me."

"Or knows of you," I amended.

There have been many times in the last few years when I was tremendously grateful and vastly relieved to arrive at Meadowdale Farm. Tonight was one of those times.

"I think we've earned a small libation, my dears," announced Horatio.

"Not me," sighed Cassie. "I'm exhausted. And I have to work tomorrow. A bath and my little bed is all I want."

"Cassie, are you okay? I mean...."

"If you mean, will I wake up in the middle of the night screaming, I don't know, Mom," she admitted.

"I love you, sweet pea," I told her, feeling the guilt ooze through my body like something oily and foul.

Mother opened the French doors and stood aside as we trudged tiredly into the library. Cassie kissed her grandmother goodnight and waved a weak farewell to Horatio before she went to her room.

I plopped down on the sofa and stared down at the stains of cherry coke and blood on my tee shirt. It was only a second or two before I started bawling. Mother poured me a cup of hot tea from the tray she had hastily prepared, and Horatio topped it off with a generous tot of brandy.

"Here, dear, drink this. You'll feel better."

"No...uh, uh," I sniffed. "How could I have let my sweet baby help me hide a dead body?" I cried. "A naked dead body at that!"

"How, indeed?" muttered Horatio. "I am feeling somewhat guilty myself," he said clearing his throat. His hands were shaking as he filled his pipe. He got up and walked over to the window to finish his task.

I took a deep swallow of tea and brandy and closed my eyes, then slumped back against the sofa cushions and tried to relax as the sweet smell of Horatio's tobacco smoke wafted across the room.

"Wussies!" muttered Mother under her breath.

"What's that, my dear?" asked Horatio.

"Wussies!" she said aloud.

I opened my eyes and turned to look at her in surprise.

"The lot of you—all wussies!" She straightened her smart tailored jacket and adjusted her pearls. "Paisley had no choice. It was something that simply had to be done. We don't have any idea what we're dealing with here. For all we know, we could be in very serious danger, and besides, Horatio's reputation had to be protected. His father and grandfather would turn over in their graves if anything happened to that funeral home. It's too bad that Cassandra had to be involved, but there was nothing for it. Andy Joiner was already questioning the reason Rudolfo called out for Cassie from his deathbed. He...."

"How's that?" I asked coming out of my stupor. "He asked for Cassie? Whatever for?"

"I don't know, dear. The ER doctor called here for Cassandra, and when I told him I didn't know where she was—that we had only just arrived ourselves, he said we'd better come right away. He didn't know anyone else to call, and the man was dying."

"Was Rudolfo dead when you got there?"

Horatio sat back down on the sofa. He appeared to have regained his composure and was ready to take up the narrative.

"Not quite gone," he said. "But he had lost a great deal of blood and could barely speak."

"He spoke to you?"

"Two words only—a woman's name—Effie Díaz."

"Who the hell is she?" I asked crossly. Dead or not, Rudolfo could have given us a better clue, I thought.

"His injuries were lethal. There was no way anyone could have saved him. He died shortly afterwards."

Mother took over the story. "There was nothing in his pockets. No identification or personal items. Quite tragic, really. The poor man! Who could have had a reason to end his life? What manner of threat did he pose to anyone?"

"Cassie says he was a Mexican government agent."

Horatio didn't raise an eyebrow, but I felt him focus on me with the intensity of a laser beam.

"I guess we should have told you earlier," I admitted with a faint attempt at a smile. "Rudolfo told Cassie he was posing as a migrant worker and on the trail of someone he'd been after for nearly two years. He showed Cassie his identification and a letter from the Attorney General. "

"My goodness!" said Mother. "We have to let Andy know. He'll want to inform the Mexican government right away."

"Not so fast, my dear Anna. We cannot allow sentiment to sway us. I admire young Joiner for many things, but finesse is not one of them. If we want to uncover our murderer we must cause him some discomfort—perplex him, as it were. That will take a great deal of careful thought."

"How?" I asked tiredly. It was beginning to sound like a game of chess to me, and I lacked the patience for chess.

"He will expect the police to find Wanda's body where he left it. And he will expect them not to find the body of the gentlemen Chief Joiner brought in this morning."

"Fatty! By the way, where is he, Horatio? He wasn't in the morgue."

"No, but a certain Mr. Harold Hemmings was. Harold was one of Rowan Springs's homeless, an unfortunate gentleman without friends or family. At Joiner's request, I put the first body—your Mr. Fatty—in the refrigerated storage cooler. Mr. Hemmings died later this afternoon. They were both of a size—er, somewhat corpulent, that is, and in the vinyl body bags it would be hard to tell the difference."

"But...but...," I sputtered.

"He wasn't there tonight? I was not unaware of that, Paisley. I checked before I left. Wanda's murderer took the only other body there, thinking, no doubt, that it was the man Joiner transported to the morgue this morning. But why the killer would want to steal the body...."

"Because Fatty was a Texas Ranger!" I sat on the edge of my seat, my exhaustion all but forgotten. "Rudolfo told Cassie they were working undercover together. As soon as Andy checked Fatty's fingerprints he would have found out who he was. That's why his body had to go missing."

"My goodness!"

"Well put, Anna my dear, well put, indeed," agreed Horatio with a sagacious nod.

CHAPTER TWENTY-EIGHT

I found Cassie sound asleep in my bed when I finally bade Mother and Horatio goodnight. Aggie was snoring quietly from a comfortable nest between her mistress's knees. I knew better than to try and move her.

I slipped out of my clothes and splashed some water on my face to get rid of the stickiness from Cassie's spilled cherry coke, then dabbed some first aid ointment on my chin and the scrape on my knee and pulled on my pajamas. Despite the fact that it was after midnight when I crawled in beside my daughter I couldn't sleep. I lay wide awake for hours, listening to the soft pitiful moans of Cassie's nightmares before I finally fell into an exhausted slumber myself.

When I awoke at ten the next morning, my hair wet with sweat and my arms and legs caught in a mad tangle of sheets, I felt as though I had been in a wrestling match all night.

Cassie had already left, so I pulled myself out of bed along with the wrinkled linens—much to the displeasure of the puppy, who was still sleeping peacefully. Aggie growled fiercely and tried to bite me. I just managed to tip her off the bed before she did any real damage.

"Stupid dog! You're not really in charge here, you know. You don't pay rent and you eat for free, so don't give me any more grief. AND STAY OFF MY DOWN PILLOW!"

Aggie gave me a look of such royal disdain that I had to laugh. It felt good. I laughed some more when she turned tail and trotted off to the kitchen, pausing once in the doorway to throw me another dirty look over her shoulder, and I felt even better. It had been a long time between laughs. I even sang loudly, and way off key, as I took my hot soapy shower and washed the night sweats out of my hair. I shouldn't have counted my grins before they hatched.

Mother was having a very sparse *petite déjeuner* at the kitchen table. I was starving. I offered to fix her something more substantial as I rummaged around in the refrigerator.

"No thanks, dear. I didn't sleep very soundly, I'm afraid. Tea and toast is quite all I can manage."

I didn't tell her that I tossed and turned all night, also. She might criticize my need for a big slice of baked ham and a biscuit or two. I busied about fixing my plate, trying hard not to react to her frequent and dramatic sighs. When I sat down to eat, she upped the ante.

"Oh, dear. Oh, my!"

I put my fork down and swallowed my first big hungry bite with difficulty. "Okay, Mother. Out with it. What's the matter?"

"Nothing, Paisley. Don't mind me," she said with another deeply exaggerated exhalation.

"Okay, fine! Glad nothing's wrong." I said chomping down angrily.

"Except maybe...."

I got up and put my plate in the sink—biscuits and all—and filled my cup with more hot tea. "Out with it, Mother," I said crossly as I sat back down. "Or do you want to wait until lunch so you can ruin that for me, too?"

"Well, I never...!"

"Please, Mother, dear," I said with a sarcastic attempt at politeness. "Whatever is troubling you will be less disturbing if you share. How's that?"

"Better," she acknowledged with tight little nod. "It's Cassie."

I nodded in agreement. "I know. I feel terrible about last night, too," I sighed.

She looked up at me in surprise. "Last night?"

"Yeah, don't you remember our little debacle with the dead body?"

She got up from the table in a swirl of pink satin. Her dressing gown looked better on her slender figure than most of my regular clothes looked on me. "Not that! I don't mean that," she said angrily. "That silly little job she has at the coffee shop. That's what I'm talking about."

I looked at her over the rim of my teacup in astonishment. I was getting as mad as she apparently was. "Let me get this straight," I said with firm deliberation. "Our little game of musical chairs with the deceased didn't phase you, but your granddaughter's choice of occupation does?"

"Exactly!" She stomped her dainty foot so hard some of the ostrich feathers on her bedroom slipper came loose and floated about the kitchen. "That business at the funeral home was unavoidable. We had to protect Horatio. Or rather, you did. After all, you started this whole thing."

"I did? Well, that's news to me!" I dumped the rest of my tea in the sink on top of my uneaten breakfast, and turned to face her with fire in my eyes. "Perhaps you'd care to explain just how I accomplished that."

"Gladly!" She sat back down at the table and began to enumerate my sins one by one on her beautifully manicured fingertips. "Firstly, if you had taken proper care of our darling puppy she never would have gotten lost. Then secondly, Mr. Rudolfo would not have found her and brought her home, prompting us, thirdly, to hire the Mexicans. And fourthly, if you hadn't gone out to the trailer park in the middle of the night and nearly killed your daughter, Wanda Blake would not have been caught up in this misadventure and gotten," she stuck out her little finger, "killed herself."

"For Pete's sake!"

Mother held up her other thumb, Persian Passion Pink gleamed from her freshly lacquered nail in the morning sunlight. "And number six...?"

I marched out of the kitchen before I heard number six. I did, however, hear Aggie barking her own displeasure with me from under the safety of Mother's skirt. Someday I would get even. Someday I would have the last word. I solemnly promised myself that elusive pleasure as I quickly dressed and left the house.

Main Street was busy. The mayor had been threatening to hold a referendum on streetlights for over a year. I could see his point. I had to circle the block twice, and dodge two tractors pulling wagonloads of hay before I found a parking place in front of Celestine's Coffee Shop.

Cassie was behind the counter brewing a pot of Jamoca Chocolate Cherry Supreme when I entered. The place was cozy and charmingly decorated, and smelled of freshly ground coffee, cinnamon, and nutmeg. My resilient daughter seemed to have recovered completely from our nocturnal activities.

"Mom! I'm so glad you came," she said with a huge, welcoming, grin. "Sit down and I'll make you some tea, unless you've already had your cup for the day?"

"No," I sighed, "as a matter of fact I haven't. And I would love some. Just plain old English Breakfast, if you have it."

I settled myself on one of six comfortable stools and rested my elbows on the long gleaming walnut bar. "This is beautiful. Who did the wood work?"

"Tommy, Celestine's husband. He remodeled the whole building, even the apartment upstairs."

I raised my eyebrows. Mother would hate to hear that. I would have to remember to tell her. "I thought the upstairs was designed by some grand pooh-bah architect back in the thirties?"

"Yep!" grinned Cassie. "Granstaff Armstrong-Jones, himself. Tommy didn't touch the original design, but he did update the wiring and plumbing—new hot water heater, new kitchen appliances, that kind of thing. It's really nice," she added wistfully. "I'll miss living there."

"You're not moving?" I tried to cover my own quick happiness by taking a big sip of tea, burning my tongue in the process. I didn't fool my daughter.

"You don't have to pretend, Mom. I know you're beside yourself with joy at the prospect of my staying on the farm with you and Gran."

I grinned openly. "You got me! Besides, your presence might be needed to stop another homicide."

Cassie sat back on the stool behind the counter and smiled back. "You and Gran already at it so early this morning? What's it about this time?" She stopped smiling. "It's my job, isn't it? She's still being a snobby pain about my working."

I hated seeing the smile fade from her pretty face so I lied—a little white lie. "No, sweetie. She's mad at me, only me. She blames all our problems on me. According to her, I started it all by leaving Aggie out in the storm."

Cassie pursed her lips. "Well, that was pretty...."

My heart began to sink. An argument with Mother was one thing—sometimes it could even be invigorating—but an argument with Cassie could ruin my day. I was saved by the telephone.

While Cassie took an order, I looked around at the assortment of gifts and goodies for sale. I was pleasantly surprised. Celestine had very good taste. I picked out a pretty apron edged with handmade crochet for Mother as a peace offering, and a box of Demerara sugar cubes for myself. I loved raw sugar and didn't find it for sale very often. I got another box, just in case.

"Mom, can you watch the store for a few minutes? I have to make a delivery to the courthouse."

"Why, I...."

"Great! I'll be back in a jiffy." She took off her own apron and pulled it down over my head. "Better get in back of the bar. Coffee's already brewed. Everything's labeled. If there's a problem, tell the customer to wait for me." And she was off with four cups of latte.

I positioned myself behind the coffee bar, laughing all the while. Mother would really be furious if she knew I had joined the ranks of the underemployed.

I snooped around and found everything to be clean, neat, and very practical. There were five regular coffees and one special flavor of the day—the aforesaid Jamoca Chocolate Cherry Supreme. A small wooden chest held the varied assortment of teas available, and large glass jars filled with biscotti and buttery shortbread lined the back wall. I put a dollar on the counter and fished out an anise-flavored biscotti to dunk in my tea. When Cass returned she found two more dollars in the pile and her mother happily slurping down her second cup.

"Looks like I don't need any more business with you around," she laughed. "Stay awhile and keep me company." She winked. "You can even leave me a tip."

I relinquished the apron and grabbed a napkin to wipe away the crumbs. "Umm, those cookies are great. They seem vaguely familiar somehow."

"They should! You've had them often enough."

"Dora Nick's housekeeper!" Dora was our neighbor. Rosie had lived with her for years—thirty to be exact—since Dora's sixtieth birthday. Rosie was a marvelous cook, and had provided the little Sterling girls with many an afternoon tea party over the years. "Here's some more money. Please pass me another."

By the time I was full, the little pile of bills on the counter had grown and my belt was considerably tighter. I was Cassie's only customer that morning. We spent a pleasant time talking about nothing for a while, then I broached the subject once more.

"So you've decided to stay with us. May I ask what made you change your mind?"

Her face clouded up and I wished I had kept on talking about the weather.

"If you don't want to...?"

"No, Mom, it's okay. Rudolfo—he's the one who made me change my mind. We talked a lot that night before we ended up at Miss Lolly's. He admired you and Gran tremendously. He couldn't understand why I would want to leave home." She wiped a nonexistent spot off the gleaming counter. "It's that Latin thing, I suppose. Just like when we lived with Dad's parents in San Romero."

"It would have been an insult not to live with them," I said softly. "It most decidedly is a Latin thing."

"Well, I've decided it's my thing, also." She held up her hand so I wouldn't interrupt. "But I'm one-half American, too, so I want some privacy—and maybe even my own outside door. That way I can come and go as I please."

I couldn't stop grinning. "I'm sure that can be arranged."

"And don't look so pleased with yourself. I could change my mind again anytime I want."

Cass decided it was safe to close down for a thirty-minute lunch break, so I drove her out to the Dairy Queen and treated her to the burger she had missed out on the night before. I ordered a root beer and added it to the tea sloshing around in my middle.

"That's funny," she said with the last bite.

"What?" I asked, leaning back in the booth.

"Did you watch the girl make change when you paid for our lunch?"

I tried to remember. "No. Did she pay me too much?"

Cassie shook her head impatiently. I had missed the point. "No, not that. She counted the money under her breath. I couldn't hear, but I saw her lips moving."

I was confused. I couldn't see where Cassie was going.

"I do the same thing," she explained. "I think everybody does. And when I went to the courthouse and delivered the coffee to Mr. Newton, he did it, too—only it looked odd—like he was counting in Spanish. You know—*uno, dos, tres, quatro....*"

"I have a vague recollection," I sniffed. Cassie always underestimated my language skills.

"I remember hearing somewhere that people can learn to speak a second language as well as their native tongue, but they always count in the language of their childhood."

"Okay, so maybe he's Latin."

"I asked him," she admitted. "It scared him to death. He got so nervous he spilled one of the cups of coffee. Then he got mad and blamed it on me. I offered to give him some money back, but he just ordered me out of his office." She looked down at the empty ketchup packets and French fry crumbs, and then back up at me. "But I think I'm right, Mom," she added defiantly. "I think Mr. Frank Newton is hiding the fact that he is Hispanic." She shook her head. "Now why would he do that?"

CHAPTER TWENTY-NINE

After lunch, I took Cassie back to the coffee shop and left her to her work. Since I really was not in the mood to go home and risk exposing myself to more of Mother's carping about her granddaughter's job, I decided to spend some time at the courthouse. I had several questions shelved away in the back of my mind, and this afternoon was as good a time as any to satisfy my curiosity.

I had seen old sepia-tinted photographs of the original seat of Lakeland County which burned down in the thirties and always thought the Victorian cupolas and turrets much more attractive than the concrete Art Deco mausoleum built to replace it.

The only charming thing about this grey monolith was the statue of a Confederate soldier on the south lawn. Every decade or so, some smarty-pants prankster, thinking he had an original idea, would come up with an article of clothing for the lonely Rebel sentinel.

Last year, the week after high school graduation found him sporting a bright fuschia bra around his concrete chest with matching lace panties over his head. I thought it was hilarious, but our mayor's reaction was to insist that Andy Joiner post a twenty-four-hour guard in order to put a stop to any future shenanigans. Andy was delighted. The mayor raised his budget and kept Andy from having to let one of his men go. Once, in an unguarded moment, he confided to me that he had some extra underwear waiting in the wings just in case the mayor deemed the guard a necessity no longer.

There were forty-one steps leading to the south entrance. I climbed them all in one breath, congratulating myself for sticking to my treadmill routine for the last three months.

The courthouse hallways were dark and dreary. A few dusty ceiling lights were all that kept visitors and employees alike from running into each other or falling down the stairwell. I was not very familiar with the floor plan, and it took me a few minutes to find my destination in the gloom.

The County Surveyor's office was in the basement at the other end of the building. I vaguely remembered going there once with my grandfather Sterling. It was a long narrow room with lots of shelves and enough dust to choke an elephant. On the way I passed a restroom and decided to take advantage of the opportunity. I had, after all, downed approximately a gallon or more of liquid refreshment since I left home.

As I was coming out, I almost ran into a tall, elderly gentleman dressed in a resplendent white suit and black string tie. His abundantly wavy hair was as white as snow and his eyes the hue of a bluejay feather.

"Little Paisley Sterling! Is that really you? Why, I swear if it isn't John Sterling's first-born in the flesh. My word, child, but you are the spittin' image of your daddy." Judge Hershey's voice was warm and deep, and left me no doubt that his sentiments were heartfelt. He was the genuine article: a real live Kentucky Colonel.

"Hello, sir," I said with a broad smile. "I haven't had the pleasure of seeing you for a long time. You haven't changed a bit."

"Ah, ha!" he laughed. "Your handsome daddy's looks and your beautiful mother's charm—what a truly devastatin' combination." He reached down, took my hand in his and leaned closer—his words for my ears only. "I met your daughter early this mornin' when I stopped in for coffee. She's a beauty, that one. And smart as a whip. When I found out she spoke Spanish like a native, I asked her to consider an appointment as the county's official translator. With more and more of these foreign fellows coming in to town we certainly have need for one. Try and convince her to accept, will you? We need some young blood around here."

"You don't have anyone else on your staff who speaks Spanish?" I asked remembering Cassie's remarks about the Judge's assistant.

"Nope!" he declared with certainty, as he let my hand go to straighten up. He was taller than I was by a good twelve inches, and thinner than I remembered. I wondered if he had been ill.

"I know a few words in French," he continued with a twinkle in his eyes. "But none that I could repeat in the company of ladies. And the rest of the folks who work around here only speak Kentuckian— possum up a gumtree, and all. Comes from the purest Elizabethan English. Remind yourself of that when you think you're surrounded by country bumpkins."

I laughed. I knew what he was talking about. "Oh, I learned the hard way never to underestimate the locals. The fool who does that could wind up without the shirt on his back."

His smile was as warm and broad as his own accent. It was like summer sunshine in the darkness of the hallway. "I'm glad you came home, Paisley. It did your momma good. Grace us with more of your presence, will you, child? The sight of you makes an old man glad."

I was somewhat taken aback by his emotional sentiments, but I had no doubt they were honestly meant. "Why, er...," I began.

"Tell your momma I send greetings and salutations. And don't forget to encourage that lovely daughter of yours to accept my offer." And he was off.

I stood and watched as Judge Hershey walked, ramrod straight, down the dark hall towards his chambers. I felt ashamed of myself for the suspicions that had brought me here in the first place. "Oh, well," I sighed, curiosity over coming remorse, "I've come this far—might as well finish the job."

The surveyor's office hadn't changed at all in the last thirty-five years. The room was still long and narrow and crammed with shelves of big unwieldy plat books. A constellation of dust motes hung suspended in the narrow beams of light that managed to filter though the dirty basement windows. Placed just below the ceiling and looking out to the sidewalk, they afforded a view of nothing more than the passing ankles and feet of my fellow townsfolk.

A fly-specked notice pinned to ancient cork bulletin board spelled out instructions for locating the correct plat book. It wasn't rocket science. I found what I was looking for right away.

Judge Hershey did indeed still own the land where the trailer park sat, as well as the over five hundred acres surrounding it. The land bordered Bass Bay on all sides and, except for the trailer park, was completely undeveloped. An old dirt logging road ran back into the acreage for five miles and then petered out. I was willing to bet it was probably unused and overgrown with brush and brambles. The lane to our own back field got that way unless it was bush-hogged every month or so.

I was just about to close the book and put it back in its dusty niche when I came face to face with Effie Díaz. She wasn't a person at all. Effie Díaz was a map coordinate: F-10. On his deathbed, overcome with pain and suffering, Rudolfo would have spoken the numbers in Spanish—his last words ("*efe diez*") would have sounded like "Effie Díaz" to someone unfamiliar with that language.

According to the map, F-10 referred to the far northeastern corner of Judge Hershey's land. The plot was nestled against heavily forested foothills and adjoined the National Wildlife Preserve. There was no more inaccessible area in all of Lakeland County. I wondered why in the world Rudolfo would have used his dying breath to bring it to someone's attention.

Cassie was closing up when I walked back by the coffee shop on the way to my car.

"You want a lift home, hun?"

"I'll take you up on that, Mom. If I have to depend on a taxi every day, I won't make any money at all." She smiled a little hesitantly and lifted one dark eyebrow. "I might have to take you up on that offer of a small, inexpensive car. Although, at the rate I'm going, it may be ten years before I can pay you back."

"No big tips today, huh?"

"Nary a one; except for the pretty lady who drank three cups of tea this morning." She handed me a large brown shopping bag with the coffee shop logo on the side, and turned to lock the door. "I wrapped Gran's apron in some pretty gift paper. It might help to get you back in her good graces."

"What say we sweeten the pot even more and chug down to Cloudt's for some barbeque? We can call Horatio when we get there and tell him to meet us at home. He'll help tame your grandmother. And to top things off, you can tell her about the offer you got to join the county payroll."

"You saw Judge Hershey! Isn't he just the sweetest old love?"

I started the engine, using that opportunity to avoid responding. I wasn't sure at that moment just what I thought of Judge Hershey.

I considered telling my daughter what I had discovered all the way to Cloudt's. All day long I had carefully avoided mentioning anything that might remind her of last night and our awful trek back to Wanda's house. Cassie hadn't mentioned it either, but I could almost feel the secret sitting between us like an unwelcomed guest. And ignoring it wasn't going to make it go away—ever. While we waited for the waitress to wrap two pounds of sliced pork, two and a half pounds of beef, and a quart of the best barbeque sauce in the western world, I made up my mind.

The best part of a trip to Cloudt's was always the drive home when we nibbled on the tender succulent meat with crispy smoked edges. That's why I always got an extra half-pound of my favorite beef.

"Ump, Mom. This is still the greatest," mumbled Cassie over a mouthful.

"Could you dunk some in the sauce without spilling it on the seat?"

"Sure thing!"

"And, by the way, I found out about Senorita Díaz," I blurted out abruptly.

Cassie turned toward me so fast she spilled about three tablespoons of dark orange sauce on Watson's seat.

"Damn it, Cassie! Watch what you're doing."

"It's your fault," she accused, as she dabbed at the widening spot with her napkin. "You startled me." She went through three napkins and gave up. "It's useless; but Gran has some upholstery cleaner at home that will do the trick. Don't be mad, Mom, please. Tell me about Effie. Who is she?"

I laughed. I had a hard time being mad at Cassie. I wish my mother could say the same about her daughter. "You mean *what* is she?" I corrected.

"*What?*" said Cassie, her pretty face drawn up in a frown.

"Yeah, 'Effie Díaz'—think about it. What does it sound like to you, oh mighty official Lakeland County Translator?"

"F-10! Of course! But what is F-10?" she asked, her eyes dancing with excitement "A new military aircraft? A spy plane, maybe? Or a secret formula?"

"Wrong on all counts. I'm not really positive, but I think F-10 refers to a map coordinate. If I'm right, your 'sweet old love' is up to his neck in some kind of nasty trouble. Map coordinate F-10 is on Judge Hershey's land, a few miles north of the trailer park on the other side of Bass Bay."

"Wow!" was my college-educated daughter's only response. My mother's was predictable.

"Impossible! Jimmy Hershey is a fine, upstanding, man. He was a very dear friend of your father's, for goodness sakes." She sat back, crossed her ankles in the most lady-like manner, and folded her hands in her lap. She was ready for an edict. "Paisley, I'll have to insist that you not speculate any further about Judge Hershey's possible involvement in this dreadful affair as long as you're in my home."

"Well," I grunted. "I'll just have to go outside to finish my conversation because if I'm right, he's up fudge creek without a paddle."

"Anna, my dear—Paisley, child," said Horatio as he sought to mediate. "Let's take this new information under consideration in an objective manner." He placed a hand on Mother's arm. "Now, Anna, calm your self, m'dear. I do not for a minute think James Hershey is involved in our recent epidemic of murders; however I do think Paisley may have discovered our elusive 'Effie Díaz.' And a fine bit of deduction that was, my dear," he said with a bow in my direction.

I blushed like a ninny. "It was nothing, really," I said in an embarrassed, little girl voice. "Quite an accident, I assure you."

"Nevertheless, a duller wit and less observant eye might not have put it all together. Congratulations, my dear. You are your mother's daughter. Anna was always very good with puzzles."

Mother appeared somewhat mollified. She even rose to the occasion and produced a bottle of chilled *Pinot Grigio* when Horatio called for a toast to my discovery. I went along with the game because I realized it was his way of taming the shrew. It didn't take Sherlock Holmes to figure that one out.

Cassie wanted to see "Effie Díaz" for herself, so we scared up the old county map once again and spread it out on the coffee table. This time I had no trouble pointing out the spot.

"You're right, Paisley. I don't think anyone has set foot out there since the Indians called this 'a dark and bloody ground'."

"Why did they call it that, Horatio? Is it because of some war, maybe?" asked my daughter.

Horatio took a small sip of wine and began the ritual of lighting his pipe. "No. This was their hunting ground, a killing field of sorts. There was such abundant game—deer, turkey, wild duck—they had no difficulty tracking down meat for their larders. Sometimes they would kill, and then gut the animals on the spot. Hence the dark and bloody ground."

"Oh." Cassie was disappointed. I knew she would have preferred a more exotic and colorful story. She stood up and stretched. I thought she was going to excuse herself and go to bed, but she surprised me. "So, Mom. When are we going to drive out there and see what we can find?"

"Wh...why...?" I sputtered guiltily, wondering if she could read my mind. "I don't think we should go out there at all, and certainly not by ourselves! I'm never opposed to a little snooping when it's safe, but don't forget that somebody has murdered four people. I'd hate to give whoever it is the chance to make it five or six."

"Your mother is right, Cassandra—and she's being surprisingly cautious for a change. I applaud you once again, Paisley," saluted Horatio raising his glass. "Your newfound discretion is admirable. May I suggest that we sleep on this information and see if we can find out something more tomorrow—perhaps from the rangers in the park, or in some roundabout way from Andy Joiner? The map we have here is quite out of date, and I would assume the one in the courthouse was not very new, either. Perhaps we could locate a more recent version at the newspaper office or in the library."

"I seem to recall," said Mother, "that the state Department of Transportation made some aerial photographs of the county last year when they were considering making another exit from the highway. Perhaps we could find out who has copies."

"Or even better," said Cassie with an impish grin. "Why not fly over the area and see for ourselves?"

CHAPTER THIRTY

Cassie said goodnight to all and took Aggie out for a walk before she went to bed. Mother and Horatio decided to finish off the bottle of wine, but I was still full of barbeque so I announced my intention to retire and left, taking the map with me. I hoped no one noticed. I had my own agenda.

I put on my pajamas and hopped up on the bed where I spread out the map. I had to memorize as much as I could. Mother would be suspicious if I took it with me when I left in the morning. My plan was to get up with Cassie, drop her off at work, and drive out to area F-10 by myself. If all went well, and I had no reason to think it wouldn't, I could be back in town by early afternoon—maybe even in time for a late lunch with Cassie. If not, then I would certainly be there in time to take her home. No one would be the wiser, and I could have my own little adventure without involving Cassie or anybody else.

Last night, when I said a visit to the area might be dangerous, I had been trying to keep my daughter from knowing about my plans. I didn't think for a minute it was—unless there was poison ivy in the woods, but Cassie would have insisted on going with me and I couldn't let her. I was determined to never again put her at risk, even from poison ivy.

I didn't know quite what I expected to find out there, but I felt Rudolfo's dying words could not be ignored. Maybe he had discovered a gold mine. That would be unlikely in these parts, but we were close to some government installations. Maybe he had located Cassie's spy plane. My curiosity was growing by the minute and I found it hard to fall asleep, although, if the truth were told, my insomnia was more than likely due to Mr. Cloudt's bold and spicy barbeque sauce.

Much to my dismay, Cassie wanted a big breakfast the next morning. I tried to talk her out of it until she began to wonder why I was in such a hurry.

"Gee, Mom. You always said that breakfast was the most important meal of the day—'eat like a king in the morning, a prince at noon, and a pauper in the evening.' If you said it once, you said it a million times. What's up with you this morning? You act like you have ants in your pants."

"Cassandra, dear," admonished Mother. "Don't be disrespectful to your mother."

"Why?" asked my daughter with a wicked leer. "Is that your job, Gran?"

Mother pursed her lips with disapproval. I could tell she had a complete sermon on the tip of her tongue; but she wisely refrained from answering. Perhaps she was being cautious because of our unpleasant argument the day before. Sometimes I had to admire her, even against my will.

"Okay, Cassie," I sighed, resigning myself to at least a thirty-minute delay. "I'll cook. What do you want?"

"Oh, no!" she insisted. "I'm hungry, not crazy. The last time you cooked breakfast, it took a week to clean up the kitchen, and we had to live with the smell of burnt toast almost that long. So, what do *you* want?"

The western omelet, country ham, red-eyed gravy, and biscuits were so delicious that I almost forgot about my secret plans. Mother even forgave her granddaughter for her sharp tongue.

"My, Cassie, dear, you are quite a fantastic cook! You even knew to put coffee in the gravy!" Mother's sigh was exaggerated and full of regret as she looked in my direction. "I guess culinary talent skips a generation. I tried to interest your mother in the gentle household arts, but she was much too impatient and, well, to put it in a word—messy. You're quite right, cleaning up after she's has been at the stove is a monumental task."

"Hello!" I said, my voice heavy with sarcasm. "Don't mind me. And certainly don't take my feelings into account! I do try, you know. It's just that, well...things seem to go wrong when I'm in the kitchen."

"I know," laughed Cassie. "The cake burns, the flour spills, and the eggs break themselves."

I couldn't help it. I laughed with her. This was an old joke. When we learned to speak Spanish, we particularly liked the reflective verbs. One didn't drop the ball—the ball "fell itself." The glass "broke itself," and so on. We always said it was a great way to avoid responsibility.

I dropped Cassie off at the coffee shop only fifteen minutes later than my scheduled plan. I kissed her goodbye with a promise to be back either for lunch or dinner and headed out on my adventure with a full stomach and a light heart.

The day was bright with summer sunshine and boasted the sweetest of breezes to kiss away the heat. I put on a tape of classical country and hummed along, happily off key, with the likes of Gid Tanner and his Skillet Lickers and Uncle Dave Macon and his Fruit Jar Drinkers.

My Grandfather Howard had grown quite deaf as he aged, but he always had a song on his lips. I liked to imagine that somewhere in his head he still heard the tinny strains of the fiddles and banjos as they had come across the radio waves from Nashville and the early Grand Ole Opry so many years before. When I was just a little girl, he instilled in me a lifelong love of that music. Some people, including my mother and daughter, thought it hokey and overly sentimental. I firmly believed it was an oral paean to the hardy men and women who settled our country. Each song was a complete story—an opera in miniature: a tale of life and love and death. I admired the composers—most of whom could not read a note of music—as much as I admired Puccini or Verdi. And I liked the tunes a whole lot better. These songs were something you could whistle and tap your foot to, and they were as honest and true as the day is long.

I was in hog heaven as I drove down the highway feeling good. Pippa was right, I thought, "God's in his heaven—All's right with the world."

The flat tire came as a complete and totally unwelcome surprise.

"Damn!" I swore, as I felt the car pull sharply to the left. I slowed down and eased Watson over to what little shoulder there was on the narrow two-lane highway that led to the trailer park and—according to my memory of the county map—to the dirt road and "F-10."

I opened the door and got out to survey the damage. The breeze that had been so pleasant was gone, and the heat from the morning sun caused the air to dance and shimmer over the asphalt road.

"Damn, damn, damn!" There was not enough space on the side of the road for me to change the tire unless I wanted to run the risk of turning up on one of Horatio's tables with a tag on my toe labeled "road kill."

I carefully looked both ways, then walked down the middle of the road about fifty feet. I was in luck. Off to the left was a dirt track that led to nowhere but would serve my purpose handsomely. I ran back to the car, huffing and puffing in the heat, and backed cautiously down the slight embankment until I came to the spot.

When I turned off the engine, I could hear the birds singing and the steady hum of summer insects. I climbed out of the car and listened for a moment, entranced. If I hadn't had to change a tire, I would have enjoyed my little side trip.

Ancient oaks spread their sheltering limbs overhead, protecting me from the hot summer sun, and just beyond the little glade where Watson was parked, a stream rippled merrily through the forest. It looked like the scene for a fairy tale. I halfway expected to see an elf pop up at any moment.

"I wish an elf would change my damn tire," I said with a sigh as I opened the rear gate and tugged on the tire well. I broke two nails and skinned my knuckle before I managed to retrieve the spare and all the rest of the paraphernalia I needed. A thumbnail went as I jacked up the car. By the time I had finished my task, I had only one unbroken nail left, and I was sweating like a stevedore in spite of the shade provided by the trees.

I caught a glimpse of my reflection in the rear window as I replaced the jack and closed the hatch. My face was smeared with dirt and grease, and my brand new aquamarine polo shirt was filthy. Cassie would have to eat lunch without me. I looked like a bum.

I grabbed a roll of paper towels from under the car seat and walked back to the little stream. After a few minutes I realized that it would take more than water to clean me up, but I was cooler and more refreshed by my efforts.

Thanking God that I had the presence of mind to bring a bottle of Evian and some fruit, I climbed on the hood and lay back against the windshield to enjoy my snack and the scenery.

Two male bluejays argued noisily back and forth in the branches above me about some stupid bird thing, and it occurred to me for the first time that I seldom saw a lady bluejay. Maybe the feminine fowl were so embarrassed by the irritating antics of their male counterparts they hid from sight. Or maybe....

I fell asleep before I could finish my thought, and dozed away the morning dreaming of the birds and bees. I woke up abruptly when I tried to turn over, and upended the bottle of Evian in my lap.

"Arrggh!" I grabbed ineffectively at the bottle, then watched helplessly as it fell to the ground. I licked my dry lips as the water gurgled out into the grass.

"Drat!"

The noonday sun was directly overhead. Above me the green leaves danced lightly in a breeze no longer sweet and cool. The polo shirt stuck wetly to my body, and the damp seams rubbed painfully against the skin of my armpits. I was miserable.

I thought quite seriously about returning without completing my quest, but I finally decided, like the man said, that failure was not an option. Besides, it would be difficult to arrange another time when I was free to roam around without anybody questioning my whereabouts. And since I was still certain I could be back in town around two, I decided to trek on.

The asphalt highway took me past the trailer park and about thirteen miles beyond before it suddenly petered out into a bumpy dirt track.

Surprisingly, the road wasn't the least bit overgrown. As a matter of fact, the track looked like it had seen some recent heavy travel. I drove slowly, trying to avoid the deep ruts and tire tracks left in the dried mud. The road was a lot rougher than I had counted on, and once again I considered turning around. Stubborn to a fault, I kept driving but rolled up the windows to keep from breathing the fine powdery dust.

I wasn't making very good time. The sun had already passed its zenith and was on the downside of its journey towards the horizon.

"Goodbye, lunch," I muttered. I had eaten both apples before my nap, and breakfast was a distant memory. Just as I made the decision to call it quits, the spare tire went flat. Watson wiggled and wobbled at the edge of the road, then slowly slid sideways, and stalled abruptly in a deep rut.

"I can't believe it!" I shouted as I beat my fist against the steering wheel. "Just one little adventure on my own—is that too terribly much to ask?" After a minute or two, I grew tired of my own theatrics and slumped despondently in the seat, well aware that Mother and Cass would never let me live this down.

The car was leaning at an angle, and I took care not to turn an ankle as I got out. I tried to slam the door, but gravity had the last word. The heavy door fell back open just as I turned around and knocked me face down in the dirt.

"That's great! That's just great!" I shouted as I picked myself up. Now I really looked like a filthy bum. Not a single solitary soul would give me a lift, and the walk back to town was a footsore journey of at least fifteen miles. Dinner seemed as far away as breakfast felt, and I was terribly thirsty.

After locking the car, I headed towards town, stumbling over the deep ruts in the road. Dry powdery dirt and small bits of gravel managed to get in my shoes as I walked, forcing me to stop and sit down every fifteen minutes to shake them out of my socks.

The afternoon sun shone down from a sky devoid of any clouds that might have provided a respite from the punishing heat. Sweat rolled down my scalp and into my eyes and ears, and the dust made a gritty, grinding noise between my teeth. All I could think of was a long, sudsy bubble bath and a tall frosty glass of sweet iced tea. Being miserable was becoming a habit I didn't want to get used to.

I walked with my head down to keep the sun from shining in my eyes, and consequently, the van was almost upon me before I noticed the approaching cloud of dust. I climbed awkwardly over the ruts to the edge of the road and waved my arms around like a windmill in a hurricane.

"Hey! Hey!" I yelled, just in case the driver didn't see the filthy scarecrow in the nasty clothes. "Help! Please! Help!"

Unbelievably, the van showed no signs of slowing down. In a final act of desperation, I jumped back down in the roadbed, held up my hands, and closed my eyes. I heard the van skid dangerously close in the dirt. I felt the heat of the engine as it came to a halt just inches from my body. When I opened my eyes, the dust swirled around me in a dense cloud making it impossible to see. I felt my way around the car and pulled on the door handle.

The cool air from inside the van felt like heaven. I didn't wait politely for an invitation, instead, I climbed inside quickly and shut the door.

"My, my," observed Ruby Dawn Coleman, shaking her head. "But you're sure a mess, Miss Paisley. I didn't recognize you at first sight. Almost didn't stop. Pardon me for saying so, but you look like you could use a bath."

She was dressed in a sleeveless pink tee shirt and very short spotless white denim shorts. Her hair was teased and lacquered into a small dry haystack on the top of her head and her thin lips shone wetly with neon-bright pink lipstick. She looked like a gaudy dime-store angel to me.

"Thanks a million for stopping," I panted. "I was almost out of steam." I looked around the cab of the small van. "You don't, by any chance, have something cool to drink, do you?" I asked hopefully.

"Why, no, honey," she answered, her pink lips a glossy contrast to the dingy teeth. "But I'm taking groceries to some friends of mine. It's not so far from here. If you don't mind going along with me, they'll be more than glad to give you a cold drink when we get there."

I sat back in the seat and tried to relax—tried to keep thoughts of cool, frosty libations from the forefront of my mind. I never once considered what sort of friends a woman like Ruby Dawn Coleman could possibly have out in this isolated part of the county.

"Damn!" she swore loudly. "What idiot left their car in the middle...?"

I opened my eyes to see that we had arrived back at the spot where Watson sat blocking the narrow road.

"Sorry. That idiot would be me," I admitted sheepishly. "I had a flat."

With some difficulty and a lot of swearing, Ruby Dawn managed to drive the van up over the edge of the road and around my Jeep.

"I'll have to send somebody back here to get your car off the road," she said a bit peevishly as we drove past Watson. "You got a spare, honey?"

"No. I mean, that was the spare," I answered in a voice that sounded exhausted even to me. I was so dispirited that I didn't even hesitate when she asked for my car keys.

"Never you mind," she said with another big tobacco-stained smile. "Maybe the tire can be patched. You just relax, honey, and let little ole Ruby Dawn take care of everything. You're plumb near tuckered out."

I felt a sudden uncomfortable rush of guilt for ever having disliked this woman. Jumping to instant conclusions about people was one of my biggest shortcomings. I vowed right then and there to be more tolerant from now on. After all, crooked brown teeth and big hair notwithstanding, Ruby Dawn had just saved my bacon.

CHAPTER THIRTY-ONE

The van lurched to a stop in front of a rusty, doublewide trailer. I sat up straight and wiped the drool from the corner of my mouth. Somehow I had fallen asleep and missed the last part of our journey.

I looked around, dismayed at the sorry sight before me. Ruby Dawn's friends had to be in dire straits. Propped up by concrete blocks under each corner, the dilapidated trailer leaned drunkenly to one side where the blocks were slightly askew. The windows were, without exception, cracked, and so dirty they were opaque. The whole scene filled me with a vague sense of *déjà-vu*. I pondered for a moment until I remember the trailer park on the bluff overlooking the lake. This trailer was bigger, but in the same miserable state as Rudolfo's. I wondered if the resemblance ended on the outside.

"Here we are, honey," Ruby Dawn announced unnecessarily. "Hop out and help me with the groceries, will ya?"

I opened the door and scrambled out on legs that were stiff and awkward from sitting too long. Ruby held the back doors of the van open while I reached inside and grabbed a large box full of bags of rice and pasta and cans of tomato sauce. I started to make a crack about Chef Boyardee, but Ruby Dawn impatiently motioned me aside and reached in the van for another load.

My arms and back protested against the weight of my burden as I stumbled over the broken paving stones that led to the minuscule front porch. Ruby Dawn was right behind me. Sweat dripped from my scalp, and damp hair fell lankly across my face as I turned to speak to her. "Should I knock, or what?" I asked, blowing hair out of my mouth.

"They aren't at home," she answered. "I have the key. Let me go ahead and open up."

"But, I thought...."

"Just move aside, sweetie," she said brusquely. "And quit thinking. It'll give you a headache."

I moved away from the door and leaned against the side of the trailer to ease the strain of the weight I was carrying while I reassessed my opinion of my new best friend.

I had just about arrived at the conclusion that her slight lapse of manners was due to the fact that she might be as tired and hot as I was, when she managed to unlock the door.

"Okay, girlfriend," she said, standing aside. "You go first."

I turned and peered inside, squinting my eyes against the late afternoon sun, trying to make out anything in the shadows of the dark interior.

"I said, go ahead!" shouted Ruby Dawn as she shoved me viciously with a foot placed in the small of my back.

I stumbled forward across the threshold in an awkward running gait until the weight of the groceries and my own momentum brought me smack up against a wall. The box of food came up painfully hard under my ribs, forcing the air from my lungs. I dropped everything and fell to my knees gasping for breath. Bags broke all around me—scattering rice and pasta in a loud clatter over the linoleum. I heard the crunch of Ruby Dawn's sneakers on macaroni as she walked slowly towards me. I looked up, but all I could see was her skinny silhouette against the backdrop of the open door.

"What the hell...?" I managed to gasp.

"My, my! You did take a nasty fall, Miss Paisley Sterling DeLeon! I do believe I see blood on your face. I hope you didn't break your pretty little aristocratic nose. Now, GET UP!"

I wiped my upper lip. My hand had blood on it, but my nose didn't hurt—it was numb. "What the hell...?"

"You sure do have trouble expressing yourself, hun. That must be quite a handicap for a writer. I think I'll do a much better job when I get around to it. Darn it! I just don't seem to have the time. And you're wasting it right now. GET UP!"

I wiped my nose on my sleeve, thinking vaguely how Mother would object, and struggled to my knees. As I pushed myself up, my hand came down on a number two can of tomato sauce. Ruby Dawn was nothing more than a scrawny runt of a woman, I thought. An accurate throw to the old noggin should settle my predicament quite nicely. That was before I got a better look at her and the wicked looking hunting rifle she had aimed at my middle.

"For Pete's sake, Ruby Dawn, there's no need...."

"You have no idea what there's a need for, Miss High and Mighty 'my family's had money for generations'! You and the rest of your fancy friends walk by people like me every day and don't even give us a second look. We're scum because we don't have the right last name, or because we do our drinking at the road house out on route sixty-two instead of at the country club."

"Look, Ruby, I don't even belong...."

The cold metal of the rifle bore pushing against the soft hollow of my neck cut off the rest of my protest.

"Haven't you got it, yet?" she asked in a soft voice, her words dripping with sarcasm. "I'm the queen bee now. This little ole gun gives me the power. I GOT THE POWER!" she shouted. "Just like that crazy old preacher down at Bethel Baptist says." She laughed. "Now turn around and open that door behind you, and drop whatever that is you have in your hand. My daddy was a crack shot and I'm twice as good as him. I could blow your head to bloody smithereens before you even thought about throwing something at me."

I promptly obeyed and dropped my can of tomatoes. For now, I had better do exactly as Ruby Dawn said. I was still optimistic enough to think I would get another chance to defend myself. Groceries weren't the only possible weapons at hand—I might even use the chip on her shoulder, if I could get close enough.

The door Ruby Dawn told me to open led to a long, narrow hallway. I hesitated for a moment because it was dark and I could barely see where I was going. Another prod with the rifle made me less cautious and I propelled myself forward, stumbling occasionally on the joints where one length of flooring met another. The hall was like the mobile tunnels at airports that take you to your plane—a series of lengths of flooring bolted together, if somewhat unevenly.

At the end of the hallway was another door. I didn't need another prod from Ruby Dawn. I tried to open it, but it was locked. She motioned me into the corner and held me there with the rifle underneath my chin as she used the same key to unlock this door.

"Open it," she ordered. "And get inside."

I obeyed as quickly as I could. The room I entered was lit by a bare overhead bulb and smelled like a kennel. Ruby Dawn laughed as my hand went up to cover my nose. I had to force myself not to gag.

"You'll get used to it! If you live so long, that is," she said with a nasty grin. "As a matter-of-fact, when you see where you're going, you'll beg to get back in here."

She gave me a nudge between the shoulder blades and directed me through another doorway into what was being used as a kitchen. A small, dark-skinned, young woman stood behind an old dry sink where she was washing dishes in a plastic bucket. She cried out in fright when she saw us and tried to hide by pressing her thin body into the corner.

"Will you look at that!" snorted Ruby Dawn. "See! She knows not to mess with me. You'd better get the message, Miss Paisley Fancy Sterling. From now on, you don't do squat unless I say so."

The kitchen opened out to a small, screened, porch. Bars had been added all around, making it look like a cage. It was hotter out here, but the fresh air was delicious after the stench inside.

Ruby Dawn pushed me down into the corner of the porch and reached for a pair of handcuffs hanging on a nail by the door.

"Here, put these on. And no funny business, either."

I crossed my legs and found the most comfortable position I could on the rough wooden floor before I snapped the cuffs on my wrists. Ruby Dawn leaned down and tested them.

"Terrific! Nice and tight. Now I don't have to punish you, but I will just the same—because I like it!"

She smacked me as hard as she could with the flat side of the rifle butt. If she had been any stronger she might have knocked me unconscious. Instead, she sent me to a place somewhere between awake and sleeping—a place filled with pain and brightly colored shooting stars.

I lay as still as I could for a very long time, willing the pain to fade, praying it away, until finally, blessedly, it eased enough for me to sit up. I swayed for a moment, waiting for the swell of renewed agony and nausea to go away, then leaned back in the corner until I saw only one of everything.

It was totally dark now, and I could hear the quiet sound of night birds in the trees. A soft sweet breeze lifted my hair and fanned my face. I had felt better, but I was going to live—and I was sure it could have been worse. Ruby Dawn, for some unknown reason, hated me and the horse I rode in on. She would be more than happy to see me dead. I wondered why she hadn't gone through with it.

I tested the handcuffs by pulling my hands apart as hard as I could. They were old and rusty, not fashioned out of steel like Andy Joiner's, but they were strong enough to keep me from causing much trouble.

I squirmed around on my bottom until I was facing outwards and pressed my forehead against the screen, wincing with pain as the tender spot on the side of my face protested.

It was dark—really dark. The windows at the back of the kitchen were blacked out, and the moon wasn't up yet. All I could make out were a few tall blotches that could be trees, and a shorter, thicker blotch that might be an outbuilding. I squinted until my eyes hurt, then gave up with a sigh. I would find out more when morning came.

My tummy growled, reminding me that I had not eaten since early that morning. I worked up as much spit in my dry mouth as I could and was pleasantly surprised to find that it didn't taste like blood. I could go another day without food, but I had been thirsty for what seemed like an eternity. That thirst made me brave.

I had no idea how much time had passed since Ruby Dawn had chucked me out on the porch and whacked me with the rifle butt, but some instinct told me she had been gone for a while. I called out.

"Hey! Hey you in there—in the kitchen! Hey! I need a drink of water, please."

There was no answer. I scooted across the rough wooden planks on my butt, tearing the fabric of my jeans on a nail head, and getting a splinter in my thigh for my efforts, but I got close enough to the door to kick it with my foot.

Bang! Bang! "Hey, you in there! Water! I need water! Please!"

The door opened a crack and I could see a dark brown eye peering fearfully out. *"¡Señora,"* said the girl in a small frightened voice, *"silencio, por favor! El Jefe viene está noche. Por favor, no hagas un escándalo."* The door closed once again.

"NO!" I cried. "Please! *¡Agua! ¡Necesito agua, por favor!"*

The door stayed shut and I realized that the girl—she could have been no older than sixteen or seventeen—was too terrified to help me. Whoever "El Jefe" was, he had certainly made an impression. And he was coming tonight! That must have been the reason Ruby Dawn had left me alive and well and shackled.

I sat back in the corner, my thirst forgotten as I tried to put a lid on the fear that slithered up my spine like a cold serpent, making it difficult to think. "Leonard," I whispered. "What would Leonard do?"

That was easy. Leonard would have a gun hidden in his ankle holster. Leonard would have taken out Ruby Dawn with a well-placed karate chop. Leonard would never have come out here on a wild goose chase in the first place.

What was I thinking of? Some little adventure this turned out to be. By now, Mother and Cassie would be worried sick about me. And nobody would have a clue as to where to start looking.

"Unless," I whispered to no one in particular. "Unless, Horatio remembers Effie Díaz." If he recalled our discussion about the map coordinate he would guess where I had gone. He knew me well enough to know I might sneak off by myself to snoop around. And he would be more circumspect than Mother. She might just go to Judge Hershey and ask him if he had seen me, but Horatio....

"Judge Hershey!" This time I didn't bother to whisper. Why hadn't I thought of it before? Judge Hershey and El Jefe—the boss—must be one and the same. There was nothing on the map to indicate that anyone lived way out here, but this house trailer was on Judge Hershey's land, of that I was certain. What was he doing with a beat up old trailer, an imprisoned Mexican girl, and a partner like Ruby Dawn Coleman?

CHAPTER THIRTY-TWO

I finally gave up trying to find a comfortable position on the rough, uneven floor of the porch and fell into an exhausted sleep—for all of about twenty minutes. I woke up when a rabbit screamed somewhere in the woods behind me. The sound was unmistakable if you had ever heard it before.

When I was eleven or so, and in the excited throes of my first experience with the Girl Scouts, I camped out in the back yard every night in a tent made of two quilts and a tarpaulin. A horrifying shriek from the woods had sent me running into the house in the wee hours of the morning. Dad was lying awake in the big bed next to my mother who was snoring quietly.

"We must never tell her she snores," he laughed softly. "She would be so embarrassed. Not ladylike, you know."

The sound from the woods had also awakened Dad. Owls hunt at night, he explained, and baby rabbits—their favorite entree—always screamed as they were dying. Even as young as I was, I had known that scream haunted him, just as it haunted me now.

I was cold, but the handcuffs kept me from hugging my arms. I pulled up my legs to my chest and rested my chin on my knees. I visualized wearing my new red hooded sweatshirt, the one Mother attempted to dissuade me from buying because she thought it was tacky. For a moment, I could almost feel the warm fleecy newness of the inside—the kitten softness that would disappear after a washing or two.

It was funny, I thought, the way Mother and I were so different. I wondered, and not for the first time, if I had spent my life working it out that way. I loved my new red sweatshirt; I wished fervently that I really were wearing it right now.

My tired mind wandered over the past—skipping and hopping over memories of happy birthdays and childhood friends until I began to focus on more recent events. I remembered the night Cassie and I climbed the cliffs and broke into Rudolfo's trailer. How surprised we had been to find his stash in the bathroom. I laughed quietly when I recalled the sight of her finger stuck in the towel rack. There was something else about that towel rack that tickled my memory, but I couldn't think what. The next day Cassie had disappeared and everything else had taken a backseat to my worry about her, except my anger with Winston Wallace and his wandering stethoscope.

That towel rack...there was something inside besides money...that was the reason Cassie got her finger stuck in the first place. Where was the towel rack now, I wondered?

The tiny sliver of a new moon peeked up over the treetops, painting a narrow path of light across the porch—winking on a shiny object in front of the kitchen door. Boredom and curiosity impelled me across the floor once again. "Damn, damn, and drat," I swore, as I felt the pinch of yet another splinter. It was a weak oath, without much passion behind it. I was tired, hungry, and way beyond thirsty. Ennui had replaced fear, and I was even getting accustomed to the physical discomfort. "Maybe this is why hostages give up so easily," I whispered to no one in particular. Then my fingers closed over the stout metal hairpin and hope surged in my heart with a powerful beat, chasing away the cobwebs of fatigue and filling me with strength.

I had no idea how to start, but Leonard used hairpins and paper clips all the time to unlock doors and padlocks—surely I could open the puny hasp of these dime store handcuffs. I scooted around again so I could take full advantage of the meager moonlight, and set about poking and prying at the tiny keyhole. Thirty minutes later, all I had to show for my efforts was a bruised thumb and two deep scratches on my left wrist.

"Well, you know what, Paisley, baby?" I told myself. "You've got all night, so settle down and take it easy. Sooner or later you'll figure this bloody thing out." And that said, the cuff on my left wrist suddenly popped open with a rusty little squeak.

I stared at it for a moment, and began to giggle. The slightly demented sound frightened me. I took a deep calming breath and went about the painful business of standing up on my stiff cramped legs.

I reached for the knob of the door, then stopped myself. I had no idea what I might find on the other side. It was quiet—there was no sound coming from the kitchen, but there never had been. For all I knew, El Jefe could be waiting in the next room, machete in hand, to whack my head off.

There was no other way out. The screen on the porch was old and friable, but the bars were strong and placed too close together to permit escape. The door to the kitchen was my only option.

I turned the knob slowly, listening intently as I did so. A radio was playing softly in the background, but that was all I could hear. I stepped inside. The only thing that greeted me was the strong odor of a kitchen with no ventilation—olive oil, garlic, and the stench of the overflowing garbage can fought for my olfactory attention.

I tiptoed around the corner into the main room. The light bulb overhead had been turned off, but a light coming from down the hall allowed me to see a filthy, sagging sofa resting against one wall and a small card table with four folding chairs against the other. The table was bare except for a beer can holding a single wilted wild flower.

I tried to figure out what seemed so odd about the place, and then it came to me. This was a trailer with the insides gutted. It was as cozy as the raw interior of an eighteen wheeler. It made Rudolfo's place look like the Ritz—and the smell! As I edged closer down the hall towards the light, the odor grew stronger. It was the stench of unwashed bodies, dirty bedding, and bad plumbing—poverty and hopelessness.

A stained sheet hung across the end of the hall blocking my view. Light danced and flickered around the edges and across the bottom. I had to guess it came from an open flame. I peered through the narrow space between cloth and wall and saw four young women huddled on a bare mattress. Three were sleeping, cradled by each other with the innocent abandonment of children. The fourth girl dozed precariously close to the edge. The flickering light of a candle highlighted her naked breast where a tiny infant lay nursing.

I don't know what I expected to find, but this was the last thing I would have guessed. My hand flew up to my mouth in surprise, the loose chain of the handcuffs clinking metal against metal.

The baby protested loudly as the startled girl sat up pulling her nipple out of his mouth.

"¿Quién es?" she shouted when she saw me. The others roused and opened sleepy eyes, which in turn widened in alarm.

"¡Por Dios!" cried one. And they huddled together as if that would protect them from harm. The baby's cries grew louder and more insistent.

I hastened to reassure them, but had trouble thinking of the Spanish words. "No problema," I finally managed to spit out. "No problema. I won't hurt you, I promise." I held my hands up to my mouth, "Shhhh, quiet, please," I whispered. I tiptoed around the mattress and pointed at the squirming, red-faced baby, smiling as benevolently as possible. "Go ahead, please. Feed the baby. I held my arms up to my chest in a rocking motion. Finally, the girl seemed to get my drift and lay back, holding the squalling infant protectively against her. When the baby found his dinner once more, his cries stopped abruptly. I smiled again, and this time the girl smiled back. "¡Bueno!" I said softly. "Muy bueno—very good." I held my arms at my sides and tried to look benign. "You speak English?" I asked. "Any of you, any English?"

The girl on the far end of the bed separated herself slightly from the huddle and spoke shyly. "I speak little," she said. "Little English, only."

"Terrific!" I forgot my trepidations about touching the curtain and pulled it aside to cross over near the girl. She immediately pulled back against the others in alarm.

"Sorry! I didn't mean to scare you. I'm harmless, honest." I knelt down by the edge of the mattress. "*Mi nombre es Paisley.* What is you name?"

The girl looked at me from under lowered eyelids and answered in a voice I could barely hear. "Clementina. Clementina María García."

"Goodness," I laughed softly so as not to frighten her again. "That's a very musical name."

"The girl looked at me steadily for a moment, then the meaning of what I had said sank in and she laughed with delight. She turned and spoke rapidly to the others in Spanish explaining my little joke. The girls smiled timidly and relaxed a little in their vigilance. The baby had fallen asleep.

"You go," said Clementina firmly. "If he find you, he hurt us."

"He who?" I asked. "Who will hurt you?"

She looked furtively around, as if someone were hiding in the shadows, "*El Jefe,*" she whispered, "*El Juez.*"

"The Judge? Oh, my God!"

The girl nodded and looked at the others to back her up. The mother of the sleeping child smiled and held her baby close. It wasn't a happy smile. It was sweet and tragic, and there were tears in her eyes. "*Sí, Señora, El Juez. El ladrón de los niños.*"

"What does she mean, Clementina? What is a '*ladrón*'?"

"A thief, Señora," she spat. "A thief who takes our babies."

I was astounded. "Wha...whatever for? Why does he steal your babies?"

"He sell to *norteamericanos*. Very big money." She hid her face, but I could hear the sniffles.

Suddenly my knees felt weak and wobbly, and my head was spinning. I needed to sit down. I stumbled back through the curtain into the other room and sank down on the sofa, heedless of the filthy stains. I dropped my head in my hands and closed my eyes against the encroaching darkness of fatigue and shock. I barely felt the small hand on my shoulder.

"Passlee, you okay?" Clementina inquired. "You okay," she decided. "Please, you go. We no want trouble."

"A drink," I mumbled. "I need something to drink, please."

Clementina padded to the kitchen on little bare feet. I looked up when I heard her return. She was wearing a faded cotton gown that had been repaired so many times it was mostly patches. She was tiny—as small as a child. Her long black hair was woven into a single braid that hung down her back, and her face was sweetly plain with big brown eyes that held a world of sadness. She gave me a can of generic carbonated cola. It was hot, but I gulped it down in four big swallows. It tasted like the nectar of the gods.

"Oh, thanks!" I gasped. "I was so thirsty. You just don't...."

"Shhhh!" whispered the girl, urgently. "I hear door outside! He comes! You go, please!" She pulled and pushed at me to get up from the sofa.

"Where? Where do I go?"

Sheer terror paled the girl's face and widened her eyes. Her neck jerked spasmodically as she shook her head and shrugged her little shoulders. Then her eyes registered something more than fear, and she grabbed my hand. "*Ven! Ven!*" She pulled me into the kitchen and pointed at an old refrigerator. "In, get in! *No functiona.* It broke. You get in. I let you out when he go." She hastily removed the two shelves and an empty egg container, and thrust them in my hands. "You hold," she ordered.

All the warnings of my childhood came tumbling back in a rush. Newspaper photographs of little children found dead in old refrigerators—children suffocated while playing games of hide and seek—flashed through my mind. Every muscle and nerve in my body protested, but I ignored them and forced myself to climb into the empty metal box. I bent over, making myself as small as possible, deliberately shutting my eyes so I wouldn't see Clementina close the door.

CHAPTER THIRTY-THREE

I panicked when the door closed. There wasn't even a tiny chink of light around the edges. Once, I had gone on a vacation trip with my parents to Mammoth Cave. When we arrived at the lowest depth, the park ranger turned off the lights and told us this was the blackest black we would ever see. I had never expected to experience that darkness again. It was all I could do to keep from screaming.

I took a deep breath and started counting backwards from five hundred. I gradually relaxed and got control of myself. I counted again. And again.

The air was stale and smelled of mold, but the terrifying thought that there might not be enough of it to last until Judge Hershey had gone sent me into another panic. I called on every mental resource at my command to quell my fears.

I just about had everything under control when I heard the scream. It was faint and sounded very far away, but I knew it had to come from one of four young women—my guess was Clementina.

"My God," I thought selfishly. "What if he kills her and no one else knows I'm in here?"

Sweat dripped into my eyes, and I was surprised to find that my arms and legs—my whole body was wet. It was hot in the refrigerator—very hot—and getting hotter. In a few more minutes I wouldn't be able to stand the heat. And I was finding it harder to get my breath.

"That's enough," I whispered. "I'm getting out of here." It never occurred to me that it might not be possible. Those newspaper stories—those accidents involved little children, not adults. I pushed on the door, but it was unyielding. I put my shoulder against it and squirmed around until my knees rested against the back wall to provide more leverage. Again I pushed, but nothing happened. "Oh, God," I gasped. "Please don't let me die in here!" There was a loud roaring in my head. I didn't know exactly when it began, but the sound blocked out all thought and reason. I covered my ears with my hands, but it only got worse. My chest began to burn. The pain started in the middle under my breastbone and worked its way outwards as the air grew fouler.

My head rested—my neck limp as a noodle—against the door. Hazy pictures of Cassie and Mother and Rafe passed through my mind. They had something important to tell me, but I couldn't hear because of the roaring sound in my head.

Something fell against the side of the refrigerator and brought me back to groggy consciousness. There was another, even more forceful blow—and the door opened just an inch—only the latch keeping it from opening all the way. Fresh air—sweet fresh air, even if it did smell of stale food and garbage—flowed in through the crack. I breathed deeply and thankfully.

Then I heard more screams, the sound of fists against bare flesh, and pitiful cries. The sounds grew fainter, then stopped. A door slammed, and it was quiet once more.

I wiggled my finger through the opening in the door and tried to find the latch. I had no doubt that sooner or later I would be able to get out, but I was impatient—not to mention hot and miserable. I pushed against it as hard as I could. Suddenly the door opened and I tumbled out on the floor, barely missing the bruised and battered little body that was already there.

Clementina lay on the floor crying silently. Her face was a war zone. Her lips were torn and bleeding, and her eyes puffed and bruised.

"*Señora*," she whispered. "You are not dead?"

"No, dear, I'm not dead," I assured her.

She tried to smile, but the torn lips would not cooperate. She moaned and pulled her knees up to her stomach. "*¡Ay, Dios!*" she cried aloud. "*¡Me duele!* It hurts very much."

I tried to pick her up from the floor, but the movement seemed to hurt her even more. She would have to stay where she was. I looked around for something to clean her wounds and saw nothing but a dirty kitchen towel.

"Clementina? Water—where is some clean water?"

The girl raised her right arm with some difficulty and pointed towards the room where I had first seen her.

"I'll be right back," I promised.

My legs felt like spaghetti, but I managed to make my way back down the length of the trailer. The curtain was gone and the other girls were nowhere to be seen. The baby was gone, too. I looked around, kicking aside dirty bundles of clothing, and finally found two plastic bottles of water they must have held in reserve for the baby. I also found a couple of clean cloth diapers and some Vaseline.

Clementina was curled up in a fetal position when I got back. I sat

172

down on the floor next to her, and lifted her head gently into my lap. I wet the diaper and dabbed softly at the cuts and abrasions on her face. A couple of the lacerations were deep enough to leave ugly scars, but we could fix that later. I promised myself she would have the best plastic surgeon money could buy. I bit my own lip to keep from crying as I ministered to her.

Clementina opened her eyes. "Passlee, you run and hide quick. I think he will come back soon."

"I can't leave without you! I won't!" Tears poured freely down my cheeks and splashed on the floor as I shook my head.

"Go! Go! Please! Only you can help us. Please, Passlee." Her voice faded off into a quiet whisper as she lost consciousness.

Clementina was right. I had no choice. I had to go for help—some big time help. And right after that, I had to convince a few people—including my own mother—that the great, wise, and wonderful Judge James Hershey, respected southern gentleman of Rowan Springs, Kentucky, was scum of the lowest order.

I lowered the girl gently to the floor and covered her as best I could with the dry diaper cloths. It wasn't much, but it would have to do for now. I placed the bottle of water within her reach and spread some Vaseline on her lips. She moaned slightly at my touch, then was quiet. I had to get help quickly. I was sure she had internal injuries.

Clementina seemed to think I would have no trouble leaving. I hoped she knew something I didn't. Maybe she noticed that the Judge had left the door unlocked when he left. I kept my fingers crossed as I tried it.

The door opened effortlessly to the long, dark hallway. Not allowing myself the luxury of a second thought, I ran as fast as I could over the uneven floor towards the other end. That door was also open, and I burst outside under the bright stars of an early summer morning.

I held tightly onto the rickety banister of the makeshift porch while a wave of dizziness washed over me. My own physical condition wasn't what I would prefer. I had a long way to go, and not much energy to go on. I consider for a moment returning to the kitchen for something to eat, but the thought of Clementina lying there in pain until I returned spurred me on.

The only car in the driveway was a rusted chassis on cinder blocks. Watson was nowhere to be seen. I wondered if he was still parked in the middle of the road. I hoped so. Just seeing my Jeep would give me comfort—and I thought I remembered throwing a cardigan in the backseat. That would be welcome right about now. Goose bumps from the pre-dawn chill stood up big and proud on my arms, and my hair was soon cold and damp with early morning dew.

The road to town ran in an easterly direction and I could see a rosy golden glow in the distance as the sun started to come up over the hills. It would be a beautiful day. And I was free.

The next few days would be chaotic. No one would believe me at first, but with Clementina's help I would slowly convince everyone that Hershey was a villain, make sure the girls and the baby were cared for—and then possibly send them back to Mexico—if that was what they desired. If not, maybe we could find them a home.

My mind wandered through paths of fancy and imagination as I walked. By the time the sun came up, the goose bumps and my desire for a sweater were gone.

"Man, oh, man," I mumbled. "I bet I smell like a barnyard."

I began to fantasize about a bathtub filled with hot lavender-scented water, about big thick terry towels and sweet-smelling hair that was brushed and shining. When I was squeaky clean, Mother would bring me luncheon on a tray. She would insist on consommé because I hadn't eaten in so long, but would relent and uncover a plate of medium rare prime rib with duchesse potatoes and baby peas. Cassie would sneak in later, when Mother wasn't looking, with a big bowl of lemon custard ice cream, and then we would share a whole box of my favorite cookies—Nabisco sugar wafers. With all that in my stomach, and all I had been through—especially "the saving the girls and the baby" part—no one would mind if I took a nice long nap. Cassie would keep Aggie from barking, and Mother would unhook the telephone so no one would disturb my sleep—especially with that loud honking noise.

I looked up when I realized the noise wasn't in my daydream. A car was bearing down on me. I stood in the middle of the road and stared like a dummy. I didn't know whether to run or wait. Then my legs betrayed me and I fell in a dirty, disheveled heap to the roadbed. I couldn't move. I was completely spent.

The car stopped about ten feet away in a cloud of dust. I coughed and tried to wave it out of my eyes so I could see who was coming for me—friend or foe. I said a swift prayer, and watched as a tall lean man with a boldly handsome face climbed out and hurried toward me.

"Are you Paisley Sterling?" he asked, with a tentative grin.

"I used to be," I managed to quip.

"I'm Frank Newton. Your mother asked my help in finding you. We've been looking for the better part of two days. She'll be overjoyed to know you're okay."

He extended a hand to help me up, then started to brush me off.

"No, please," I said standing back. "I'm too filthy to touch. Just put a towel or something in your car seat so I won't ruin it." I looked up into his face and felt even more like the nasty scarecrow I knew I resembled. Newton was one of the best-looking men I had seen in a long time.

"Just my luck," I mumbled.

"Pardon?" he asked politely, as he helped me into the fancy, low-slung, sports car.

"Luck," I prevaricated. "Just my good luck that you found me when you did. I'm about to die for a drink. Do you have...?"

Newton reached around in the back seat and lifted a bottle of water from a cooler. "There's more where that came from," he smiled. "Just let me know when you want another."

I tried to twist the top off as he walked around the car to climb in the driver's seat. By the time he got in, the tears of frustration had started to fall. I couldn't get the cap off. He took the bottle gently from my hand, opened it effortlessly, and passed it back without a word.

I leaned back in the seat and drank deeply as we drove off. The cool water gurgled and sloshed down my parched throat, and splashed into my empty stomach with a nauseating plop.

"Please," I gasped. "Can you stop?"

"Why," he asked somewhat suspiciously.

"I'm...I think I'm going to be sick."

He slammed on the brakes and watched every humiliating minute as I opened the door and vomited on the side of the road. When I was through, and as embarrassed as I have ever been, I got back in the car and wiped my face on the tissues he held out to me.

"Here's another bottle of water," he said. "Take it easy this time. Little sips, maybe. Okay?"

His smile was dazzling, his teeth white and even in a tanned "Town and Country" face. Dark-lensed, gold-rimmed sunglasses hid his eyes, but he could easily have been a model in an Armani ad in any one of Mother's fashion magazines. His clothes were simple and casual, and obviously very expensive. The watch on his wrist was a stainless steel and gold Cartier Santos—worth more than Watson—and the tip of a pricey Mont Blanc pen peeked out from his Polo shirt pocket.

The only jarring notes were the heavy gold chain nestled in the dark hair at his throat and the large gold and diamond cluster ring on his little finger. I had seen enough men with fancy jewelry and macho outlooks in San Romero. Too bad, I thought, that flashy fashion statement seeping into North American men's wardrobes. But on the whole, he was one terrific looking dude. It was a shame I had to meet him when I looked like Godzilla's red-headed stepchild.

I took the water in short, quick sips like he suggested and felt better almost immediately. I relaxed in the soft leather seat and breathed a sigh of relief.

"Can I call Mother?" I asked as I noticed the cell phone in a holder on the dashboard.

"We're out of range," he smiled. "I tried to use it when I first saw you. Just a few more miles and you can talk all you want."

"How far away from town are we? I need to get some help for a friend. How long will it take for us to get there?"

"Whoa!" he laughed. "What's the big hurry? Don't you like my company?"

The question sounded somewhat inappropriate considering the circumstances, but I didn't want to seem ungrateful. "I'm just anxious to get home, that's all," I explained humbly. "I'm really, really ready for a nice long bath."

"Sure," he laughed. "I can understand that. I go hunting sometimes. I love it when I'm out in the woods smelling like my prey, but I'm always ready to get back to the niceties of civilized life."

The guy was weird. There's always something wrong with them, I thought sadly. This one looks like a dreamboat, but he's a putz. He acts like I've been on safari. I dismissed his country club looks and gave up being dismayed because of my own sorry condition.

"You said you had more water? I'll get it," I offered, raising up to lean over in back for the cooler. His hand looked soft, but closed over my wrist with the strength of a steel band. He stopped the car and pulled me deliberately back around to the front.

"Let me," he insisted with an edge to his soft voice. "I wouldn't want you to strain yourself." He reached back and handed me a bottle, then placed one more in the seat between us. "Just in case," he said with another winning smile.

A toothpaste ad, I mused. He's a walking, talking, breathing, toothpaste ad.

CHAPTER THIRTY-FOUR

Newton put on a Frank Sinatra CD. Pretty soon "Old Blue Eyes" was asking Joe to "set 'em up," at top volume in my ears.

"GREAT SOUND, HUM?" yelled Newton. "JUST HAD THESE NEW SPEAKERS INSTALLED. TERRIFIC BASS, DON'T YOU THINK?"

I nodded and smiled weakly. The sound pierced my brain with a numbing effect. I tried to think of a polite way to ask him to turn it off, or at least down a bit, but he was, after all, rescuing me.

I leaned my head against the window and surreptitiously stuck my finger in my right ear. That was when I noticed we were going in the wrong direction. Newton had never turned around—he was headed back towards the trailer.

"You're going the wrong way," I told him.

"HOW'S THAT?" he yelled with a smile, as he directed Frankie's back-up singers with his free hand.

"THE WRONG WAY!" I shouted. "ROWAN SPRINGS IS BACK THAT WAY."

"OH...RIGHT YOU ARE! I'LL JUST TURN AROUND UP HERE IN THE DRIVEWAY. WOULDN'T WANT TO HURT THE UNDER CARRIAGE OF THIS LITTLE BABY." He gave the polished wood dash a fond pat, and grinned amicably. His white teeth flashed in the sunlight. I didn't smile back. I was tired of smiling.

I pressed my head back against the leather headrest and tried to block out the music. I had never particularly liked Frankie—he was too skinny when he was young, and too jaded when he was old. Kenny Rogers—now there was a man who could age gracefully. And Toby Keith—he had a sense of humor as well as....

Something Newton said finally penetrated my thoughts. How did he know about a driveway up ahead where he could turn around? And he said he tried to call Mother when he first saw me on the road, but he didn't know for certain who I was until he asked, "Are you Paisley Sterling?"

Don't be a dummy, I thought to myself. It was a pretty damned good guess that the bedraggled, dirty woman he found stumbling down a country road was the woman he had been looking for; but what about his knowing where the driveway was?

I closed my eyes and pretended to be resting, but my mind was going a hundred miles an hour. Newton was Judge Hershey's assistant. Andy Joiner told me that when he came out to the farm with the injunction. He had even hinted that it was Newton who signed the order and not the Judge. What the hell was going on?

The blast of music stopped with a mind-lurching abruptness as Newton turned off the tape player.

"You've figured it out, haven't you?" he asked quietly.

I opened my eyes and turned to face him. I smiled as innocently as I could. "What do you mean, figured it out? Figured what out?"

"Good thing you didn't go in for theater. And forget about playing poker. Those big green eyes will give you away every time."

I grabbed the door handle. We weren't going that fast. Maybe I could throw myself out of the car and come up running. The edge of the woods wasn't so very far off the road. Maybe I could make it to the trees before he could stop the car and come after me.

"Don't try to open the door—handy little thing, child locks—I've got all the buttons I need over here to keep you all to myself."

"What the hell?"

"Now, now, mustn't curse," he chided. "It's so unattractive in a woman. American women know nothing about femininity. You could learn a lot from the fair sex in my country."

"And just what country is that?" I asked with a pounding heart. As long as I was a captive audience, I might as well get my money's worth. "Cassie said you counted in Spanish…."

"Ah, yes! The lovely girl with the coffee. That was a silly little slip-up on my part. She quite took my breath away. You must be very proud of her—so tall and slim—such lovely breasts. I shall have to console her after all of this is over and she is grieving over the loss of her mother."

"You scum-sucking pig!"

"Oh, my! Ruby said you had a very ordinary vocabulary. Frankly, I was hoping she was making that up. Poor Ruby," he mused. "She did have a tendency to stretch the truth. That was her undoing," he sighed. "Just like yours is stubborn curiosity. If only you had left well enough alone, neither of us would be out here in this neck of the woods looking for a good place to hide your body."

I turned to lunge at him, but stopped short at the sight of a wicked looking Saturday night special.

"Don't make me ruin this beautiful interior," he begged. "I had to wait an extra month to get this color scheme. And please take me seriously. No one ever seems to believe that I really will blow their brains out until I actually pull the trigger."

"Why do you have to kill me? I don't know anything," I added as persuasively as I could.

"True. You don't know very much, even though you may think you do. But you're creative, and sooner or later you would come up with all the answers. This way, I'll have a head start. By the time they find your body, if they ever do, I'll be well on my way to establishing a new identity in another state. I won't make the same mistakes I made here. Believe it or not, after the thrill of the first few times, this killing business gets kind of old. I don't look forward to it like I used to. I much prefer little sessions like I had with that little whore last night."

"You beat Clementina up? I thought that was Judge Hershey!"

Newton laughed so hard he almost dropped the gun. "Hershey? That old fool? What made you think it was him?" he gasped.

"Clementina, and the other girls...they said the judge stole their babies. You mean he didn't...he isn't?"

"I'm the judge, you silly bitch! To them anyway. I was a judge in México—the Distrito Federal. They had all heard of me—heard horror tales of the judge who steals babies. It wasn't really true, but my countrymen can spin as good a yarn as you, probably better. Actually, I simply took babies from mothers who were prostitutes, mothers who already had too many children, and young unmarried girls who were foolish enough to get pregnant. I arranged for the children to have good homes in the United States—comfortable homes with rich parents who could afford to give them everything, parents who could afford to make me rich, as well. What's the harm in that, I ask you?"

"Well, nothing, I suppose, unless you're a mother whose baby was torn out of your arms."

"My, my! Such hyperbole! Do you really make a living writing books?"

I ignored the question and asked one of mine instead. "So, what's a renowned baby-stealing judge from Mexico City doing in Rowan Springs? Run out of children in Mexico?" He started to grin and I couldn't help myself. I had to wipe that smile off his face. "Or did they run you out?" I added wickedly.

The blow took me by surprise. Stars burst behind my eyelids, and I slumped forward, barely conscious and unable to move. I don't remember how much farther Newton drove, but he passed the trailer and pulled up in front of an old tobacco barn. I was totally unable to fight back or even resist when he dragged me out of the car and into the building.

Half of the shingles on the barn roof were missing. The missing shingles allowed the early morning sun to shine brightly on the lifeless body tied to one of the center support columns. Ruby Dawn Coleman's wrists were tied together over her head and her arms were almost pulled out of their sockets where she had tried to get free before she died. Her face was swollen and purple, and her tongue flopped over her lower lip where she had nearly bitten it in half. Ants were swarming over her face, eating the blood and mucus. Soon, they would be eating her flesh.

The first movement I made was automatic. I retched and vomited all the bottled water Newton had given me. I got immense pleasure out of the fact that he didn't move quickly enough and I managed to splash it on his expensive loafers.

"Bitch!" he yelled, slamming me hard against the second support column. He snapped the handcuffs back on my left wrist, and then tied my hands together just like Ruby Dawn's. He made me stand on tiptoe while he hooked the rope and the chain over a big nail. One more length of rope went around my middle and held me close to the beam. Now, Ruby Dawn and I were like bookends. Only one thing kept us from matching: I wasn't dead yet.

Newton found an old burlap sack in the corner and wiped off his shoes, then he sauntered back over and faced me. "I let Ruby off easy, because of our little relationship. I didn't even hurt her. I just left her alone to die. Same thing with that little waitress. She was getting out of the shower when she saw me at the window. Guess I just scared her to death. But you, Paisley Sterling—you have been nothing but trouble from the very beginning. I'll have to think of something special for you."

"How can you say that?" I gasped. "I never even met you until forty minutes ago?"

"Oh, you've met me, you just didn't know it. That day you came driving back to the airport through the field...."

"You were the one who shot at me? Why on earth?"

"You were getting too close to Ramón Valdez. If you had seen his body before I got to him, you would have told the police he was already dead before I slit his throat—that he died when I forced him to jump from my Cessna. Since I was the only one who landed at the airport that afternoon, they would have known it was me who killed him. I couldn't have that. I wasn't ready to leave Rowan Springs, yet—too many loose ends, and one more baby to sell."

His words chilled my blood. I forgot the pins and needles shooting through my arms and the cramps in my calves from standing on the balls of my feet. All I could think of was the certain knowledge that this man would make me feel more pain than I had ever felt before I died.

I took a deep breath and tried to find some anger. Anger would get rid of the fear and give me strength. I remembered Clementina's battered face and the terror on the faces of the other young girls. Anger would see me safely through this ordeal. I had to save Clementina, and I couldn't forget that he had threatened to "console" Cassie after I was gone. I had to make sure I didn't "go" anywhere.

"Was Ramón Valdez part of Rudolfo's posse? Is that why you killed him?" I asked, trying to put some muscle in my voice. "Was he a Texas Ranger, or a Mexican Federale?"

Newton smiled broadly as he took a long cigar from a case in his pocket. "See what I mean about creative thinking? Somehow you figured out I killed Rudolfo and the portly Texan. Maybe I *should* read one of your books. You're a smart lady."

"I really appreciate the fan mail, but you haven't answered my questions."

"Okay," he said. "Why not?" He took a moment to snip the end off his cigar—his expensive Cuban cigar. The fear came rushing back as I saw the little domed end fall at his feet. Now I knew who had killed Wanda.

"You're not going anywhere," he told me politely. "I might as well enlighten you."

He brushed off the top of an old wooden barrel and sat down carefully, extending his long legs casually in front of him. The shine on his shoes was only a little dimmed by my watery vomit, and I marveled at the way he could look so much like an ad man's dream while speaking of death.

"Ramón Valdez was a hired killer. He brutally murdered my entire family—my wife and two children."

I stared at him, the surprise evident in my face, but still I wasn't ready to sympathize with this monster.

"Oh, don't feel sorry for me," he laughed, his voice imbued with arrogance. "Isabel was a pious whining cow! I couldn't stand the sight of her—on her knees day and night begging God to forgive me for my pleasures—for my love of other, more beautiful women, and for the vast amount of money I received from powerful men willing to pay me for my silence." He lit the cigar with a slim gold lighter and politely turned away to keep the smoke from getting in my eyes. Under the circumstances, his good manners made me want to vomit again.

"I'm glad she's dead. Sooner or later I might have killed her myself," he admitted calmly. "She bored me beyond belief."

"And what about your children? Did you want to see them dead, too?"

He took off his dark sunglasses and stuck them through the neckline of his shirt. Beautiful, dark—almost feminine—lashes framed his cold amber eyes. The depth of loathing in them was evil incarnate.

"They were just like her. Always whining and begging for a piece of my life." His voice was flat and unemotional when he added, "I found them unpleasant and disappointing. I shall not miss them."

He took a long puff from his cigar, obviously relishing the taste. "I am glad they are dead," he continued. "But the killing—that was an insult to me. That was an attack on my family honor—*pundonor*. You know what that means? It means I had to avenge the assault on my family name—to find the one responsible and make him pay for what he did. Not to mention the fact that he also interrupted a very lucrative business enterprise, and my very special relationship with a lovely lady named Carmencita.

It took three years, but with the help of some people I know, I finally found him and flew him back here under the pretext of hiring him to assassinate someone else. Just before we touched down, I revealed my identity and gave him the choice of jumping from my plane as it landed, and possibly surviving the fall as a cripple, or getting a bullet through the heart. The stupid fool chose to jump—exactly as I knew he would. The memory of the fear on his face will give me pleasure for a very long time."

"Man, you are some piece of work! What do you do for fun?"

He turned and looked at me, then he began to laugh heartily, almost uncontrollably. "Believe me," he said wiping the tears from his eyes, "you do not want to know." His feral smile chilled me to the bone.

He stretched his legs and recrossed them at the ankles, then resumed his self-congratulatory litany. "Thanks to my own creative initiative, I was able to resume my business operations here in Rowan Springs. I hated living in this miserable little town, but it served my purpose. With the money I made, I will be able to move to a bigger community and live more to my own taste.

"I love your country, Paisley Sterling. Life here is so comfortable, and one is always innocent until proven guilty. And that seems to be quite difficult to do. More often than not, the victim is under more suspicion than the perpetrator. Yes, justice is indeed blind here, especially if the one dispensing it is your golfing partner."

"Judge Hershey?"

"He leaned closer. The cigar had a sweet strong smell. Amazing enough it made me think of Rafe. Newton had Rafe's dark good looks, and as he talked, his voice took on the rhythm and structure of his native language.

"Believe it, Chiquita, because in about one hour I will be playing golf with him and you will be food for the ants like poor Ruby over there."

I had to keep him talking. I was Scheherazade, only in this case, the caliph was telling the tales. As long as he wanted an audience, I lived. It wasn't difficult. I had a lot of questions.

"How come you speak English so well? You have no accent at all. And you don't look...."

"Like a wetback?" he sneered. "I know what stereotypes people have about Mexicans. I've even used them to my own advantage. But to answer your question—my mother was *una norteamericana*—a silly little flower child who fulfilled her destiny and became a Tijuana whore. She taught me every dirty thing there is to know about life. I even acted as her pimp until she got too old and flabby to bring home money."

"I guess the concept of family honor didn't come up until you married Isabel. What was she, very rich, with influential parents?"

Newton's smile was slow and lazy. "As a matter of fact, my dear wife paid my way through law school. And she bought my seat on the bench, although she didn't know it at the time."

"Why did you leave Mexico? Wouldn't a judge have a better chance of avenging his family's honor than a man on the run trying to hide his identity?"

"Ah, but you don't know one very important fact. The night of the killings my houseman, Manuel, came to Isabel's aid. The killer destroyed his face, poor man. He was, perhaps, the only one for whom I felt pity. He was mute, you see, and could not cry out. Manuel often wore my cast-off clothing, and therefore his dead body was mistaken for my own. I had spent that night in the arms of my mistress, and did not hear the news until the next morning. I immediately decided it was prudent to play dead until I could determine who the killer was. You might not imagine it to be so, but I had made quite a few enemies over the years."

"Oh," I scoffed, "I don't have much trouble imagining that at all. You're a real prince, you are."

The blow came out of nowhere. He moved faster than I had thought possible. The pain brought tears to my eyes and filled me with dread that there was more to come.

Newton ran his hand through my hair and pulled my drooping head up. "Don't try that again, literary lady. As you may have guessed, I don't enjoy being insulted." He let go of my hair and tried to pull his hand back, but the heavy gold ring on his little finger was caught in my hair. He yanked out part of a tangled red curl, swearing softly as he checked to see if any of the diamonds were loose.

Despite the pain, I didn't even hesitate. "Then try this one on for size," I sneered. "You're nothing but a child-stealing punk with delusions of grandeur!"

"Such fire and passion!" he said with a dangerous smile. "Are you good at pleasing a man?" He held my chin up and folded back the neck of my shirt to expose the tops of my breasts. "Yes, I think you must be."

I tried to pull away from the iron grip of his hand.

"Aren't you going to thank me for the compliment?" he asked, raising his eyebrows.

"Won't Carmencita mind your attentions to another woman?"

He let go of my chin and stepped backward. "Carmencita, poor thing, won't mind anything ever again—not even the cold hard ground where she has been feeding the worms."

"You killed her, too," I gasped.

"Of course," he stated matter-of-factly as he took up his seat on the barrel once again. "Well, not right away. She was a great help at first. She went to the morgue and identified poor Manuel's body as that of Francisco Villanueva, then withdrew all of her cash and sold some of her jewelry. It was she who made the arrangements for the burials. A grieving mistress is not an uncommon sight in my country. Actually she was quite the belle of the ball—standing by those four graves dressed in resplendent black silk—she was magnificent in her make-believe grief. But when she began to realize the life I had provided for her was over—that coming with me would mean being on the run, and staying would mean giving up her apartment and her beautiful clothes—she decided to sell me out to highest bidder. When I found out what she intended to do, I made love to her one last time. At the height of our passion I slipped a very sharp, thin, knife under her lovely breasts and pushed until I felt it pierce her heart. That's when I discovered how easy it was to kill—much easier than leaving a witness. It has gotten even easier since then. You will be no trouble at all, Paisley Sterling—quite like squashing a pesky mosquito."

CHAPTER THIRTY-FIVE

I searched my mind for an appropriate oath and came up with a word I had heard my father-in-law's gardener use one summer afternoon long ago when he found a snake in the bougainvillea. I wasn't exactly sure of the meaning, but from the rapid change in Newton's complexion, I knew he did.

"Ay, ya, ya," he said shaking his head. "Where did a lovely lady like you learn a word like that?" He walked around the column, examining me from head to foot. "I think you need to be punished. What is it that American mamas do? Ah, yes, they wash their children's mouths with soap." He looked around in mock dismay. "No soap? Well, then we will have to find another punishment."

He grabbed my chin again, then brought the end of his glowing cigar close to my cheek. I tried to move, to free myself, but it was useless. He held the burning ash against my hair. I heard the sickening sizzle, and coughed as my nostrils filled with the stench.

Newton backed away and waved the smoke out of his own eyes. He was obviously very pleased with the fear he saw on my face. He came toward me again, puffing the cigar to make the end even hotter.

I was terrified. Death was one thing, but torture was quite another. I was chicken, pure and simple, and I had a very low threshold for pain. I reacted completely out of the instinct to survive. I kicked as high and as hard as I could, my foot landing squarely in the hollow of Newton's throat—crushing his sunglasses and driving the metal earpiece into his neck. He stood there, eyes bulging out—fury written on his face. He opened his mouth to speak but no words came, only a flood of bright red. He gagged and coughed and fell to his knees, tugging on the metal. When he pulled it free, blood spurted from the wound, pouring freely from his open mouth. Newton stared at me—arrogant disbelief in his eyes—and fell forward at my feet. His legs jerked twice, then he was still.

I cried. Tears poured down my face and into my mouth. I sobbed. Finally the ache in my arms and the burning in my wrists brought me back to the problem at hand. I was still a prisoner in an abandoned barn in the middle of nowhere with two dead bodies for company.

My nose was running freely so I didn't smell the smoke until I saw the flames. Newton's cigar had landed in a pile of debris. Several burlap sacks and some shingles from the fallen roof had caught fire. I had no desire to imitate Joan of Arc. I had to find a way to escape.

I pulled against the nail holding my wrists, but if it were like the big shiny one still holding Ruby Dawn up, no doubt it would survive in one piece after the building burned to ashes.

The smoke drifted lazily in my direction, reminding me that I had very little time. I looked around, searching for anything that might be of use. Newton's dead body was the only thing close by. He might have a knife in his pocket, but there was no way to get to it. I kicked him as hard as I could. At that moment, I hated him more than I had ever hated anyone. Not until I stomped on his hand did I realize that standing on him might give me the extra height I needed to get free.

I stretched my right leg out and hooked my foot under his armpit. Pulling his body slowly forward with my toes took an enormous effort. The fire was getting bigger and closer. Arid black smoke billowed upward through the hole in the roof, obscuring the bright blue of the summer sky. "Damn you, Frank Newton!" I shouted. "Help me get out of here, you bastard!"

I gave Newton's body one last tug, then stepped on his bloody face. My foot slipped off twice, but I finally managed to gain enough purchase to stand up straight. I raised my arms as high as I could and was rewarded for my efforts by the sound of the handcuffs sliding over the nail. My unfeeling arms dropped heavily forward and I lost my footing on Newton's head. The rope around my middle caught my fall, forcing the breath from my body as I sagged forward from the waist. I gasped for breath and choked when my lungs filled with smoke.

I tried to make my hands work—to untie the rope that still held me—but my fingers were numb. I could feel nothing but the pain of blood surging back into my veins. I cried with the unfairness of it all. I was so close to freedom. I rocked back and forth, pulling against the rope. The column suddenly came loose from the damaged roof and toppled over dragging me with it. I tried to bring my arms up to protect my face, but it was no use. Shingles and rafters tumbled down on top of me, blocking out the sound of the approaching fire truck.

When I came to, a fireman was standing over me with a huge axe. I screamed as he brought it down with a solid thump that cut through the rope around my waist, freeing me so the paramedic could pick me up and carry me out of the barn.

By the time they got me outside, the building was completely ablaze, the flames reaching high into the summer sky. Hundreds of displaced barn swallows circled overhead, crying out their distress and berating us for our careless destruction of their home.

"Poor little birds," I mumbled.

"She's out of her head," said the paramedic, as he stretched me out on the stretcher.

"Damn. I was hoping she could tell me what the hell happened here."

"Andy Joiner, is that you?"

He slid in beside me in the ambulance. "Paisley, are you okay?" he asked.

"Nice of you to worry," I observed sarcastically.

"I guess that answers my question." A relieved smile stole across his face. "I radioed your mother and Cassie. They've been half out of their minds with worry. And Horatio Raleigh has been about to drive me out of mine."

"So Horatio's been on the case, hum?"

"Big time!"

"Andy," I began, licking my dry cracked lips so I could speak, "I hate to appear ungrateful, but do you have the faintest idea how hungry and thirsty I am?"

"Nothing by mouth, Miz DeLeon," interrupted the paramedic. "Not until we get you to the hospital and the Doc gives you the once over."

"But I'm dying for a drink!"

"Actually, you're in pretty good shape. Your heart rate and pulse..."

"Screw my pulse. I want a drink of water! Is that so difficult to understand?"

"I'll radio the Doc, and see what he...."

"You mean I have to wait until that miserable Winston Wallace, says I can have a drink?"

"Well, no," answered the paramedic, blushing to the roots of his fair hair. "The new doc, Dhanvantari, is on call weekends."

"Oh, terrific! THEN ASK HIM!" I shouted, raising up from the stretcher.

"Take it easy, Paisley," soothed Andy, as the ambulance started up. He steadied the stretcher as we lurched from side to side over the ruts in the dirt road.

I could hear the paramedic speaking over the radio. When he finished, he climbed back over the front seat and squatted down next to Andy. From the look on his face, I could see I wasn't going to get my drink. I started crying—softly at first, and then in great big hiccoughing sobs.

"Doc says to start an IV—get some fluids in her that way, and maybe something to calm her down. Can you help me, Chief Joiner?"

Andy nodded, and talked to me in a quiet voice while the other man cleaned off my arm and inserted the needle in my vein. I didn't understand a word Andy said, but after a while, I didn't care any more. The only thing worrying me was where the barn swallows would nest tonight.

I slept for two days. Mother and Cassie, and even Horatio, came at various intervals to hug and kiss me, and make sure I was going to be all right. On the morning of the third day, I convinced the plump little Indian nurse who was Dr. Dhanvantari's assistant, that I was strong enough to take a shower. When I didn't come out after five minutes, I had to convince her again. She was wringing her hands and babbling curses in Hindustani when I finally exited twenty minutes later, skin glowing and hair squeaky clean.

"You should not do that!" she cried. "Your body is very weak. Doctor will take me to task when he finds out!"

"Then let's make it our little secret," I said with a winning smile.

"Oh, no!" she cried. "No secrets! Honesty is the best policy, is it not?"

I let her help me back to bed and fuss endlessly over the sheets and blankets because I was clean again, and feeling more like myself. Whether she and Dhanvantari liked it or not, I was out of here. Tonight I would be in my own little bed. I was through with the watery slop the hospital nutritionist called soup. I wanted some of Mother's bisque. I told her so when she came for the morning visiting hour.

"Do you think that's wise, dear?" she asked, as she put yet another dozen roses in a vase she found at the nurse's station. "What has the doctor said?"

"I don't know. You tell me?" I looked at her suspiciously. "I can't hear what you two mumble about out in the hallway."

Mother blushed the color of the roses, and gave them one final pat before she came to sit by my bedside. She reached over and took my hand in hers. The contrast between the two—her beautifully manicured nails and smooth skin, and my rough, scratched fingers with the torn nails and ragged cuticles—made me uncomfortable. I pulled my hand away on the pretext of scratching my nose.

"You've been through a terrible ordeal, Paisley, dear. Give yourself time to heal."

"I don't have time," I protested. "That's just the problem."

"What is your hurry?" she asked calmly. "What is so pressing, that you can't get the rest and the nourishment you need?"

188

"Nourishment, hah! Poison is more like it! And you know perfectly well what I have to do. Find out what happened to those Mexican girls, and that poor little baby, for one thing! Not to mention, making sure that Clementina is being taken care of properly!"

Mother bit her lip and lowered her eyes. I could tell she was trying hard not to cry. I raised up in alarm.

"Don't tell me something's happened to them! Not like what happened to Ruby Dawn! And Clementina? What about her?" I cried. "Please, Mother! Tell me, please!"

The nurse came running into the room clucking like a distraught mother hen.

"Little Mother, you must go, now," she ordered, lifting Mother bodily out of the chair. "Our daughter must not be disturbed. It is not good for her." She ushered Mother out of the room before I could say another word. Mother looked back over her shoulder and smiled tentatively. "I'll be back later, dear," she called as the door closed behind her.

"Damn it!" I shouted throwing back the covers. "I'm blowing this joint. I have places to go and things to do!"

The nurse threw up her hands, "No! No! Daughter, you must behave! If you do not, I have orders to calm yourself."

"What in the hell do you mean by that?" I asked as I bent over to look under the bed for my shoes. The painful needle stick in my bottom answered my question. I was out like a light before I even hit the bed.

CHAPTER THIRTY-SIX

Two more days passed before I got my wish to go home. Dhan-vantari spouted words like "dehydration" and "mental confusion" when he explained why he wouldn't let me out of the hospital. I almost began to wish Winston Wallace were on my case. But as the hours passed, and my progress pleased him, the good doctor's smiles grew bigger with every visit.

"You are almost quite done with your healing," he announced one sunny afternoon. "And," he added with a twinkle in his eye, "Nurse Indira has threatened to leave my services if I do not send you on your way. She has quite met her match! Yes, I do believe it."

When we drove up in the driveway, the sight of Meadowdale Farm brought a happy tear to my eye. While I snuffled into one of the new handkerchiefs Mother had gifted me with, Horatio pulled the car close to the walkway and parked.

"Is this close enough, my dear?" he asked. "Do you think you can walk from here to the library door?"

"For Pete's sake, Horatio. I'm not an invalid!" I grumped.

"Quite right, my dear, quite right. But do you think...?"

"Yes, I can make it."

Cassie came running down the walk to open the car door for me. "Mom, it's great to have you home! And when your hair grows back, your cuts heal, and you gain a few pounds, you'll look just like yourself again."

"Gee, thanks, Cassie."

"Gran has a bed made up for you in the library. She thought you would want a place to stay during the day where you could be around the rest of us and see outside, too."

She helped me in the library, babbling on about the little things that I had missed. "...a brand new baby groundhog. Aggie cornered the poor thing, but I managed to rescue it just in the nick of time."

"Where is the mighty dog?" I asked as she helped me into bed. "I missed her."

"You did? Wow! Things really must have been bad!" She fussed over the sheet until I brushed her hands away. She wasn't Nurse Indira, and I could fix my own bed now, thank you very much. "I'll go get her," said Cassie with a big smile. "You can take it from here."

"Finally! Thank you, Cassie. At least you still think I'm capable of taking care of myself."

"We all do," said Horatio quietly from the wing chair by the fireplace. "But on occasion, some of us need special care. We were simply making sure you have that care, Paisley."

"I'm sorry for acting like such a brat, Horatio, really I am," I offered, my voice full of remorse. "I gave everybody a hard time didn't I?"

"From what I hear," he chuckled, "Nurse Indira Amana very nearly became one of Mother Theresa's nuns last week. Her bags were packed, and she had reservations on a plane to Calcutta. God only knows what Saijad Dhanvantari had to promise just to convince her to stay in Rowan Springs."

Mother came in bearing a tray brimming over with all the tiny finger sandwiches I loved. "Cassie and Aggie are behind me with the tea," she announced. "And I have some nice gossip for our little party. Doctor Dhanvantari and his sweet little nurse are getting married this afternoon. Isn't that lovely?"

Horatio and I were still laughing when Cassie and Aggie burst into the room.

I let Aggie sit in my lap and sneak bites of my sandwiches while I listened to the pleasant sounds of my family. I was home again, and the nightmares were almost gone.

"Clementina....," I began, but Mother cut me off.

"Don't worry about her, dear. She's quite all right. The plastic surgeon from Wieuca City promised us there will be little or no scarring."

"But does she really have to go back to Mex...?"

"Mom, you promised the doctor you wouldn't worry about things like that if he let you come home. Especially things you can't help." She patted my knee and passed the tray of sandwiches. "Try one of these sausage and cheese pastries. They're absolutely divine."

If Mother hadn't insisted I take the little white pills the doctor sent home with me, I would have stayed up all night trying to figure out what to do about Clementina and the other girls. Somehow, I felt it was up to me to save them.

The next morning after I finished the magnificent breakfast Mother brought in on a tray, I announced my intentions to get up and get dressed.

"But, Paisley, dear...."

"No arguments," I stated firmly. "I'm fine, really I am. I may look scary, Mother, but I'm okay. What's on the agenda?" I asked with a reassuring smile. "Surely you have something you've been wanting me to do. Clean out the attic? Polish that king's ransom of silver you have in the maid's pantry?"

"Butler's pantry, dear."

"Whatever. What can we do? It's a beautiful day. Let's make the most of it."

"Well, "she began.

"Well, what? Whatever it is, I'm willing. Just let me out of this sickbed."

"Miss Lolly...."

"Oh, no," I said, making a face.

"You did say 'whatever,' dear. And Miss Lolly called every day after you disappeared. As soon as she found out you were all right, she made me promise to bring you over to see her just as soon as you were up to it."

Cassie was right. I had lost a few pounds. My jeans sagged on my hips, and even my new Cole-Haan moccasins were loose. "Well," I said to myself, "we'll just have to stop at the Dairy Queen on the way home."

Mother decided to wait in the car and let me face my old nemesis alone. I argued with her, but it was no use. I trudged up to the back door and found a note. "I'm in the front parlor," it read. "Come on inside."

The old lady was sitting in a dainty maple rocking chair by the big bay window when I entered. She turned and gave me the benefit of an unexpected smile.

"Don't just stand there with your mouth open," she said in a not so gruff voice. "Have a seat before you fall down, Paisley, child. You look like something the cat dragged in."

Oh, geez, I thought, here comes the Mr. Whiskers speech. I should have stayed home and cleaned the bathrooms.

But I was wrong.

"You know, Paisley, my papa took us to Louisville one year to see a play about three sisters. They were silly things, those young girls— always yearning for something they couldn't have. I can't remember their names because they were Russian, but they reminded me of Hannah and myself."

She stopped and smiled, remembering. "Just like the girls in the play, we were educated by the best tutors in French and German and taught things we would had no use for in this little town. We traveled

192

with Papa to Paris and Rome and attended wonderful parties in London."

She looked at me and whispered in a wondering voice, "Did you know, we even met the Duke and Duchess of Windsor?"

She turned back, her profile frail and delicate against the afternoon sun.

"But just like the sisters in the play, we always had to come back home—to Rowan Springs, where according to Papa, no one was good enough for us. Nevertheless, Hannah fell in love with a young man who was the foreman of Papa's lumberyard. They were planning to run away together when he had a tragic accident in the millrun. He lost his leg. When he was well, he moved away from Rowan Springs and bought a bar in another town with the 'insurance money' Papa gave him. Hannah never spoke to Papa after that. This old house was filled with angry silence until he died. Then at first we thought we were free—that we could invite people over and make up for all the lost years of isolation—but we discovered there was no money left. The lumberyard was heavily mortgaged, and we owned nothing but our furniture and the house. There was no money for entertaining. Indeed, there was barely enough for us to survive."

She shifted her body in the rocker as though the hard wood was painful to her brittle bones, and continued her story. "We stayed to ourselves after that—only seeing Doctor Baxter occasionally when it couldn't be helped, and after he passed away, no one except the delivery people from the grocery and the druggist. Our choice to remain secluded wasn't challenged until your Cassandra came along." She smiled sweetly at the memory, "That child wouldn't take 'no' for an answer. She was determined that we rent the apartment over the garage to her young man. It was hard to refuse. She was so beautiful—it was a pleasure just to look at her."

"I know," I smiled. "I say the same thing very often, myself."

Miss Lolly ignored me and went on, "She was so sweet. So fond of that young man. The two of them reminded us of what we could have had. Hannah and I were quite lovely, too, once upon a time—not as beautiful as Cassandra, but lovely—pale and lovely in our own way, like pearls."

She sighed, "Now, Hannah, my dearest sister is gone, and I am truly all alone."

"We're...," I began half-heartedly.

"I am all alone," she repeated. "For the rest of my days I will be taking up space in someone else's bed and infringing on someone else's time. I dread that. But while it is still mine to give, I want your Cassandra to have all that I have left—the house and all of its contents.

If the law insists that I am too dangerous to the community to live on my own, then let the state pay for my keep. I'll leave this house with nothing but the clothes on my back."

She saw the surprised look on my face. I was struggling to find the right words to argue without offending her, when she held her hand up to quiet me.

"Don't argue with me, my girl. I've thought quite long and hard about this, and I will have my way. I've already taken care of the legal necessities with young Hawkins. There will be no loopholes or unanswered questions. He's quite competent, that young man. I have you to thank for that, Paisley Sterling. I guess you turned out to be good for something, after all. Now be on your way. The afternoon sun doesn't stay long on the parlor window at this time of day, and I want to sit in my rocker and soak up the warmth in my old bones while I still can."

I was closing the door behind me when I heard her whisper, "Tell Cassandra I've loved knowing her more than I can say."

CHAPTER THIRTY-SEVEN

After I left Miss Lolly's I realized that I was still on an emotional roller coaster. One minute I was crying over the generosity of the old woman's gift to Cassie, and the next I was in a rage because the Dairy Queen was out of hot caramel sauce.

"Paisley, darling," soothed Mother. "Try to get hold of yourself. Perhaps you should rethink your decision not to fill that prescription."

"Tranquilizers? Hah! What's wrong with me is perfectly natural. The only way to get over it is to find a perfectly natural solution."

"But, how, dear? The problems seem to be insurmountable: a pitiful old woman who's committed a foolish act and four young Mexican girls without visas? The only good news is that the baby can stay. She's an American citizen. She can be adopted by a nice family. But the others—there's really nothing we can do. You must face up to it sooner or later." She smiled and patted my hand. "Are you sure you don't want to go by the drug store and...?"

"Mother!"

"Very well, dear. I haven't said a thing."

I was quiet for a moment, engrossed in thought. Something Mother had said was the answer to everything. For the first time in days, I felt my body relax. The answer was there, and it would come to me sooner or later. Everything was going to be fine, after all.

That afternoon I moved my pillow and blankets back to the bedroom. The library was back to normal—just like me, I thought happily.

"Why don't we invite some people over?" I suggested to Mother. "I'm sure you have something on hand we can serve."

"Why, of course, I do. That lovely country ham from Broadbent's, and those beautiful ripe pears Billy picked this morning—we could have a cheese platter, ham and biscuits, and fresh fruit."

"Great! Who'll we invite?"

The Joiner girls were practicing for the annual high school musical and Connie had promised to play the piano during the rehearsals, but Andy said he would be here shortly after seven. Horatio was the only other person who could come on such short notice.

I refused to be depressed by such a small turnout. "Next time we'll give people fair notice. I think we should entertain more, Mother. Our social life is the pits."

Mother looked puzzled, and just a tiny bit worried. "Paisley, I went ahead and had that prescription filled. Don't you think...?"

"Hooray!" I interrupted, "Andy's here, and there's Horatio's car, too. I'll go out and say hello, then I'll help you bring in the food."

Andy was leaning against his car speaking softly and earnestly to Horatio. They broke apart like two naughty little boys caught with their hands in the cookie jar when I approached.

"Telling secrets, gentlemen? For shame!" I teased. "Well, we'll just have to ply you with food and drink and make you tell all."

"Eh, good evening, Paisley," mumbled Andy. "We're not...."

"Careful, my boy," interjected Horatio with a chuckle. "The women in this family possess unusual powers. I'd think twice before I misspoke if I were you. They can make a rock sing."

"I promise to go easy on you, Andy," I laughed as I took Horatio's arm and ushered the two men into the friendly confines of the library.

"My, what smells so good?" inquired Horatio. "So sweet...it reminds of something long, long ago."

Mother pointed to a big vase of delicate white flowers in front of the empty fireplace.

"Gardenias, Horatio, dear. They probably remind you of our high school tea dances. All the girls wore gardenias pinned to their party dresses. Billy had to cut down the rest of Paisley's damaged moon garden today," explained Mother. "These flowers are the only ones we'll be able to enjoy for quite a while, I'm afraid."

"Damn tornado!" I groused.

"I'll have to admit it sure stirred up a lot of trouble," admitted Andy with a grin. "I was busier than a bucket of red ants there for a while."

"And I suppose my being kidnapped and nearly murdered was just all in a day's work?"

"Paisley, don't be rude to our guest. Andy, dear, please forgive her...."

"Forgive, hell! I was nearly a paragraph in the obituaries of yesterday's Rowan Springs Times. I'd like to think I was at least item number one on Andy's 'things to do' list!"

"Paisley, "whispered Mother, "those little pills are in the kitchen...."

"Bother the stupid pills!"

"Country ham biscuit anyone?" interrupted Cassie, with a pointedly wicked look in my direction.

"Sorry, everybody," I mumbled with a wan smile. "I guess I'm not quite house trained, yet. What would you like to drink?"

"Eh, do you have a beer?" asked Andy, blushing slightly.

"Why, of course, Andy, dear," said Mother graciously. "Beer goes so well with ham. I think I'll have one, too. How about you, Horatio?"

Horatio smiled and nodded.

"Beer all around, it is then. Paisley, will you be all right...?"

"Of course, Mother. I'll behave while you're gone. And Cassie will help you bring the drinks back," I said casting my own wicked grin back at my daughter.

Mother left the room, glancing uneasily over her shoulder. I gave her a big reassuring smile, and then focused it on my two friends.

"Fess up, you two! I want to know everything! After all, I think I deserve it—if for nothing more than saving the county the cost of a murder trial."

Andy grinned and scratched his head. He had lost some hair in the past year and was self-conscious when not wearing his uniform hat. "I guess you're right, Paisley. What do you think, Mr. Raleigh? Think she's up to it?"

"In my considered opinion...."

"For Pete's sake, you two! Mother's going to be back in a minute, and she'll end this conversation in a heartbeat." I made a face. "And maybe even hide one of these killer pills in my sandwich for good measure."

"Very well," began Horatio. "For a start, James Hershey had absolutely nothing to do with this unfortunate affair—except perhaps when he made the mistake of taking Frank Newton's references and resume on face value when he hired him."

"Is that right, Andy? Hershey's as clean as a whistle?"

"Yes, Paisley, cleaner, even. Of course, he doesn't think so. Blames himself for the whole thing. By the way, he wants to see you sometime tomorrow afternoon."

"Whatever for?"

"To apologize, I should imagine," answered Horatio. "I do know this whole affair has hit James very hard. He was a great admirer of your father, and if he feels responsible for everything that happened, including what happened to you. He will want to make amends."

"Oh, geez! Just what I need, another blubber fest!"

Horatio threw back his head and laughed. "Oh, my dear! You are quite something. Does anyone ever really please you?"

I grinned back. "You and Andy will, if you fill me in on the rest of the picture. I have a million questions, and I want answers to them all."

"Paisley," warned Mother as she entered with Cassie, who was carrying a tray loaded with frosty mugs of Heinekens, "Not now."

I winked at Horatio, and smiled at Andy. "I'll save it for dessert, gentlemen. Answers always go better with coffee and Cointreau."

I behaved myself impeccably throughout our jolly repast. Even Mother finally relaxed when she saw that I was being good.

Andy decided he would have another beer instead of Cointreau. I kept him company, but poured for Mother and Horatio while Cassie brought our coffee and dessert.

"Now, Mother," I began soothingly. "If you don't want me to embarrass you, you'd better let Horatio and Andy finish the story they started earlier.

"Yeah, Gran," seconded Cassie as she set down the heavy silver tray. "I haven't figured this out either. I'd like to know what was behind it all. For instance, why did Rudolfo come looking for Newton in the first place?"

Andy took a deep breath and started telling his story. "Rudolfo Ramírez and Captain Louis Arledge, the man you called Fatty, were on the trail of one Francisco Villanueva who was wanted for murder in Mexico, Arizona, and Texas. He was also charged with kidnapping, statutory rape, transporting illegal immigrants, impersonating an officer of the court, and a half a dozen other charges—including soliciting for prostitution."

"Wow! He looked so self-satisfied and innocent in that picture with his family. It's hard to believe he was such a bad ass."

"Cassandra, please," reprimanded Mother.

"Wait a minute! What picture is that, Cassie?"

"The one stuffed in the towel rack, Mom. I found it under the seat of the car the day after you disappeared." She hopped up and retrieved the tattered photograph from the bookshelf and handed it over. A stouter, mustachioed Frank Newton stared backed at me. Surrounded by a smiling family—his wife Isabel and their two children—he looked for all the world like any proud and loving papa.

"Mom, you look a little green. Are you sure you're...?"

"Fine, fine, I'm fine!" I insisted impatiently. "Please go on, Andy."

"Arledge and his Mexican counterpart got wind of Newton's possible whereabouts earlier this year. That's the only picture they had to go by," explained Andy. "They decided to blend in with the immigrant workers here in Lakeland County—Rudolfo as a tobacco picker and Arledge as a foreman—to make sure Newton really was Villanueva." Andy took a sip of beer and continued with a wry little grin. "At first they didn't know who to trust, including the local law. After all, their quarry was chummy with some of the most respected people in Rowan Springs. They made the decision to work on their own, but when push came to shove, and Arledge was found out and murdered, Rudolfo came to the only person he could trust for help."

"Me?" asked Cassie in a very small voice."

"Yes, you, my dear," smiled Horatio. "And you took quite a chance when you went off with him. Nevertheless, I'm very proud of you."

"What about the body in our back field? Didn't that raise any red flags? I mean, even to my untrained eye, he looked a bit squashed."

"Paisley, dear, must you?"

"She's quite right, Anna. The gentleman's body in question did appear to be somewhat distorted."

"That was my fault," admitted Andy. "With the tornado and all, I just assumed he had been picked up by the force of the wind after his throat was slashed. I had no idea Newton had made him jump from his plane."

"It's ironic, isn't it?" mused Horatio. "Newton sought to cover his crime by disfiguring the corpse, when it would have gone completely unnoticed if he had left well enough alone."

We were all quiet for a moment, thinking.

"Poor Ruby Dawn," said Mother shaking her head. "She was completely taken in by that monster."

"Poor Ruby nothing! She wasn't exactly an innocent bystander. I still have a knot on my head where she whacked me with that rifle butt!"

"I have to agree with Paisley, Miz Sterling," said Andy. "After reading Ruby Dawn Coleman's journal...."

"Journal? She kept a journal? Wow! What did it say?" asked Cassie, her eyes shining with excitement.

I forgave her for forgetting to sympathize with my bump and seconded her question. I was as excited as she was.

"Well, I really shouldn't be talking about police evidence...."

"Evidence against whom, for what? Everybody's dead! Ruby Dawn can't be tried for anything now," I argued.

"Neither can Frank Newton," added Cassie. "You saw to that, Mom," she added with a pat on the back.

I swallowed hard, forcing my mouthful of beer down a second time, and grinned weakly. I didn't want Mother to bring up the subject of those damned little white pills again. "That's right," I acknowledged in a steadier voice. "Newton's gone, too. As a matter-of-fact, nobody's left, so you might as well tell us what Ruby said in her diary."

"Well, she hated you, for one thing," admitted Andy, with an embarrassed laugh. "She was jealous. She was convinced you got to be a famous writer because you came from what she called 'a good family.' She was determined to become as famous as you, and Newton fed that desire. He made all kind'a promises I'm sure he never would have kept. Ruby Dawn was probably just one in a long line of women he used and then discarded."

"You've got that right," I agreed, remembering Isabel and Carmencita.

"Anyway, according to her journal, Newton brought a kind of dirty excitement into Ruby's life. When he found out she was thrilled by tales of his less than perfect past, he let her take part in some of his activities. He even told her she would make a fortune one day by publishing his life's story. What he didn't know was that she was already putting pen to paper and recording everything he said and did. That was ultimately her undoing. When he found out she had compromised him, he killed her. But she had the last word, because she left the journal in her safe deposit box with instructions to give it to Judge Hershey in the event of her death."

"Exactly what did she do for this man, besides kidnapping Paisley—before he found her out, that is," asked Mother.

"For one thing, she told Newton that poor Wanda Blake, the only person who had seen him in the vicinity of the trailer park the night of Fatty's murder, was hiding in my upstairs apartment."

"But I honestly don't think she knew he meant to kill the Blake woman, Mr. Raleigh," interjected Andy. "The journal is somewhat vague on that point, but I believe she was stunned when she found out Wanda was dead. Until then, she had been playing a character in a movie where the blood was made of ketchup."

"Well, she certainly didn't hesitate to whack me a good one when she had the chance!"

"Like I said before, Paisley, she hated you. And by that time, she was too caught up in Newton's affairs to back out. In the diary she refers to 'my beautiful Frankie's wicked, wicked ways.' She might also have realized, after he killed Wanda, that she'd better be careful if she wanted to escape the same fate."

"I still believe she couldn't have been corrupted if she had been a fine upstanding citizen in the first place. She must have known he was keeping Clementina and the other girls prisoner. Does she mention that in the journal?"

"Like I said before, Paisley, she saw herself as Newton's 'gun moll.' She even knew he was taking the young women to the trailer park and forcing them to prostitute themselves to the migrant workers."

"Oh, my dear Lord," breathed Mother. "Those poor children."

Cassie got up from her seat by Horatio and snuggled next to me on the sofa. "Is that how they got pregnant?" she asked.

Andy had turned a bright and interesting shade of red. Horatio rescued him by answering my daughter's forthright question.

"Precisely, my dear. And that's where some of the babies he put out for adoption came from. The others he flew in from Mexico in his own plane."

"That's right," said Andy as he took on a more normal skin tone. "He still had some contacts he could trust in the interior. Ruby Dawn even went with him once. She thought it was going to be a wonderful romantic holiday, but Newton only needed her to help him with the infants. She was more than a little miffed when she found out."

Andy paused to take a bite of his dessert before he continued. "I think Paisley's right about Ruby Dawn's character. According to her diary, our Miss Coleman was angrier about not having her Mexican holiday than she was about Newton's smuggling babies into the United States in order to sell them to the highest bidder."

CHAPTER THIRTY-EIGHT

I told Cassie about her gift from Miss Lolly later that night after Horatio and Andy had left and we were alone.

"But, why me?" she asked.

"Lots of reasons, honey. The main one being, she's very fond of you." I smoothed the long, dark, hair back from her face. "I can understand that," I added. "It would be hard not to love you."

"Wow! A whole house. But what do I do with it? It's too big to live in all by myself, and you and Gran would never leave the farm. I guess I could sell it and make sure Miss Lolly goes to a nice place."

"I don't know, Cassie. She was pretty adamant about making the state pay for what she calls 'her wrongful incarceration'."

"Well, it is, isn't it? She really didn't do anything wrong."

I raised my eyebrows on that one.

"Well, maybe just a little wrong," admitted Cassie with a grin. "Any more biscuits left?" she asked, as she unfolded her long legs and stood up to stretch. "This sudden wealth has given me an appetite."

Cassie didn't say another word about Miss Lolly's gift. I knew that sooner or later she would come to the same decision that I had about what was the right and proper thing to do.

The next afternoon I put on some new jeans, a silk shirt, and the linen jacket I save for best, and went to see Judge Hershey in his chambers at the courthouse.

The place was a mess. Cardboard boxes half full of books covered almost all the floor space, leaving me only a narrow path to the chair in front of his big mahogany desk.

When I asked as politely as I could what was going on, he smiled—a sad but determined smile—and explained in his own roundabout way.

"You know, Paisley, your father was a great friend to me. When he came to Rowan Springs after the war and settled down in our quiet little town to teach high school, we questioned his motives. He was somewhat famous, you know—a war correspondent, a hero—a man whose stories and photographs had appeared in *Life* magazine. What, we wondered, could a small town like ours have to offer such an icon. You see, we were still too young to know that peace and quiet and good neighbors were such precious commodities."

"At first, I was jealous. He was dashing—handsome, with a supremely confident air. What I didn't know was that the unseen—the hidden aspects of your father—were far more admirable." The old man looked at me intently. I was shocked to see the tears in his eyes. "His courage and honesty dwarfed that of other men," he admitted hoarsely.

He cleared his throat and stared at the high ceiling for a moment. The courthouse was old, built in the nineteen thirties, and I wondered briefly what the heating bill was.

When the Judge had recovered himself, he continued. "I was a teenager back then—somewhat of a rapscallion, always in trouble, barely staying ahead of the law. John Sterling cornered me one day after class. I had behaved badly that morning, but he hadn't said a word in front of the other students, waiting instead until we were alone. 'James, my boy,' he said, 'It's like this: nothing is gray. It's either black or white, good or bad, strong or weak. Which are you? And don't disappoint me with the wrong answer.' From that moment on, I was as good as I could be for him."

I laughed softly. "I know exactly what you mean."

"I'm quite sure you do," he chuckled, as he stood and walked over to the tall windows where he could look down on Main Street.

"He was a pretty good sailor, your dad. He used to say, 'Stay on course, Jimmy, stay on course.' I know as sure as I'm standing here what he would say to me if he were here—if he knew about all of this mess."

"What's that, sir?" I had a catch in my voice, too.

"He would say, 'James, my boy, this thing, this terrible thing, happened on your watch. You are as responsible as the evil man who caused it'."

"Oh, no!" I protested. "But you're not!"

He turned around to face me, his tall, lean, body silhouetted against the bright afternoon sunlight. "But I am, Paisley. It did happen on my watch, and there are no gray areas. Your father was right. It's time for me to step down and make way for someone who is younger—more alert. Alert enough to keep a weather eye, and keep the ship on a straight course."

He came back to his desk, and sat down in the big leather chair where he had made so many decisions that had changed other people's lives. His face was a blur through my tears. I knew he would never reverse the sentence he had passed on himself. My father would have been proud of him. I told him so.

"Don't worry about me, Paisley, girl" he said with a kindly smile. "I'll be fine."

I believed him.

Two weeks later Billy came out and tilled the soil for my new moon garden. The other one had been nice, but this one was going to be fantastic. I selected a quiet corner of the yard off the east wing. The remaining trees on that side of the house were not tall—dogwoods and wisteria, mostly—and the moon would have no trouble seeking out the white blossoms and my silver gazing ball.

Mother wanted to give me something to celebrate the ground-breaking. She tried to talk me into one of those concrete children—a goose girl, or a strange little boy with a weird frozen smile holding a bunny. I told her "nothing doing." They always reminded me of those terrible pictures of people incinerated into ashes in Nagasaki and Hiroshima.

"For goodness sake's, Paisley!" was her only response. But she had a charming little white wrought iron bench delivered by two o'clock that afternoon.

I sat on my new bench with a pencil, some graph paper, and a ruler, and tried my best to make an organized drawing of my garden.

After an agonizing hour of thinking and thinking, I threw down the pencil and paper, whistled for Aggie, and hopped in Watson for a trip to the local nursery.

Just like my dad, Tony Piccolini came to Rowan Springs after World War Two. He worked in the tobacco fields until he had saved enough money to go back to Italy and marry his childhood sweetheart. He and Rosa returned and built the nursery and a wonderful life that included six children. Their eldest daughter's son had taken over the day-to-day operation of the nursery from his grandfather a year ago.

Xavier Piccolino Martin had devoted his young life to the propagation of antique plants. Roses were his specialty. I wanted some for my garden.

"Exactly which ones?" he asked with a huge grin. "They're my pride and joy, you know." He was short and darkly handsome, with a big handlebar mustache and wavy black hair. His wife, Sylvia—blond and blue-eyed—worked by his side, keeping an eye on their three children who played in a nearby sand pile.

"Don't get him started on those silly roses," Sylvia said with a smile. "Sometimes I think he loves them more than me!"

"Foolish woman!" Xavier grabbed his wife and placed a big noisy kiss on her blushing cheek. "Follow me, Paisley. You can tell me which ones call to your heart."

204

I followed him back into the greenhouse listening to him explain about the marvelous attributes of "his bambini" as we walked.

"So?" he asked, pointing proudly to the marvelous collection of bushes and blossoms. "Which one can you not live without?"

"I don't know, Xavier! Now, I'm really confused. I tried to plan it out, but that's not my thing. I'm too impulsive, too disorganized. All I know is that I want everything to be white and smell great."

He didn't hesitate. "You must have a climber. I suggest a *Sombreuil* which has large, very fragrant double blooms with creamy white blossoms, or a *Cherokee*—single pure white flowers. And then an *Iceberg,* and a *Madame Joseph Schwartz* for background."

I left with considerably more than that.

Billy helped me set up the trellises and plant the climbers before he left for his wife's birthday dinner. I worked on alone into the evening.

Mother brought my dinner out on a tray, and afterwards I turned on the outside lights so I could finish. Bruce Hawkins found me covered with dirt—and happy as a hog in mud as I planted the last rose bush.

"Wow! This is really something."

"Wait until everything blooms in the moonlight. It's like magic!"

I pointed to my new bench, and Bruce sat down. I turned a bucket upside down and perched. "What can I do you fer?"

Bruce smiled. "Farming is good for the vocabulary as well as for the soul, I see."

We laughed at his joke, and I got up awkwardly on stiff knees to pour him some sweet iced tea from the tray Mother brought. "I'm not so sure about the body," I admitted ruefully. "I'll find out for sure tomorrow, I'm afraid."

"I hope you'll be well enough to attend the ceremony. Tomorrow's going to be a big day," he announced with a satisfied grin.

I plopped back down, almost knocking over the bucket. "It worked?"

"Like a charm!"

"Tell me all about it!"

"Judge Hershey cleared Miss Lolly of all the charges, including social security fraud. She had received only one check for Hannah and hadn't even cashed it, so she's okay with the government. And he declared her to be competent and mentally capable of making any and all decisions regarding her self and others."

"Hooray and hallelujah," I sang triumphantly.

"She's signing the adoption papers in Hershey's chambers at eleven o'clock tomorrow morning. It's the Judge's last official act.

Miss Lolly's going to be a mother times four."

"And a grandmother times one—don't forget the baby," I laughed.

"How could I? The baby's new name is Hannah Maria Parsons."

"And my baby? What did she decide? I haven't seen her all day." I pointed at the mess of empty plant flats and fertilizer sacks.

"That's a wonderful young woman, you raised," observed Bruce.

"Sometimes I think she raised me!"

"She asked me to set up a trust fund with the revenue from the baseball memorabilia we found when we emptied out old Papa Parsons' closet. There's enough money to take care of the operating expenses for the Parsons House for Visiting Workers for the next twenty years."

"My gosh! All those old pieces of cardboard were really worth that much?"

Bruce threw back his head and laughed. "Just ask my nephew how much he wants for his Mark McGuire baseball card. Some of those 'pieces of cardboard' were seventy years old—they're priceless. Not to mention the autographed baseballs from Shoeless Joe Jackson and Babe Ruth. Old man Parsons was quite a fan, and he had more than enough money at one time to indulge himself in his favorite pastime."

"Thank God!"

"You're right, Paisley. That old house would have been nothing but a problem for Cassie without the money to renovate. And I must say, I'm very impressed that a person so young has such a fine head on her shoulders. She knew exactly what she wanted to do with the house and the money. I followed her wishes to the letter. Miss Lolly will take up residence again in a special apartment set aside for her. She'll be the titular head of the enterprise—with Cassie doing the work behind the scenes until she trains Clementina and the other girls in bookkeeping and purchasing supplies. All the migrant workers will register with the county when they arrive, at which time they will be referred to the Parsons House. They will be eligible to room and board for a very nominal fee—really just enough to cover laundry costs—as long as they have a job in the county. Clementina and the other girls will do the cooking and housekeeping for their own keep and have a nice little salary as well."

"Sounds great!"

"And Hershey has ordered the trailer park cleared. He's donating the land to the county for a park. He plans to build a pavilion under those big beautiful cedars—says he used to picnic out there years ago."

"So I've heard."

"You haven't heard what he's going to call it," added Bruce with a twinkle in his eye.

"What?"

"The John Sterling Memorial Park."

It was perfect. Even the intrepid Leonard Paisley couldn't have written a better ending.